Taylor took a deep breath. The man looked to be her age—thirty…maybe a little older.

"I'm sorry, I didn't mean to scare you."

"What do you want?" Tall, dark hair… She'd seen him somewhere before.

"I'm Jack Parker. I came to see your mother."

"Why did you want to see my mother?"

He turned to face her. "It's…business."

He had a smooth speaking voice, with a Texas accent. "It's six in the morning. You have strange business hours, Mr. Parker."

He smiled, and she relaxed somewhat. If it weren't for the intense green eyes, his olive complexion and dark hair would make her think he was Italian, or Hispanic, maybe. Handsome…and very sexy.

Not that it mattered. She wasn't in the market for sexy or anything else.

Dear Reader,

We've probably all been through the search for identity as adolescents; and, as a result of the process of maturation, we usually come to understand who we are and what we want out of life. But what if, after finally coming into your own, you discover something that makes you question all that you've built your life on? That's what Taylor Dundee, the heroine in *The Man from Texas,* must face when Jack Parker shows up.

Jack Parker has had a similar experience years earlier when he learned the identity of his biological father. But it's only recently that he sets out on a quest to find out more about the man. What Jack discovers sends him on another course of action that disrupts him as much as Taylor. But like any of us who deal with uncertainties in our lives, it's what we do in times of trouble that defines who we really are. Jack and Taylor are no different, and the decisions they make not only define who they are, but will also determine whether they have a future together. I hope you enjoy Jack and Taylor's story.

Be sure to watch for my next book, *Going for Broke,* in December. It's part of the new TEXAS HOLD 'EM continuity series featuring five cowboys from River Bluff, Texas. *Going for Broke* is the third book in this exciting new series that begins next month.

I love hearing from readers. You can reach me at P.O. Box 2292, Mesa, AZ 85214, or e-mail me at LindaStyle@LindaStyle.com. To read about my upcoming books, I invite you to visit my Web site at www.LindaStyle.com.

May all your happily-ever-after dreams come true,

Linda Style

THE MAN FROM TEXAS
Linda Style

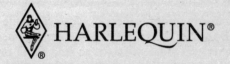

HARLEQUIN®

TORONTO • NEW YORK • LONDON
AMSTERDAM • PARIS • SYDNEY • HAMBURG
STOCKHOLM • ATHENS • TOKYO • MILAN • MADRID
PRAGUE • WARSAW • BUDAPEST • AUCKLAND

ISBN-13: 978-0-373-71443-8
ISBN-10:   0-373-71443-2

THE MAN FROM TEXAS

ABOUT THE AUTHOR

If you could own any horse it would be... Fury, the stallion who starred in *Black Beauty*. **Favorite Western?** It's a tie between *The Magnificent Seven* and *Butch Cassidy and the Sundance Kid*. Oh, *Tombstone* was great, too. Oh, and *High Noon* and *Shane*. Oh my gosh, there are too many. **Favorite Western state?** Arizona—because I live there. (Trivia: more Western movies are made in Arizona than in any other state. If you see a saguaro in a Western, the movie is made in Arizona...because saguaros don't grow anywhere else.) **Zane Grey or Louis L'Amour?** I should say Zane Grey, since he wrote his books in a cabin in Arizona, but... **Cowboys are your weakness because...**still waters run deep! **Best title of a Western?** *The Good, the Bad and the Ugly*. **What makes the cowboy?** The whole package...but if I have to pick one thing, it's the jeans. Followed by a sexy Texas drawl.

To Victoria Curran, with deep appreciation for being an extraordinary editor, and for having the patience of a saint. Thank you for your understanding and support through a most difficult time.

And to my wonderful family... always the wind beneath my wings.

CHAPTER ONE

DON'T THINK. Just do it and get out.

Taylor Dundee sucked in a deep breath of mountain air, waited a moment, then shoved the key into the lock.

Six months later and she still got that empty, gutted feeling whenever she thought about sorting through her mother's things. Taylor steeled herself against the heartache, turned the knob, then slowly pushed open the door and stepped inside.

The lingering scent hit her first. Apples and cinnamon. Every day when she'd come home from school, the house had smelled as if there was something baking in the oven.

Sunlight and shadows played over the pale green overstuffed sofa and love seat. Her mom's paintings hung on the walls, the scrapbooks she'd made were stacked on the table, along with a dried floral arrangement and the pottery her mother had fired in a kiln in the back.

It was almost as if Margaret Dundee was still there.

But she wasn't. Her mother would never be here again. Taylor swallowed over a lump in her throat. Tears welled behind her eyes. She blinked them back. It would be so much easier if the dull ache in her chest would go away. Somehow she had to do this. Just do it and go.

Maybe if her mom's death hadn't been so sudden, the

accident so…strange…. She simply couldn't understand how her mother had missed a turn on a road she'd driven hundreds of times—couldn't understand why her mother was on the road at two in the morning or why she'd called earlier that day to tell Taylor she *had* to talk to her.

From the coffee table, she picked up one of the ceramic miniatures that her mother had so carefully crafted, holding it in the palm of her hand. A little girl, kneeling in prayer, every tiny feature hand painted. Her mom had said she'd patterned the figurine after Taylor as a child when she'd kneel by her bed to say her prayers.

She closed her hand around it, then stuck it in her Taylor Made purse. She headed for the kitchen to make coffee. Leaving Phoenix at five that morning to beat the heat, she'd been too preoccupied to stop for breakfast. It had taken all the courage she could muster to finally go home to her mom's. Several months later than she should have. She ran some water in the coffeepot. As she shut off the faucet, she heard a thump.

She froze. There was a loud scratching sound. Then nothing.

Maybe it was a tree branch scraping the house or a squirrel on the roof. Nothing bad ever happened in Prescott, Arizona, right? Taylor edged down the hall.

Reaching the open door to her mother's bedroom, she gasped. The dresser drawers were pulled out, some upside down on the floor. The sheer white curtains floated high on the summer breeze through the open window. She swung around, making sure she was alone.

Something moved to her left. Her heart leaped as a blur of silver and gray streaked across the room and landed on the windowsill. "Oh, jeez!" The neighbor's calico hissed and arched his back like a Halloween cat. Adrenaline pumped through Taylor's veins. "Dammit, Lion, you scared me half to death. Shoo. Go home. Scare someone else." Taylor pulled out her cell phone and then tapped in 911. "There's been a…a break-in at 7508 Kokopelli Drive," she said and started for the front door.

"Your name, please?"

"Taylor Dundee. My mother's house has been broken into. Everything's a mess."

"Is anyone there? Are you in danger?"

"I…don't think so. Not as far as I can tell, anyway." For all she knew, this could have happened right after the funeral. Wasn't that when thieves and scam artists preyed on unsuspecting families?

"Your phone number, please."

She rattled off the number as she walked past her mother's office, stopped and took a quick glance inside. Papers everywhere. File drawers ajar. But…the computer was still on the desk.

Taylor glanced from one side of the room to the other. Though it was a mess, nothing appeared to be missing.

"Can you please send someone now?" The vandals might be long gone, but as far as she was concerned, the police couldn't get there fast enough.

"I'm getting the information into the system as we speak, ma'am. They're already on their way."

"Thank you," Taylor said, then hung up. Who could have done this and when? The obituary had been in the paper, thieves could have watched the house and realized it was empty, taken advantage of the opportunity.

She thought about checking the other rooms, but decided against it. It had been twelve years since she'd gone off to college and the last she knew, her old room was still the same as when she left…a constant reminder of her depressing high school years. If someone had trashed it, that was fine with her.

The floor squeaked behind her. A hand landed on her shoulder and she swung around—a scream in her throat.

"Miss Dundee?"

She took a deep breath. The man looked to be about her age, thirty…maybe a little older.

"I'm sorry, I didn't mean to scare you," he said.

"What do you want?" She moved to the side, keeping the window in her mother's room in mind as an escape option.

Tall, dark hair… She'd seen him somewhere before. He had to be someone from town, but she couldn't place him.

"I'm Jack. Jack Parker," he said. "The door was open."

"Do you know my mother?"

"No, I don't."

She felt dwarfed by him, he was a head taller, over six feet. "Then what are you doing here?"

"I came to see your mother earlier, but I discovered from a neighbor that she, uh, passed away," he said gently. "I'm sorry. You have my condolences."

Taylor hitched herself up. He didn't seem dangerous, but there was no way to know. "I called the police. They'll be here any second," she said.

His forehead furrowed as he glanced toward her mother's office. "I think the police are a little too late." He stepped around her, still assessing the situation. "Did you check the rest of the house?"

"Why did you want to see my mother?"

He turned to face her. "It's…business."

"It's six in the morning. You have strange business

hours, Mr. Parker." She took another step back toward the living room and the front door.

"Actually…I hadn't planned on talking to anyone right now. When I was here before, a neighbor said I should get in touch with you. I was out for breakfast and drove by on my way to the hotel. I wanted to leave a note for you to contact me…when it was convenient. But I saw the open door and got concerned." He peered behind her. "I just wish I'd come earlier. Caught whoever did this."

He had a smooth speaking voice with an accent like Abigail, Taylor's neighbor in Scottsdale who'd grown up in Texas. He was also quick with answers. "Well, as you can see, this isn't a good time."

He gave her an apologetic look. "Right, and I'm sorry about that. I can come back another time…but maybe it would be better if I waited with you for the police."

He wouldn't stay if he'd had anything to do with the mess. "Thank you, but it's not necessary."

He didn't make any move to leave, so she asked, "What kind of business? Did my mother sign up for some book-of-the-month club and forget to pay the bill?" She was trying to lighten things but instead it probably came off as flip. It was true though. Being an artist, her mother had no head for business and frequently forgot what she called "the unimportant things."

He smiled, and she relaxed a little. If it weren't for the intense green eyes, his olive complexion and dark hair would make her think he was Italian, or Hispanic maybe. Handsome…and very sexy.

Not that it mattered. She wasn't in the market for sexy or anything else.

"It's a bit more complicated than that," he said, frowning

and gesturing toward the living room. "Did you check in there?"

"I came in that way. But—" She waved a hand at her old room. "I didn't look in that room."

He strode past her, glanced inside and said, "No mess." He smiled reassuringly.

"Good," she said, then headed back down the hall toward the living room. Sweat dampened the back of her neck under her hair, and she felt her camisole top sticking to her back like a second skin. "What did you mean?" she asked over her shoulder. "More complicated than what?"

"It's about an old crime I'm...looking into."

She stopped abruptly and turned. He was so close behind, he stumbled into her, then grabbed her by the shoulders to steady them both.

"Looking into?" She gave him the once-over. In jeans, a Houston Astros T-shirt and cowboy boots, he didn't look like a police officer. And the Mickey Mouse watch on his tanned wrist wasn't exactly cop attire, either.

He took out an official-looking ID from his back pocket. "I'm with the *Houston Chronicle,* and I'm writing a story about a crime that occurred thirty years ago."

Texas. She'd been right. "What does that have to do with my mother?"

"I wanted to ask her some questions."

"And, obviously you can't do that."

"Can we sit?" He walked slowly toward the couch. "Maybe you can help by telling me some things about her."

An alarm went off inside her. "No. I can't do that," she said without hesitation. He could be a serial killer for all she knew.

"Mind telling me why not?"

"Because I don't know you, Mr. Parker. I'm not going to share information about my mother with a stranger."

He crossed his arms and shifted his weight from one foot to the other. "I understand. If you let me explain, you might think differently."

His earnest tone gave her pause. The police were on their way, so… "I don't know what you think my mother could have possibly known about your story, but…okay. Explain."

The okay was barely out of her mouth before he launched into it. "Thirty years ago your mother worked for a wealthy family in Houston where the crime was committed. I wanted to talk to her about some of the people she'd worked with, but since that's not possible now, I started wondering if maybe your mother ever mentioned any of them to you. And, if so, what she might have said about them."

Taylor's mother had never mentioned living in Houston, much less working for someone where a crime had been committed. "When did you say this happened?"

"Thirty years ago."

"Who was the employer? What happened?"

He clenched his hands. "The employer was Seymour Hawthorne, a prominent citizen in Houston. His wife, Sunny Hawthorne, was murdered and a lot of money and jewelry were stolen."

"But I think you've mistaken my mother for someone else. My mother never lived in Texas. And, believe me, if she'd known about something as serious as a murder, she would have mentioned it to me some time in the past thirty years."

He frowned. "Your mother never said *anything* about working for the Hawthornes?"

"I've never heard a word. I think you might need to do more research to get your story straight." She raised a brow.

He didn't bat an eyelid at her assessment. He didn't head for the door, either. And in a way, she didn't mind. Having someone there delayed her from sorting through her mother's things.

"That's what I've done, Taylor. A lot of research...and it led me here. I'm certain your mother knew the Hawthornes very well. She lived with them and I believe she knew something about what happened that night."

Taylor's skin prickled at the way he'd so casually used her first name. As an advertising/marketing major in college, she knew salespeople did that all the time to make them seem more personable and to develop a quick intimacy. She knew all the tricks. Unfortunately, she wasn't always this good at spotting them. Her ex-fiancé, Reed, had been an expert in the art of manipulation.

"Well, I don't know what else to say, except that my mother never mentioned anything."

Parker came over and stood in front of her. "How about Margot Cooper? Is that name familiar?"

"No." Taylor shook her head. "Why?"

"Well, Margot Cooper worked for the Hawthornes and the night of the murder, the same night the money and jewels were stolen, she disappeared."

Taylor pinched the bridge of her nose. "I'm not making the connection. Do you think my mother knew this person?"

At her question, he reached into his pocket and pulled out a photograph. "This is Margot Cooper."

Taylor glanced down. Her heart stopped.

He handed her the picture. "It's thirty years old, but I'm sure you can tell who it is."

Taylor's hand shook as she clasped the photo. The resemblance to her mother was uncanny. In fact, Taylor remembered seeing a similar photo. She turned it over, squinting to read the faded writing on the back. It looked like Mar…something and Cooper. "Where did you get this?"

"In Houston. It's from an old personnel file."

Taylor's heart pounded. Texas again. But she would know if her mother ever lived in Texas. They were close. As close as a mother and daughter could be. She would know. "I can see the similarities, but…this *isn't* my mother."

One side of his mouth lifted slightly.

She couldn't tell if it was a condescending smile or not, but it made her blood rush in anger. What he was inferring was ridiculous. "I'm done talking, Mr. Parker. Now, please leave." Taylor walked over and held open the front door.

He started to go out, but stopped in the doorway. "They arrested someone for the murder, but the money and jewelry were never found. The police thought Margot Cooper might have known something about those things because she disappeared that same night. They looked for her for a long time. Eventually, when they had no new leads, they stopped the investigation."

He stared at Taylor. "People don't disappear for no reason, Taylor."

Her head started to pound. "So, you're saying my mother was not only using an alias, but she was a thief as well?"

"No," he said softly. "And I'm sorry if it sounded that way. What I believe is that your mother knew a lot of the people in the household—and others who came and went—and maybe she knew something that could be important to the case, and maybe sometime in the past thirty years she'd said something to someone that might give me a clue. Since you've spent the most time with her, I was hoping you might give me some insight."

She heard the plea in his voice. This was obviously important to him. But surely he could write his story even if he didn't talk to Taylor.

"She may have said something that you wouldn't even think is significant," he continued before she could get in a word. He reached out and picked up the photo of Taylor and her mom on the table next to the door. He studied it briefly, then set it back. "You know, from the damage to this house, I'd say I'm not the only one who wants to know something about your mother."

The thought that someone had been in the house creeped her out. "If you're trying to scare me, it's not working."

He tipped his head toward the entertainment unit in the living room. "I'm telling you to be careful. They weren't looking for electronics."

Yeah. She'd already realized that.

"Thieves usually take stuff that's easy to fence," he said. "So, it's logical to think someone went through your mother's things for a reason other than robbery. Could be someone thinking she has the money…or maybe the jewels. Jewelry is hard to get rid of. And I'm not saying she had them, but someone might think—"

"If you don't leave right now, I'm going to start screaming rape and then the police will arrest you."

His mouth flattened. He raised his hands. "Okay. I'm gone." Down the steps, he turned. "I'm simply looking for answers, that's all, and I hoped you might be able to help."

Something in his eyes made her soften. But then she remembered how easily Reed had wormed his way into her heart. She was a pushover for men with problems.

"It seems to me you want more than simple answers. I think you decided my mother's resemblance to this Cooper woman is your license to rake her through the muck…and answering your questions might give some credence to your story."

He stiffened. "My only goal is to uncover the truth—whatever that may be."

"Then you won't want to waste any more time here."

She saw steely determination harden his gaze.

"If you're so certain of that, then answering questions can't hurt."

The guy wouldn't give up. Did he actually believe what he was telling her? If so, he was wrong. Her mother was the most honest person Taylor knew. She'd never lie to anyone, especially her own daughter.

Taylor had had her fill of liars, and to say that her mother had been one…well, if that were the case, there wouldn't be much to believe in anymore. "If you're some scam artist preying on the grieving family of a dead person…"

He looked surprised, but only for a second. "Again, I apologize," he said. "I know this has to be a difficult time for you, and I'm sorry for that."

He stretched up to hand her a card with his cell phone number. "In case you want to get in touch. I'll be in town for a few days."

She didn't take it, so he climbed the three steps again, reached past her and set the card on the table. "Please think about it."

On his way to his car Jack was sure he heard something about hell freezing over. He had to give the woman props. She was as stubborn as he was.

He liked a woman who could hold her own.

But he wasn't going to stop searching for the truth just because he liked her.

Climbing into the gray Taurus he'd rented, he glanced in the rearview mirror and spotted a police car a half block away. He'd read the thirty-year-old police reports. He'd seen the police interrogation videos. He swallowed, bitter. If he hung around they'd probably arrest him for the break-in at Margaret Dundee's house and throw him in jail.

Like his father.

CHAPTER TWO

JACK HIT the gas and headed in the other direction. After a few blocks, he cruised through the center of Prescott, passing an old courthouse and bandstand. Several restaurants, a turn-of-the-century hotel and a couple of saloons lined the street. He needed to find a hotel. His all-night driving stint had made the insides of his eyes feel gritty, as if he'd been caught in one of the Arizona dust storms he'd heard so much about. He had to catch a few winks before he tried to meet with Taylor Dundee again.

Everything would have been a hell of a lot easier if Cooper was alive. But that small hitch wasn't going to stop him.

As he turned onto Montezuma Street, his cell phone jangled. "Jack here."

"Jack, it's Lana. Are you okay?"

"Of course. How are you?"

"Worrying about you."

He shouldn't have asked. "How's Ryan?"

"Your nephew is fine. Don't change the subject. I hadn't heard anything, so I got worried. Any luck?"

"I found Cooper."

"Cooper—or the woman you were looking for?"

"I found Margaret Dundee. She's Margot Cooper. She has to be."

"But you can't be sure."

Jack's sister was the most skeptical person he knew. "Ninety-nine percent. I saw a photo of the woman and she looked so much like the picture Hawthorne's former secretary gave me, they could be twins. Only...she's dead," he added.

"Really?"

The lilt in her voice told him how she felt.

"So, what now?" she asked.

He remembered a hotel behind the courthouse and circled back. "More research. I met her daughter and I'm going to see if I can coax some information from her."

"You think she knows something?"

"She has to know more about her mother than I do."

"Well, be careful, okay? I don't know why, but I have a bad feeling about this whole thing. I know it's important to you, but I'd hate to see anyone hurt because of it."

She meant that just because Jack's biological father said he was innocent, didn't mean he was. To Lana, Henry Juarez was an ex-con who'd served time for murder. That meant he was guilty. Jack had plenty of his own doubts and didn't need more. "I'm always careful. Worry about your boyfriend instead. He's the one riding bulls and wild horses."

"He's just a friend. You're my brother."

Adopted brother. Not that Lana ever thought that way. Jack's feelings about his place in the family were his own. "I thought you two were a thing."

"I don't do *things*. When do you think you'll be home?"

"As soon as I get some answers."

"How do you plan to get them?"

Damned if he knew. "Whatever way I can."

"I still think you should just forget it. It's not going to change anything. He's already served the time."

It might not change anything for Henry Juarez, but it would for Jack. He hadn't started out to prove anything, much less whether Juarez was innocent or not. He'd started as a teenager desperate to know where he came from. To find his identity.

"I forgot it for years, Lana. I need to do this."

"I know. I just want you to understand my concerns. There's Mom and Dad to think of. Ryan, too."

Jack bit his bottom lip. "Jeez, Lana. I care about them as much as you do. I promised I won't say anything and I won't."

"Juarez is getting out in two weeks. If you pursue this, everything will come out. You can't keep it a secret."

"Yes, I can. I will. Just trust me. Can you do that?"

She sighed heavily. "Of course. I'm sorry. I shouldn't go off like that."

"It's fine. Don't worry. Now, I gotta go," Jack said. "I'll call soon."

Lana reluctantly said goodbye, then made him promise again to be careful.

Hanging up and pocketing his phone, he pulled into the drive and followed the arrows to the parking lot behind the Hotel St. Michael, parked and then headed inside the old hotel. Jack knew Lana was right. Henry Juarez had spent thirty years in prison. Thirty years that had to have made him a different person than he was before he'd been incarcerated at twenty-five.

What Jack wanted to find out was what kind of man his biological father had been…before he'd been convicted. He needed to know whether the man really was the kind of person who could take another's life in cold blood.

Jack didn't remember what had happened to send Juarez to jail. He'd only been three at the time. His adoptive parents had given him a new last name. They gave him love and the kind of security any kid would want. Growing up on the small ranch had been idyllic.

But nothing could have prepared him for the shock when he learned who his father was. Nothing could change the fact that he was the son of a murderer.

He'd thought if he could just find out what kind of person his biological father had been before he was convicted, maybe he'd feel better about the man. About himself.

His search had led to the one person who might be able to give him the answers he needed—the one person who might know what really happened the night of the murder.

And she was dead.

All he could do now was figure out a way to get the daughter to talk to him.

THE NEXT MORNING, Taylor leaned wearily against the bedpost and let the bank statements flutter to the floor among the pile of paid bills and other receipts. God, her mother was a pack rat.

She'd spent most of last night cleaning up the mess the vandals had made, but all she could think about was what Jack Parker had told her.

He had to be wrong. The idea was ridiculous. And it was even more ridiculous that here she was at six in the morning looking through her mother's papers as if there might be some truth in what he'd said. She felt like a traitor.

A stranger shows up with an old photo and all of a sudden she's questioning her mother's whole life. How stupid was that?

But even as she tried to convince herself, she couldn't get the picture out of her head. Either her mother had a twin, or that photo was of her. There had to be an explanation.

It didn't help that there had been no logical explanation for the accident, or why she'd called Taylor saying they had to talk. No explanation for why her mother was on the mountain road to Phoenix at two in the morning.

And now, there was the burglary. Except the police had said it wasn't a burglary, because there was no evidence of a break-in and nothing was missing. They called it vandalism. It all added up to a lot of unanswered questions.

Yet the thought that her mother might have had a dark past was just too bizarre to even think about.

And so what if her mother *had* worked for someone in Texas under a different name?

Taylor sighed. If it were true, it meant her mother had lied to her. She'd taught Taylor that honesty and integrity were virtues no one could ever take away—so, how could she teach Taylor and lie at the same time?

She launched to her feet and went to the kitchen. She poured herself another cup of vanilla coffee and then opened the drawer on the antique telephone table where her mother kept her address book.

At the table, she scanned the names, noting the people she knew and those she didn't. Some had occupations listed next to them. Plumber, yard work, attorney. Maybe she'd call a few to find out if they knew anything about her mother that Taylor d.... .. But what would she ask?

She stopped on *R* near the end. Rungel. Doris Rungel, her mother's best friend. If anyone knew anything about Taylor's mother, it would be Doris.

She glanced at the clock. Too early to call. Doris had

moved to Flagstaff last year, and Taylor couldn't just pop in for a chat. She slapped the book shut.

Just then, she heard a knock at the back door and saw someone with silver hair through the frosted glass. Taylor was still in her nightshirt, but it had to be her mother's neighbor, Milly Campbell, and Milly wouldn't care what Taylor was wearing.

"Hi, Milly," Taylor said as she opened the door.

The woman smiled and handed her a plate covered in tin foil. Taylor could smell the aroma of freshly baked cookies.

"These are for you, Taylor. I know you probably haven't had time to cook, but dessert was the best I could do—for now."

"Well, thank you. You know how I love your cookies. Come inside and have some coffee." The police had talked to Milly yesterday, but she said she hadn't seen anyone. It was odd since Milly was always on watch and knew everything about everyone in the neighborhood.

Milly went to the kitchen table. "The man who was here yesterday, is he a friend of yours?"

After pouring the older woman some coffee, Taylor sat next to her, clutching her own cup. "You saw a man here yesterday?"

She nodded. "A very handsome one."

Taylor smiled. She had to mean Jack Parker. He was that. "No, he's not a friend. He was here about my mother. Why?"

"I thought he might be the one your mother told me you were going to marry."

Taylor spluttered, trying to swallow her coffee, and had to put her mug down while she coughed. Her mother must have told everyone about Reed. "No, my fiancé and I broke off the engagement almost two years ago."

She frowned. "Oh, no. But I saw him here with your mother not that long ago."

Taylor stared at the older woman. Her mother knew all about what Reed had done and there was no way she would be entertaining the man who'd left her daughter nearly bankrupt. "Did you meet him, Milly? What did he look like?"

"No, I just saw him go inside with your mother. She told me later it was your fiancé."

"And when did you say this was?"

Milly waved a hand. "Oh, I don't remember dates very well anymore. But it was right around my birthday."

"And when is that?"

"March. March first. That I remember," she said, laughing.

Taylor took the piece of paper she'd been using to write down some phone numbers of people to call, and added that date. "Was it on your birthday?"

"Maybe." She thought for a moment. "No, my children came to visit then. So, it had to be the next day, because I brought Margaret some cake."

"Did you see what he looked like at all?"

Milly gave Taylor a strange look, then smiled. "I think you know what he looks like better than I do."

Oh, man. Taylor didn't know if the woman was pulling stories out of the air or what. Milly was in the early stages of Alzheimer's.

"I liked his tattoo. Charlie has a tattoo from when he was in the war."

Charlie was Milly's husband, who had died ten years ago. "What kind of tattoo did the man have?"

The neighbor frowned. "I don't remember," she snapped, then abruptly rose to her feet. "Why don't you ask your mother? I don't remember things anymore. Do you know how frustrating that is?"

Taylor's heart went out to the woman. She'd known Milly since they'd moved to Prescott when Taylor was twelve. Milly had been a vibrant woman back then, and Taylor could only imagine how it must feel to know she was getting forgetful, that she wasn't the same person she'd been when she was younger. She didn't even remember Taylor's mother was gone. The woman's unmarried son lived with her, and Taylor frequently saw him watching out the window.

"I forget things all the time," Taylor said. "Our brains can only hold so much information and sooner or later, we have to get rid of some of it."

Milly smiled. "I better go. I know you probably have things to do to get ready for that wedding."

Right. Taylor waved Milly off, then stuffed a still-warm chocolate chip cookie into her mouth, savoring the chocolate as it melted on her tongue. A man had been there. Her mother had told Milly it was Taylor's fiancé. That is, if anything Milly said could be taken as fact.

But Milly had known her birthday and that it was around that time…which was only two weeks before the accident. Who had been here with her mother? Someone with a tattoo. For Milly to believe it was Taylor's fiancé, the guy most likely looked Taylor's age. What if that's what her mother had wanted to talk to Taylor about?

She felt as if a heavy weight had just been dropped on her chest. All she'd wanted when she came here was to clear out the house, put it up for sale and try to get on with her life. Now she didn't know what to do.

She went to the bedroom, pulled her hair back into a ponytail, threw on a pair of pink sweat shorts, a white tank top and her running shoes, then headed outside. The tree-lined streets and the old stucco homes with porches looked like a scene right out of an old *Andy Griffith Show*.

Prescott would have been a wonderful town to grow up in if her high school years hadn't been so miserable.

But she wasn't into *ifs* anymore. She'd used up all her *ifs* during the first twenty-five years of her life. *If* only she didn't stutter, the other kids would like her. *If* only they wouldn't move so often, she'd have lots of friends. *If* only she was as pretty as other girls in school…*if* only she was popular.

She'd come a long way from that insecure kid—until she'd met Reed. Bile rose in her throat at the thought of how he'd coldly taken advantage of her. She was still angry at her own stupidity.

She picked up her pace, her feet pounding the sidewalk harder and harder. For two years she'd worked like a dog to clean up the debts Reed had left her, and now her boutique was in the clear again. She'd bought a small town house in the older part of Scottsdale, and she had a few good friends. Except for her dreams of marriage and a family, everything in her life was finally going as she'd planned.

She touched her stomach, remembering the one brief month when she'd been pregnant. A child growing inside her. She'd fantasized about the family she and Reed would have—four children at least, and they'd live in their comfortable home with a big yard, and they'd go to church and ball games and functions at the schools. They'd have a dog and a cat and…

But once she became pregnant, Reed suddenly said he didn't want children and he'd accused her of getting pregnant on purpose. He'd said he wished she'd have a miscarriage and then he'd walked out. He didn't even know his wish had come true.

She bit her lip and jogged faster, forcing herself to focus on the new design she'd come up with two days ago—an evening bag with a Renaissance flair. The burgundy velvet she'd purchased the week before was the perfect fabric.

As her Nikes slapped concrete, she felt the warm, dry air wrap around her like the arms of a lover. The sun crested on the horizon, and though it was early, she felt sweat beading on her face and trickling down the inside of her arms. Summer in Arizona could be brutal, and while it was always cooler in the mountains, it didn't feel like it this morning.

She wiped her forehead with her wristband as she continued toward the park down the street. A rush of energy elevated her endorphin level like a jolt of espresso, only better.

Just as she reached the bottom of the hill, a gray sedan turned the corner in front of her. There was no mistaking the driver.

She kept on running, even when he pulled up next to her. "I'd like to talk to you again," he said through the open window.

Yeah, but she didn't want to talk to him and kept on going. She heard the squeal of tires and seconds later he was cruising alongside.

"It won't take long. I just need a few minutes."

She hopped the curb and ran on the grass heading for the other side of the park—and damn if he didn't follow her over the curb and onto the grass with his car. Was he crazy?

The car gained on her halfway across the park, so she finally stopped, panting heavily. When he stopped beside her, she said between huffs, "You can get arrested for this, you know."

"For what? Driving on the grass?" He glanced around. "Maybe, but I don't see any cops."

"No…. For…stalking."

He shrugged, then pushed open the door.

"And—" she gulped air "—you're ruining the grass."

He climbed out, all six plus sexy feet of him. He wore baggy cargo shorts and an olive drab T-shirt. "Go ahead, I'll keep up with you," he drawled. "I need a little exercise."

She eyed him warily. "What do you want from me, Mr. Parker?"

"Jack. Call me Jack."

"Okay, *Jack*. Why are you stalking me?" She started jogging again.

He tagged along at her side. "I'm not stalking you."

"I know I've seen you someplace before. You came to my mother's house and now you're here again, even though I told you I can't help you. It may not be stalking to you, but it is to me."

In her peripheral vision, she could see him grinning. "You could help me and then I'll go away."

"But…you're forgetting one important thing."

"What's that?"

"I—don't—want—to." She crisply enunciated each word, before picking up her pace as she made the first turn around the park. She was getting out of breath again, and he was keeping up, step for step.

"Why not?"

"Why should I?" She stopped at the swing set in the kids' play area.

He stopped, too, but he kept jogging in place. "Because you might learn something. Because people who change their names usually have a reason."

"That's not always true. I thought about changing my name for business reasons."

He looked at her questioningly, as if to say *yeah, right*.

"What are you afraid of?"

The muscles in her chest contracted. "I'm not afraid of anything."

"If you're not afraid, and you think I'm full of crap, then prove me wrong."

She wanted him to be wrong. But she kept seeing that picture he'd showed her. "I don't need to prove anything. To you or anyone else."

Bending at the waist, hands on her knees, she tried to catch her breath, observing as she did that he wasn't even breathing hard. She caught a glance at his legs, then her gaze traveled upward. Yeah. Great shape.

"I could have information about your mother that you don't have."

Her head came up. "You mean the woman *you think* is my mother."

He stopped jogging in place and smiled. "Right."

The dimple in his left cheek made him look boyish and charming. She knew the type only too well.

But if he did know something that she didn't…

"As I say, it wouldn't take too long." This time he toned down the charm in favor of sincerity. And she had a feeling he wasn't going to give up until she relented.

"Okay," she finally agreed. "If you can tell me things about my mother that I don't know, I'll answer your questions."

His expression brightened. "Sure. When? Right now? When you're done jogging or—" He shrugged.

She didn't want him inside her mother's house again,

and she had other things she needed to do today. "How about tomorrow? And it would have to be in the morning. I'm going back to Phoenix in the afternoon."

Grinning, he said, "Whenever, wherever. You're in charge."

"Tomorrow then. There's a café downtown about a block and a half from the Courthouse Plaza on Gurley Street. The Dinner Bell Café. Say about nine?"

"Do they serve breakfast?"

"They do."

He smiled wider. "I'm all over it."

"And you'll bring this so-called information?"

He pointed a finger at her like a gun and clicked his tongue. "Absolutely."

She took off running again, but couldn't help smiling to herself.

CHAPTER THREE

SITTING AT HER MOTHER'S KITCHEN TABLE three hours later, Taylor pressed the numbers for Doris Rungel into her cell phone. On the fourth ring, Doris answered.

"Doris. It's Taylor Dundee. How are you?"

"Well, my, my. Taylor, how nice to hear from you," Doris chirped. If Doris was surprised, she didn't sound it.

"I'm so sorry about your mother," Doris said. "I'm even more sorry I couldn't make it to the funeral. But—"

"Thanks, Doris. My mom would have understood, so don't give it another thought."

The last time Taylor had seen Doris, with her gnarled hands and frail body, it was hard to believe she was the same age as Taylor's mother.

"I so miss the conversations Margaret and I used to have. She was the dearest…" The woman choked up, and Taylor felt her pain as if it were her own.

"But I don't imagine you called to hear me whine or to while away the day," she finally said. "What's on your mind?"

Right to the point. Taylor remembered that trait about her mother's friend. Some people thought she was rude and abrupt. "I love talking to you, Doris. I'm just sorry I don't have much time to while away these days." She leaned forward, elbows on her knees. Doris had a degree in psychology and was the quintessential listener. If Taylor's mother had confided in anyone, it would have been Doris.

"You know, life catches up with all of us sooner or later, and when it does, you might regret not whiling when you were able. But that's an old lady blathering. What is it that you want to ask about, dear?"

"Well, I recently learned something about my mom that has me puzzled. I thought maybe you could help me clear things up."

"I'd be happy to, if I can."

Taylor's throat suddenly felt dry as parchment. She swallowed. "Did my mother ever say anything to you about living in Texas?"

The woman took forever to answer. Taylor couldn't decide if her mom had said something and Doris was debating whether to tell her, or if Doris was simply trying to remember.

"Why, yes," she finally said. "She told me she'd worked there a long time ago."

It took a moment for this to sink in. Her mother had lived in Texas. Her mother had worked in Texas. How could Taylor not know that? "Did she say who she worked for or why she left?"

"No. She said it was a bad experience so I never asked. Why all the questions, dear?"

Taylor moistened her lips. "It's nothing really. I just heard something about when she lived there, and I didn't know the whole story."

"All I know about Texas is that she said she wasn't happy there."

Taylor felt a dull ache in her chest. That was as far as she was going to get.

"I still can't imagine why she was on the road at that time of the night," Doris added.

"She called me earlier and said she had to see me. The only thing I can think is that she was coming to see me."

"She said something over the phone that day…or the day before…about making amends for past mistakes. I don't remember exactly, but I thought maybe the two of you had had a disagreement or something."

"No, we were getting along just fine." But suddenly, bits and pieces of conversations with her mother flitted through her head, conversations and situations that alone didn't mean anything, but now…thinking back… "Did she ever mention a man coming to see her a couple of weeks before she…before the accident? A man with a tattoo?"

"No. Why?"

"The neighbor saw someone."

"Milly?"

"Yes. But she *is* forgetful. And whoever she saw could have been anyone at any time." Taylor ran a hand through her hair. "Things just don't add up. But I doubt my mother had some dark secret past." She forced a laugh. "Although we did move around a lot."

"Your mother was a fine woman, Taylor. She loved you more than anything in this world. Don't you ever forget that."

Holding the phone between her shoulder and her ear, Taylor stood, pulling at the terry-cloth shorts that had stuck to her skin. "I know. And even if there was something in her past, it wouldn't make any difference in how I feel about her."

"You know your mother's character better than anyone, Taylor."

There was an unflinching certainty in Doris's words. But Taylor didn't feel that same certainty. She wished she did.

JACK LISTENED to the clack of billiard balls in the back as he waited for his coffee. The scent of beer and stale cigarettes permeated the air, as if embedded in the dark leather and deep mahogany wood of the booths at the Palace Saloon and Restaurant on Whiskey Row. Touted as the oldest saloon in Arizona, locals and tourists alike gathered at the ornately carved bar.

Jack took out the stash of papers in his pocket, one that told about the restaurant. He also had the quarter-page ad he'd torn from the *Phoenix Magazine* that advertised "Taylor Made...A Unique Boutique."

She looked almost too young to own her own business, and a thriving one at that.

And then there was Margaret Dundee's obit. He read it again, searching his brain for some information that the woman's daughter might not know. Hell, no matter what he told her, she wouldn't believe him anyway.

Thinking about her made him smile. Even though they were at cross purposes, he'd enjoyed the fifteen minutes he'd spent with her at the park. That in itself wasn't unusual, since spending time with a pretty woman was always welcome, but he especially liked it when the woman had a brain.

"Thanks," he said when the waitress brought his coffee. Now that he'd located someone who could give him some information, he needed to find out how to get it from her. If she knew anything at all. Focus. He needed to focus. And he would if he could just stop thinking about her full pink lips or wondering if her long dark eyelashes were real. She hadn't been afraid to look him in the eye...or say what she thought. Despite being the owner of an upscale boutique, she didn't seem the type to be worried about what other people thought, whether her lipstick had faded or if every sun-streaked blond hair was in place.

A refreshing change of pace from most of the women he'd dated. If not for the fact that she was the daughter of the woman he was investigating, he might have thought about seeing her personally.

But no point in dwelling on that. He was here to get information. And if that information put Taylor's mother's character in question, there wasn't anything he could do about it.

The break-in at her mother's house could easily have been a crime of opportunity, as Taylor said. Someone who'd read the obit and knew the owner of the house was dead. He saw the bad side of people every day in his job.

Except this break-in went against everything he knew about burglaries. Either Taylor Dundee had interrupted a crime in progress, or whoever broke inside was looking for something specific.

Yeah, he was certain the break-in had something to do with Margaret Dundee's past. And he was certain her daughter had to know something, because she was so resistant. If she didn't, why the hell was she so stubbornly protective?

When Jack finished his coffee, he went outside to call Lana and was surprised at how cool it had gotten. Being 5000 feet up in the mountains had its advantages. Houston never cooled off, day or night.

He walked across the street to the plaza in front of the courthouse where a few people were strolling the square. He picked a bench farthest from the sidewalk to sit, then hit the memory button on his cell. "Lana," he said when she answered. "I've got a job for you."

"Shoot."

"Look in the files I left at your place and see if there are any facts about Margot Cooper that will make her daughter believe her mother is really Cooper. Something that would identify only her. Something unique or…hell, I don't know. Just come up with something. Okay?"

"What about the old personnel photo?"

"Won't work. Anyone can get a photo from anywhere these days on the Internet. It has to be something that's specific and couldn't have been picked up just anywhere by just anyone."

"Maybe Hawthorne's former secretary has something else," Lana said.

"I tried that already. You'd think the woman was protecting the Federal Mint. Be creative. Do whatever you can. I'm staying at Hotel St. Michael. Room number two twenty-five. I'll have to call you later with the fax number."

Finished, he pocketed the cell and walked back to the hotel, went to his room and flipped on the television. In the past year, he'd tracked down every lead on Cooper that he could find. Unfortunately, most were leads the police had already followed up on. A few weeks ago, when he'd finally found Seymour Hawthorne's former secretary and convinced her to talk to him, he'd learned a few more things about Margot Cooper—the most interesting being that she'd been a budding artist thirty years ago.

After hours of Internet research, he'd practically sprung cartwheels when he found an article in the Life section of the *Arizona Republic* about a local artist who specialized in small figurines—the kind the secretary had mentioned Cooper made. He'd thought it odd that there wasn't a photo of the woman with the article. Human-interest stories almost always used photos.

It wasn't until he arrived in Arizona to talk to her that

he discovered she'd died. He'd come all this way only to reach a dead end.

More research produced the obituary and the photo of the woman in the obit, who looked amazingly like the one Hawthorne's former secretary had given him. Even though the woman in the paper was thirty years older, he knew it had to be her.

For the first time in the past year, he actually had hope of finding some kind of proof that might or might not substantiate his biological father's claim. And no way was he going to let the opportunity slip through his fingers.

EARLY THE NEXT MORNING, haunted by Doris's words and with the scent of dry paper tickling her nose, Taylor sat on the floor in her mother's bedroom surrounded by boxes of pictures and memorabilia her mother had collected over the years. They'd been scattered during the break-in. She'd brought most of what was in the attic downstairs, too, because she was going to have to go through it anyway to decide what to do with it all.

The way things had been tossed around, it did appear as if someone was looking for something. But what? There was no hidden money. That much she knew. If there was, her mother wouldn't have eked out a living by selling her artwork at swap meets and flea markets when Taylor was little. It had only been in the past ten years that she'd started making decent money on her work.

Why had her mother never mentioned living in Texas? Maybe she'd loved some guy there and the memories were bad. But her mother had said she met Taylor's father, William Dundee, in Chicago and he'd died in a car accident before Taylor was born. That was thirty years ago, and her

birth certificate listed Chicago as her birthplace. Her
mother couldn't be in two places at once.

She shuffled through some pictures, picked up one of
her maternal grandparents and stared at it. Nana and Poppa
Harden. They'd died when Taylor was young. Nana first
when Taylor was four and Poppa six months later and,
because they'd lived so far away, she didn't have a whole
lot of memories of them.

Fingering the photo, she could see the resemblance
between her mother and grandmother. Taylor didn't look
a lot like her mother, except maybe the eyes. She'd always
figured she resembled her father. She shuffled through the
pictures and found an old back and white of her father.
Taylor was blond like he was. She put the photos away and
went back to the payment files she'd gathered together last
night. She was pretty sure she had them all.

After the funeral, Taylor hadn't had to do much, since
her mother's bills were paid by automatic deduction from
her bank account. She'd left all the utilities on, thinking
she'd return on weekends to clean out the place. But she
hadn't. She couldn't. It had been too soon. She wasn't sure
she was ready to do it. And since there was enough money
in the account to last a year or more, she wasn't going to
worry about it. What she didn't know was if the taxes on
her mother's property were included in the payment or
not. And she couldn't find the damned payment booklet.

She shuffled papers. Her mother was so organized, such
a perfectionist. Surely the break-in couldn't account for
this one thing gone missing. That didn't make sense.

Margaret had kept lists and files and everything was just
so. She kept copies of all her important papers in a metal
fire-resistant box, and she also kept copies in a safe-deposit

box in a Scottsdale bank near Taylor's home. Well, at least those papers wouldn't be messed up. Taylor wrote "check safe-deposit box," on her to-do list, right under "call attorney" and "call the insurance company."

There wasn't much left to take care of, except for the house and she still wasn't sure what to do about it. Having a second home in the mountains to escape the summer heat was enticing, but affording it was another thing.

Her business was doing very well, but not well enough to afford two homes. She continued riffling through the files and finally found the deed. She'd call the bank and get another payment booklet if she had to. She was glad now that her mother had simplified things by having the house in both of their names so Taylor didn't have to worry about it going into probate.

Clutching the paper to her chest, Taylor closed her eyes, remembering how she'd laughed and said her mother was being paranoid, that nothing would ever happen to her. Her bottom lip began to quiver. Tears wet her cheeks. God, she missed her mom so much.

Unable to think anymore, she set the deed aside. But a second later, she snatched it up and looked again. There wasn't a payment book, she realized, because the house was paid for.

Paid for. How could that be? Her mother had done well selling her paintings and pottery at the surrounding art festivals and the boutique, but Taylor couldn't imagine she'd ever made enough to pay off a house.

Taylor looked at the date—January, 1989. The year they'd moved to Prescott.

Was that the date when the payments had started? She read it again and caught her breath. Her mother had purchased it outright. The house wasn't big and had only cost $50,000 back then, but even so, where would her mother ever get that much money? And why wouldn't she have told Taylor?

She stuffed the papers back in the box, her emotions in flux. On one hand, she felt relieved, but on the other, she was hurt and angry. *"Dammit, Mother,"* Taylor said as she kicked aside an empty box. She went to the closet. Aside from the photos and memorabilia from Taylor's childhood, there seemed to be nothing else…except a box labeled Winter Clothes. As she dragged it out, she noticed a suitcase next to it. Something the vandals had missed?

She grabbed the handle, but it didn't budge. She shoved the box out of the way and tugged at the heavy piece of luggage until she got it out far enough to open. She dropped to her knees and pressed the latch. Locked. Pushing to her feet, Taylor glanced around, then rummaged through the drawers for a key. Nothing. Crap. She stood, arms crossed over her chest, wondering where to look next.

The sharp jangle of the phone made her jump. Probably someone who didn't know her mother was gone. She hated explaining to people who didn't know. But she couldn't ignore it, either. It might be important. "Hello."

"Did you forget?"

"Excuse me?"

"Our meeting at the Dinner Bell."

Oh, man. Taylor glanced at the clock on the dresser—nine-fifteen—and then at herself in the mirror. Uncombed hair, no makeup, still in her sweats. "How did you get this number?"

"It's in the phone book. You did say nine o'clock, didn't you?"

"I did. I'm sorry. Time got away from me. Can we make it some other time?"

"I'll come there."

She glanced at the suitcase. "No, I'll be there if you can wait for me. It'll take me fifteen minutes or so."

"No problem. I'm not going anywhere."

After talking with Doris and finding the deed, she was more interested in what Jack Parker had to say than she had been yesterday. "Okay. I'll be there," she said, and hung up.

But interest didn't mean she believed him. Just because her mother had once lived in Texas, or used another name—if in fact she had—didn't mean she was a criminal. Just because she'd paid for her home. She nibbled on her lower lip. Coincidences. They didn't mean anything.

But she didn't know what to make of the fact that her mother hadn't told Taylor about any of them.

And if she didn't meet Parker right away, he'd end up on her doorstep for sure. She shoved the suitcase back in the closet as best she could. The police were making regular rounds in the neighborhood now, so she doubted anyone would try to break in again. Not vandals anyway.

Taylor undressed, went to the shower and turned the water on full force. She raised her face to let the water pepper her skin. All she wanted right now was to clear up the questions and put this uncertainty behind her. She'd meet Jack Parker and get him to put up or shut up. Once he was gone she could get back to normal.

Then she realized that would be impossible. Without her mother, her life would never be the same.

Fifteen minutes later, with her wet hair in a ponytail, Taylor walked into the café. She'd forgotten how popular the place was, especially for people from the Valley wanting to escape the summer heat. The strong, nutty aroma of coffee and bacon made her mouth water. She'd been so distressed last night, she'd barely eaten a thing.

She glanced around for Parker, looking first in the upscale dining room, then back to the room that resembled a fifties diner. He was sitting at a table near the side exit. Seeing her, he smiled and motioned her over. As she slid onto the chair opposite, he made a point of looking at his watch. "I'm impressed."

"The house is only five minutes away."

"I'm still impressed. Not many women can get ready in under a half hour. At least that's been my experience."

Taylor was sure he had a *lot* of experience. He might even be married, though he wore no ring.

"Coffee?" a matronly waitress asked.

"Yes, please."

The waitress stood looking at Taylor, her expression puzzled. Then she said, "Taylor Dundee? Why, I barely recognized you. I'm so sorry about your mother."

Taylor stiffened as she recognized the woman. Angela Wilkenson's mother, a woman as nasty as her daughter. "Thank you, Harriet." Harriet hadn't been concerned enough to attend the funeral, however.

The waitress scrunched eyebrows. "You look so different, Taylor. Did you have something done?" Then, without waiting for an answer, she looked at Jack. "Taylor was such a plain wallflower. My Angela always tried to give her advice, but Taylor was so stubborn she'd never listen." Harriet turned back to Taylor. "I see you finally took Angela's advice and did something with yourself."

Taylor smiled through gritted teeth. "Thank you, Harriet. You're too sweet."

Jack loudly cleared his throat. "Can you please give me a refill?" He lifted his cup. "And I'm starving. How about we order some breakfast."

At that, Harriet smiled at Jack and said she'd be right back.

"Well, that was interesting," Jack said, and looked to Taylor for a response.

Taylor folded her hands in her lap, cool and calm. "What was interesting?"

"Were you really a plain wallflower?"

"You saw the photos on the mantel, didn't you? Glasses, skinny, zits. I wasn't winning any beauty contests. No popularity contests, either."

"I would never have guessed."

A different waitress sauntered over with Jack's coffee and a cup for Taylor. "Harriet had to go somewhere, she said. I'll take your orders."

Taylor ordered, doctored her coffee with cream and sugar and was acutely aware that Jack was watching her every move. After he told the waitress what he wanted, Taylor said, "So, what did you come up with? What can you tell me about my mother that I don't know?"

"I hate discussing business before breakfast."

She suppressed a smile. "Just as I thought. You don't have anything, do you?"

He shrugged.

"Okay," she relented. "Let's eat, and you can tell me how you came to be a reporter."

Jack tightened his grip on his cup. He didn't like talking about himself, but he'd learned early in his career that the best way to get others to talk was to share something personal. He took a sip of coffee. "I think writing picked me rather than the other way around."

"Really. How so?"

"As a kid, I read a lot of comic books and science fiction stories. Then I decided one day that I should write my own comic books, so later on, I took journalism and creative writing in high school. It just mushroomed from there. And…to be honest, I couldn't think of anything else I wanted to do." He took another drink of his coffee. "How about you? Did your mother's artistic bent influence you?"

She smiled. "Maybe. But that was the last thing she wanted, because she knew how hard it was to make a living in the arts. And since I excelled in math and science, my mother wanted me to go into medicine or something where I could make real money."

He noticed her relax. "But…? You didn't."

"No." She sighed. "All I ever wanted was to design things. Clothes, accessories, whatever. But in college, I ended up in advertising and marketing because I knew if I wanted to make more money than my mother, I'd have to know how to sell my product."

He grinned. "My mother wanted me to be a doctor."

"And your father? Did he want you to be a doctor, too?"

Jack laughed. "He was just happy I was going to college. I wasn't the most studious kid." He looked down at his mug, wondering what his real father might have wanted for him if things had been different. What would she think if he told her the truth? That he wasn't writing a story but trying to get information about his biological father. She'd probably be even more reticent if she knew who his father was.

"I never would have guessed that," she said.

"It's that obvious?"

She laughed. "Not really."

He was surprised by her candor…and her ability to see into him. "Well, it's true. I gave my parents a pretty hard time back then. I was one of those angsty teenagers trying to find my niche."

Her big blue eyes seemed to get even bigger as he looked at her. And why the hell was he telling her all of that?

"And it looks like you found it."

He smiled. "I did. No more angst." Except in one area. Had Henry Juarez ever even thought about his son, or what he wanted him to be when he grew up? A man who signed away his parental rights obviously didn't give a damn. Jack got a bitter taste in his mouth just thinking about it. "My parents were extremely grateful for that."

She got thoughtful then. "You're lucky to have them. I never knew my father," she said, tipping her head. "He died in a car accident before I was born, and I always felt like I'd missed something important in my life." She picked at the corners of the sugar packets in the dish in front of her. "My mom was great, though. When I finally decided what I wanted to do, she was my biggest supporter."

Her voice cracked when she spoke about her mother, and Jack realized that even though it had been six months, Margaret's death was still a fresh wound. And regardless of who Margot Cooper slash Margaret Dundee was, or what she'd done, the woman had been Taylor's mother— and without a doubt, Taylor's loyalties ran deep.

Had he not been so young when his family was torn apart, maybe he wouldn't have so much doubt about Juarez.

Just then the waitress brought their breakfast. Steak and eggs for him and a Mexican omelet for Taylor.

"I'll be back to freshen up your coffee," the blonde said after leaving their food.

The sizzling steak made his stomach growl. "I forgot to ask you what the police said about the burglary."

"They said it wasn't. They couldn't log it as a burglary since there was no evidence that someone broke in or that anything was taken." She picked up her English muffin and started to butter it. "They chalked it up as vandalism."

"And is that what you think?"

She frowned. "I don't know. There wasn't any real destruction…just things lying all over."

"And you didn't find anything missing?"

"Not that I could tell. It seems senseless." She cut the omelet with her fork, then took a bite. "My mother had nothing that anyone would risk going to jail for. I think whoever came in discovered that and left."

"Maybe. But I've covered plenty of burglary stories in my time and my guess is that someone was looking for something. If you could find out what it is, you might avoid it happening again."

"And how do I go about doing that?"

"You let me help."

She glanced at him, and recognizing the "no" look in her eyes, he quickly added, "I'll be doing research anyway."

Taylor leaned against the back of her chair, her mouth pinched. "Research on my mother?"

"I'm sorry, but yes."

"You're that certain that she was involved in this crime."

"No. I'm certain she worked there. Without more information, I can't be sure of anything."

She paused, drummed her fingers on the table. "So, you admit you could be wrong?"

"Of course. But I honestly think I'm on the right track."

Her eyes darkened. "Well, when you find out, why don't you let me know."

That was not what he'd wanted her to say. "Think about it. You have to have questions. Don't you want them answered?"

He saw her clench her hands. "You got me here by saying you'd tell me something about my mother, and apparently that was just a ruse—"

"I never said I didn't have anything. You said it." He reached into his shirt pocket and pulled out one of the photos he'd brought along in a file. It was all he'd been able to come up with. "Do you recognize him?"

Her face went white, but she shook her head.

She looked both shocked and surprised. "No? Are you sure?" Hadn't Cooper told her she had a brother? Or was Taylor that good at lying? "Take a good look. It's Matt Cooper. Margot Cooper's son."

Her gaze was glued on the photo, and she kept blinking, as if trying to remember something. "He was killed on a motorcycle," he added, "not long before Cooper left the Hawthorne's employ in 1977."

Abruptly, Taylor shoved herself away from the table. "I don't know who that is." She stood. "I have to go."

MINUTES LATER, Taylor stormed into her mother's house and headed for the bedroom. She'd seen the same photo in the drawer when she'd been looking for a brooch to put on her mother for the wake. She hadn't thought any more about it. And now Jack was saying the boy was Margot Cooper's son.

Her hands shook as she rummaged through some lingerie, socks and T-shirts. Pajamas. Damn. Where was it?

She was sure it had been in the top drawer. When she thought about it now, it didn't make sense that her mother would keep a photo of anyone in her dresser...unless that person was important to her. But if there was someone that important to her mother, she would have told Taylor. They'd been close. Her mother told her everything.

Except Texas. Her mother had never mentioned Texas. Taylor jerked open a drawer on the mirrored bureau. Nothing. She felt her pulse hammering in her throat as she opened one drawer and then another. Either she was going crazy, or the picture was gone.

She swung around. How could it have disappeared? The only people who'd been there since her mother's wake were the police, Jack, and whoever ransacked the house. She stopped rummaging.

Jack could have taken it when he was there. She tried to remember if she'd seen the photo when she was looking for the suitcase key. She hadn't. It had been gone then. Leaning against the dresser, she searched her brain for some other place she might have seen the picture.

Then...she crossed her arms. Was it possible Jack had taken the photo? To get her to talk to him...all the while trying to find out where this supposed money was? Was that what he wanted? How did she know he was even who he said he was?

And *she* was getting paranoid. Just because she'd been stupid enough to be taken in by one man didn't mean everyone in the world was like Reed. God, she hoped not.

Well, whether Jack was a thief or not didn't matter, because her mother wasn't and there was no money. No matter what Jack did, he wasn't going to find anything.

Pressing her hands flat on the dresser, Taylor glanced

at a photo her mother had stuck under the edge of the mirror. Taylor and her mom standing at the rim of the Grand Canyon on Taylor's sixteenth birthday. Her mom had said the plateaus in Taylor's life could be even wider than the Grand Canyon if she wanted them to be.

Heartache constricted her chest. Her tears welled as the finality of her mother's death sank in. God, she missed her so much. She would always miss her.

There had to be an explanation. That's all there was to it. And she was going to keep telling herself that until she was proved wrong. It wasn't as if two people couldn't…didn't ever…look alike. She heard once that everyone has a twin somewhere.

She glanced at the closet. Okay. She would. She went to the garage, found a screwdriver, came back and dragged out the suitcase again and plunked down on the floor in front of it. She jammed the screwdriver in the lock, trying to pry it open. After several futile attempts, she decided to get a knife and slash the damned thing open. Then she noticed the hinge looked rusty. She stuck the screwdriver underneath where the lock adjoined the suitcase. That loosened the hinge. She shoved harder, getting way underneath and broke the hinge off. She did the same to the other side, then lifted the top.

Newspapers. The suitcase was filled with old yellowed newspapers. She didn't know what she was expecting, but it sure wasn't this. The dry musty scent made her nose itch. The *Houston Chronicle*.

The same paper Jack worked for. Gripped by a sudden uneasy feeling, she read the headline. Socialite Sunny Hawthorne Murdered.

She went through the newspapers, one after the other.

They were all about a robbery and murder—and the police were looking for Margot Cooper. For questioning.

Margot Cooper who'd worked for the Hawthornes and who had a son named Matt.

CHAPTER FOUR

JACK DROVE DOWN Kokopelli Drive past the Cooper home. Taylor's car wasn't there. He'd tried contacting her again yesterday after she'd bolted from the breakfast table, then again last night. But either she wasn't answering the phone or had gone back to Phoenix.

He parked, went to the door and knocked. Several times. Finally he got back in his vehicle and headed to the hotel. He hadn't planned on Taylor disappearing. Even if he had absolute proof the women were one and the same, that wouldn't vindicate his father. It wouldn't prove Margot Cooper had anything to do with the murder they'd pinned on him. Finding out if Margaret Dundee had the jewels or the money would at least show complicity. He'd thought Taylor might help him to access her mom's bank records. But instead, she'd fled.

It had to be the photo. She'd looked shocked to see it. Though Matt Cooper had died before Taylor was born, her mother must have told her she had a brother. Maybe that was it. She realized Jack was right. If the photo of Matt was one she'd seen before...

Or was he so focused on his theory being right that he was reading things into her reactions and ignoring other possibilities? Was it possible Margaret Dundee wasn't Margot Cooper?

No, he'd seen the picture on the mantel. Dundee was Cooper. Everything he'd done, all his research had narrowed the search to this point.

He ran a hand through his hair. Hell, he was tired of speculating. He needed to do something. Taylor had to help him again. That's all there was to it.

If she wasn't at her mother's home, that meant she'd probably gone back to Scottsdale.

Mulling over his options, which seemed pretty limited, he went back to the hotel, packed his clothes and headed for the Prescott courthouse and the public records section. What he couldn't get from Taylor, he'd get elsewhere.

Then he'd head for Scottsdale.

AN HOUR AND A HALF after leaving Prescott, Taylor was standing inside the Scottsdale Bank of America with her mother's safe-deposit key in hand. After completing a form for access to the box, showing her mother's death certificate and the power of attorney papers, the teller called over a manager, who led Taylor to the vault.

The manager opened the heavily barred door that led into a room with a wall of boxes in various sizes. The woman unlocked one and pulled out a long rectangular metal container, and then carried it to a small room where she left Taylor alone.

Taylor stared at the receptacle. God only knew what she would find inside. She shoved in the key and as she turned it, the top popped opened. There wasn't much, a small white envelope and some jewelry. The brooch her mother had loved and which Taylor had searched the house to find for the funeral. It wasn't expensive, but had been one of her mother's early creations. One of her favorites.

Filled with dread she picked up the envelope, tore off the end and pulled out a piece of paper folded in threes. Inside, she found a gold cross and chain and a scrap of newspaper, which had apparently been ripped out of the Want Ads.

Taylor frowned as she read it. "Looking for Margot Cooper. Please call…" The paper was torn, so she couldn't see the full number to call. She turned it over, hoping for some clue that might indicate what newspaper it had come from. All she could tell was that it was an ad for something. "Buy now. Big discounts. Offer begins tomorrow for three days, January 3-5, 2007. Be the firs—"

Her mouth fell open. Oh my God. That was three weeks before her mother died. Taylor flipped the ad over and over, looking for the name of the paper, but saw nothing that would identify it. The ad had to be from a local paper, Phoenix or Prescott. Otherwise how would her mother have seen' it? Had Jack put it in the paper hoping for a response? That didn't make sense. He'd have to know that if her mother was impersonating someone, answering the ad would be the last thing she'd do.

Nothing made sense and all Taylor knew for sure was that her mother had kept a pile of newspapers, a photo of a boy, who may or may not be Taylor's brother, and a torn ad she obviously thought important enough to keep.

What logical reason could her mother have for saving any of those things? Unless… A light went on in Taylor's head. Unless Margot Cooper was a friend of her mother's. The boy, her friend's son. Or maybe Cooper was a distant relative who resembled her mother. And if her mom saw the ad, she would have kept it. Taylor felt a tiny sense of satisfaction.

But why keep the ad in the safe-deposit box?

Feeling sure she could find a reason for that, too, Taylor got to her feet. She couldn't sit here all day thinking about possibilities. Jack was wrong and she had work to do. Designs to create. Her business wasn't going to run itself.

She gathered the contents from the box, stuffed everything into her purse and on her way out told the manager she wanted to close the account.

Twenty minutes later she arrived at her town house, flew in through the garage to the kitchen and stopped in the doorway. The light was on. She scanned the room. Nothing seemed out of place. She could have easily forgotten the light, she'd been so preoccupied.

She dropped her keys on the granite countertop and went to the phone where the answering machine light was blinking. Just as she was going to press the button, she had the eeriest feeling that something wasn't right. Was the kitchen towel in a different place? The canisters a little to the left of where they usually were?

Her heartbeat quickened. She could see into the living room and nothing seemed wrong. She took a few steps toward the stairway and listened.

A knock at the door to the garage made her jump like a scared mouse.

"Taylor? It's me."

Taylor sighed in relief as Cara, her neighbor and good friend, opened the door.

"You left the garage door up. Are you okay?" Cara gave Taylor a hug.

"I'm fine. Just a little overwhelmed."

Her friend hoisted herself onto a bar stool. "Yeah, I can tell. So how did it go?"

"Like I expected. Sad. Nostalgic. Sad." Taylor held her feelings close, because if she didn't, she just might fall apart.

"Yeah, but it had to be done and now you don't have to think about it anymore."

Taylor opened the refrigerator. "Want some wine?"

"It's nine-thirty in the morning. But, what the hell, I'd love some."

"Never say die, huh." Taylor grinned. "I was just kidding."

"You asked and I answered. Actually, I can't stay. I've got to check on one of my rentals. I might have to evict someone."

"Bummer. What's the problem?" Taylor perched on the stool next to her friend.

"Dogs and cats. The lease says no dogs or cats. They have five." Suddenly Cara waved a hand in front of Taylor's face. "Are you okay?"

"Oh." Taylor focused back on her friend. "I'm sorry. Can you walk upstairs with me for a minute? When I came inside, it seemed like something was different."

"Sure." Cara glanced around. "Everything looks the same to me, but let's go."

They went upstairs, and Taylor looked first in the master bedroom and then the guest bedroom, which she also used as her office.

Cara shrugged. "Okay?"

"Yeah. Okay." She sighed. "I guess I'm just being weird."

"Paranoid weird. You better snap out of it. You've got a business to run."

"I know."

"And I really do have to leave, too. Are we done here?" Taylor laughed. "Yes. So go."

"I'll be in later," Cara said on her way down the stairs.

"Ciao." Cara worked at the boutique three times a week for a couple of hours each day. She didn't need to work there, but she'd begged Taylor to hire her because she liked the people contact.

Taylor watched Cara go downstairs and then heard the door close. She went into the bedroom to change clothes, her mind still churning about what to do. She hadn't finished at her mom's so she'd have to go back again. But at least she didn't have to worry about making a house payment, and maybe she should hold on to the property for a while.

Flipping on the light in the walk-in closet, she glanced around for what to wear, stopping cold when she got to the shelf where she kept her T-shirts. The shirts faced the wrong direction. She always placed them with the collar at the back. Had she done that without thinking? The line of purses on the shelf above looked okay. Except…the shoulder strap on one was hanging down. She always tucked the straps inside.

Icy fear crawled up her spine. She swung around, went to the phone to call 911, then stopped. What would she say? She went down the stairs, two at a time, then got the yellow pages from under a kitchen cabinet, all the while looking around to make sure she was alone.

Locksmith…there. She punched in the number. Maybe she was imagining things, but at least she'd feel better changing the locks. And maybe she'd get one of those security systems, while she was at it.

When she finished and was waiting for the locksmith to come, she hit the button to listen to the phone messages—one from Cara and one from her only full-time employee, Roxi, and—she caught her breath—Jack Parker…asking to talk to her again.

How had he gotten her phone number? The hair on the back of her neck rose.

She returned Roxi's call. "Hey, I just wanted you to know I'm going to be a little late."

"That's cool. Did you talk to the guy from Texas?"

Caught off guard, Taylor stuttered, "Wh-what do you know about him?"

"Just that he called and had information for you on your mother. I gave him your number because you said before if anyone called about your mom…"

"I know. It's okay." Taylor felt sick. Was he going to keep bothering her? "I wasn't here anyway, and he left a message. I'll be there in an hour."

"Gotcha," Roxi said, always her effervescent self.

Two hours and three new locks later, Taylor arrived at Taylor Made Boutique. As she entered through the back door, Roxi practically accosted her.

"So, how was it?"

They went into the small break room, which was used for just about everything, including storage. "Coffee smells good."

Roxi handed her a TMB mug, one of their promotional items. As Taylor poured the liquid—black as dirt and just as thick—into it, Roxi sidled over to her. "You didn't answer me. How was it?"

"You don't want to know."

"That bad?"

"Not in the way you think."

"So, enlighten me." Roxi, a transplant from New York, was the most impatient person Taylor knew. But she was a good friend. Besides Roxi and Cara, Taylor had one other employee who worked part-time and two hourly employ-

ees who did the hand crafting on the purses and other creations Taylor designed.

"To make a long story short, someone broke in to my
mother's place."

"Oh my gosh. I had that happen once. Did they empty
the place?"

"That's the weird thing. They didn't take anything. They
just messed things up. The police figure it was vandals.
Teenagers most likely."

"In Prescott? I thought that was a quiet little town."

"It is. But—"

Just then they heard the bell at the front door. A
customer. Roxi turned and went out.

Taylor stayed in back, getting together the makings for
a new design. Taylor Made Boutique carried more than
purses. Once the store had started doing well and was
getting a lot of word of mouth, she'd had several artisans
contact her about consignment work. At the time it had
seemed a good way to make extra money, but now the
merchandise was quickly outgrowing the shop.

Taylor had started her business on eBay as a lark, just
to see if she could sell the purses she made. Now two years
after narrowly escaping bankruptcy after Reed cooked the
books and stole the money in her accounts and disappeared, the company was doing so well she had to decide
whether to concentrate on her own creations and stay here,
or continue to include the consignment items and expand.

Taylor reached inside her purse for a pen and felt the
figurine her mother had made. She ran her thumb over the
smooth dress and the little pokey parts. It was a small piece
of her mother she could hold on to, keep with her. Taylor
Made Boutique had carried her mother's work, but now

there would be no more Dundee crafts, and all the people who waited for the next new piece of pottery or a new figurine to add to their collection would be disappointed.

"So, where were we?" Roxi said as she sashayed back into the room. Twenty-eight, with dark curly hair and a slender figure, Roxi had style and flair. She wasn't afraid to say what she thought and wasn't afraid to wear what she liked, even though her ensembles were outrageous at times.

Taylor liked everything about Roxi. And customers seemed to like her, too. Roxi's who-cares-what-anyone-thinks attitude made Taylor want to be more outrageous herself.

"We were talking about the break-in at my mother's, but there was no real destruction, just a mess."

Her friend gave Taylor a look that said she knew she wasn't getting everything. "O-kay," Roxi said. "And did you decide what to do with the place?"

Taylor pulled out her design tablet and the burgundy red, crinkly velvet fabric she'd bought earlier, and sat on her worktable. "I thought I had, but now I don't know. I figured I couldn't really afford two places, but my mother's place is free and clear."

"Awesome. No decision there for me. A home in the mountains to escape in the summer. Every time I go outside here, I feel like someone should baste me with butter and I'd be well done in no time."

Taylor snorted. "You'll get used to it. After a while you'll be wearing a jacket when it's seventy-five degrees."

"So I hear."

Taylor stared at the fabric. The design she'd thought of when she bought the material escaped her. The excitement she'd felt over it was gone, too.

She grabbed a plastic bin of estate sale jewelry from the shelf, then sorted out a couple of Art Deco pieces, two faux gemstone brooches and two necklaces, one pearl and the other a silver chain. Usually the design came to her immediately, but now all she felt was free-floating anxiety that she should do something—except she didn't know what.

"So, what happened at your place? Why change the locks? I thought you did that after…you know."

After Reed left. Yeah, she'd changed the locks then. She never wanted his ass in her place again. But this, on the heels of the break-in at her mother's, was too coincidental. Maybe Jack was right. Maybe, like Jack, someone thought her mother had the missing money or jewelry and, unable to find it at her house, thought Taylor had it. "I forgot one of them."

Roxi looked at her askance. "Why don't I believe you?"

Her friend knew her too well. "Okay, I'm paranoid. My mother's place was broken into, so I started thinking they might have found information about me and maybe…well, I just thought why not be safe rather than sorry?" And if she believed that, Taylor was a damned good liar.

"You need a massage or something. Better yet, you need to get laid."

Taylor laughed. "Maybe you're right." Lord, she felt that all she did lately was whine to Roxi about her life. First Reed. Her mother's accident. The funeral. Her mother's house. Keep it or sell it? Yada yada.

"If you're serious, I can help. I met this guy—"

The bell rang again and Roxi headed for the front, but as she was leaving, she waggled a finger. "You're not getting off the hook that easy. I'll be back."

Taylor smiled. What could she say to a woman who

never took no for an answer. But how could she tell her anything? The encounter with Jack Parker, what he'd told her…it was all so crazy, she wouldn't know where to start.

Well, yes, Roxi, something did happen in Prescott. A man stopped by and told me my mother may have had another child she never told me about, and, oh, yes, she might also be a criminal and may have been using a fake name for thirty years.

She was lost in thought when suddenly her friend was standing in front of her and waving a hand in Taylor's face.

"There's some guy here to see you." Roxi's dark eyes sparkled with suggestion. "A ver-ry hot guy."

Taylor came to attention. She moistened her lips. "Did he say what he wanted?"

"No, but if you don't want to talk to him, I'd be more than happy to find out." She grinned salaciously.

"Is he tall, dark hair, green eyes?"

Roxi nodded. "Yes. And you forgot extremely hot."

Taylor's hands suddenly felt clammy. Parker. Who else would show up unannounced? "Tell him I'm not here."

"He'll know I'm lying."

"No, he won't."

"Yes, I will," a male voice interjected.

Both women turned. Jack Parker stood in the doorway to the break room, Stetson on his head and all cowboyed up.

"Well, I'll leave you two to…whatever," Roxi said. "I have customers to take care of." She flashed a movie star smile and sidled past Jack.

Jack removed his hat as she went out.

Taylor grimaced. "I don't know why I'm not surprised to see you, but I'm not."

"That's not good. I hate being predictable."

His smile caught her off guard. "You're not. Believe me."

The way he was looking at her, as if he actually liked what he saw, made her self-conscious. She folded the fabric on the table, placed the silver necklace across the flap, then said matter-of-factly and without looking at him, "I hope this isn't about my mother, because I don't intend to talk to you about her."

"I understand. And no, it isn't."

Taylor sat there for a moment at a loss for words. He was dressed in a pale green western shirt with pearl snap buttons, black jeans and cowboy boots. He looked more like a wrangler or rodeo rider than a newspaper writer. The shirt made his eyes look even greener, especially against his tanned skin. "Well, if it's not that, what then?"

He reached into his pocket and withdrew the photo that he'd shown her the day before. "I thought you should have this."

She wanted to ignore it, but she couldn't. "Where did you get that photo and why do you think…what you do?"

He arched an eyebrow. "I thought you didn't want to talk about…any of it."

Her mouth twitched. She didn't. She looked down again, toying with the materials in front of her, conscious only of his penetrating gaze and the crisp scent of his aftershave. Or was it soap? Whatever it was made her think of ocean breezes.

"You've got quite an interesting shop here. All your designs?"

She looked up. He was studying three handbags hanging on the wall next to her. One made from the back pocket and leg on a pair of Levi's, trimmed in lace and old pearl buttons, another in black velvet with plastic Art Deco jewelry and satin cording and the last, a tan corduroy with a variety of gold studs that used to be earrings. "Yes."

He touched the soft corduroy with two fingers. "You're very creative."

"It runs in the family. And you didn't answer my question about the photo."

He looked at the picture still lying on the table. "I got it, or rather made a copy from a high school yearbook. And I think what I do because that's what the boy's death certificate tells me."

Taylor picked up the photo, studying it to see if she could see any resemblance to her or her mother. But just looking at it made her dizzy. "It's…sad to think of anyone dying so young." Someone who might have been her brother. She'd always wanted siblings. Someone to share with, someone to talk to, someone to love and who would love her…someone besides her mother.

"It is," he agreed.

"But…the photo doesn't mean anything to me," she said. "So whatever you were hoping to get from bringing it here isn't going to happen. You'd do better to go back to Houston and rely on other people to finish your story." *And leave me alone.*

"You are distrusting, aren't you?" he said. Then without missing a beat, he added, "So, I suppose it will ease your mind to know I am going back. Today, as a matter of fact."

"Good for you," she said, acting uninterested. But she couldn't help wondering whether he'd gotten more information and if so, would it be something she wanted to know?

He reached over and wrote a phone number on the notepad on her desk. "That's in case you lose my card and suddenly decide you want to share information."

She waited a moment, tore off the paper, crumpled it into a ball, then tossed it basketball style into the wastebasket in the corner. "That's in case you didn't understand what I'd said."

He looked a little surprised, then gave a hearty laugh, saluting on his way out the door. "It's been fun, Taylor."

Taylor was still trying to compose herself when Roxi flew in a second later, fanning herself with her hand. "Hot, hot, hot. How did you find him?"

Taylor sucked in some air. "I didn't find him, he found me."

Roxi's eyes lit up mischievously. "So, have you got a secret lover I don't know about?"

"Hardly."

"You two seemed awfully friendly to me."

"He came to see my mother when I was in Prescott."

"Well, he likes you. I know that."

"You were only in here a millisecond."

"Long enough to see lust in his eyes."

Taylor laughed. "Okay, now I know you're full of crap. Lust in his eyes. Yeesh, have you been watching *Boston Legal* or something?"

Roxi sobered. "It's a good show. But that's beside the point. I could tell because I could've been a piece of furniture. He didn't take his eyes off you the whole time."

"You think?" Taylor said, feigning disinterest, but in truth, the thought made her pulse quicken.

"Yeah, I think."

Taylor had to admit, she'd had a hard time taking her eyes off Jack from the moment they'd met. The idea that he might be attracted to her, too, sent a jolt of excitement to some strategically located body parts.

All her life, she'd been the geek. When it came to guys noticing her, Taylor had always been the one who could've been furniture. Having someone like Jack seem interested in her was an ego booster, if nothing else. Even if she couldn't do anything about it.

But knowing why he'd come to see her mother squelched any notion of lust or romance...or anything remotely related. How could she be attracted to someone who thought her mother guilty of a crime? And she knew he thought that, even if he didn't come right out and say so. "Well, don't think. I'm not interested."

"You looked interested when he came in."

"Not in that way."

"So then tell me what's going on."

Roxi and Cara were her best friends and she was going to tell both of them sooner or later, so why not now. "Okay, but this is between you and me. Got it?"

"Okay. Tic a lock." Roxi made a motion to zip her lips.

"You zipped, not locked," Taylor accused her.

"Yeah, yeah. Just tell me, will you?"

Taylor began slowly, then launched into it, telling Roxi everything. "And before you ask again, yes, I was attracted to Jack, but that ended as soon as he started talking about my mother." Besides, Taylor knew her limitations. When it came to men, she was spectacularly wrong every time.

She'd trusted Reed and he'd betrayed her. It wasn't just that he'd found someone else—he'd also taken her money and nearly ruined her business. The fact that she'd trusted him again, given him another chance, was pure stupidity on her part. But what else was new? How many times had she been taken in by other guys? Three? Four?

The worst part was that Reed wasn't just a failed relationship. He'd played her. She should have known when she'd had to bail him out of financial trouble time after time. Her friends told her to be cautious, and she tried to be sometimes.

But he'd always had reasonable explanations. She'd been blinded to the truth because she'd loved him. Believed in him—and his dreams. Their dreams. She'd been blinded to the truth because she'd been so damned needy.

When she'd finally pulled herself together, she'd vowed to never let her emotions rule her life again. "Now that you know what's going on, you know why I can't even think of Jack like that."

Roxi grinned like a fat cat. "But you're already thinking like that."

Taylor frowned, then went back to work on her project. "What I think doesn't matter. It's what I do that counts."

"So, okay. Don't get emotionally involved. Just take things as they come. Like a guy."

"You want me to be like a guy?"

"Just have fun. Don't make it about anything more."

"Believe me, I wish I could do that. But I can't. I'm not like you."

Roxi wrinkled her nose.

Oh, man, open mouth insert foot. "I—I meant that in a good way," Taylor said. "You have the ability to be objective about sex and relationships. I don't." Taylor sighed. "I can't be objective because I want more—I want different things than you do. I want love and marriage. I want a family and the whole ball of everything."

Roxi rubbed the fabric on the table between her thumb and forefinger. "Nothing wrong with that," she said, her voice quiet. "I might want that, too." She looked down. "Just not now."

For one brief moment, Taylor sensed a vulnerability in her friend that she hadn't seen before. "Hey, that's cool. Everything in its own time."

"Nothing wrong with either of our choices," Roxi capitulated.

Taylor wasn't sure Roxi actually believed that, and she knew *she* didn't. "No, that's where you're wrong. I've made horrible mistakes when it comes to men. Besides, *any* choice right now is the wrong one."

Roxi opened her mouth to speak, but Taylor held up a hand. "Don't say another word."

CHAPTER FIVE

TAYLOR FLOPPED BACK on the bed and watched the ceiling fan circle overhead, the swish of air through the fan's blades and the click of the chains keeping pace with the thoughts going around and around in her head.

What she'd told Roxi earlier was true and she could beat herself up again and again for being so stupid to waste her time with Reed. Now it looked as if she'd never have the family she longed for. She'd thought about adopting, but having grown up with only her mother for support, Taylor knew how hard raising a child alone would be. Yet if the boutique continued to prosper, finances shouldn't be a problem. A child of hers would never have to wear secondhand clothes like Taylor had growing up.

A child of hers would never have to use free lunch tickets either. She'd been embarrassed using them and had always waited until the last kid had gone through the line before she got her meal. She'd mistakenly thought if the other kids didn't see her using the tickets, no one would know. But everyone did.

More importantly, a child of hers wouldn't wonder every day when she came home from school whether they might be moving again. Taylor had hated the moving and always being the new kid at school, but she'd never complained because her mother explained they had to go where she could sell her art. If she didn't, they'd have no money at all. Mostly, Taylor didn't complain, because she'd loved her mother and knew she was doing the best she could.

If she were to adopt as a single parent, she'd be doing the exact same thing. A child deserved two parents if at all possible.

And now, since Jack had arrived with his story of crime and secret identities, she had to wonder if they'd moved because of her mother's work or because she was running away. And why, after years of moving around, had her mother finally settled in Prescott…and where had she gotten the money to buy the house?

Taylor closed her eyes. Did any of that matter? What her mother had or hadn't done thirty years ago wouldn't affect anything now, would it? She flicked her hair back over her shoulder. If by some trick of fate it turned out her mother was involved, could it affect Taylor's business? Would she have to sell her mother's place to pay back the money? Was there a statute of limitations on stolen money?

Her head began to hurt. She had to stop thinking this way. Her mother was not a criminal. She got up, went into the den and turned on her computer.

She waited for the PC to boot, then pressed the Internet icon, keyed in Google and did a search for Matthew Cooper. Nothing. And if Matthew was her mother's son, who was the father? Did he have the same father as Taylor?

Staring at the search field, she placed her hands over the keyboard and, as if her fingers had a mind of their own, she typed in *H-a-w-t-h-o-r-n-e*.

Several Web sites popped up, many of them archived newspaper articles. One headline stopped her cold. Suspect Apprehended in Hawthorne Death.

Jack had said someone had been arrested. Sitting forward, she quickly scrolled through the article. Hawthorne Gardener Arrested. Henry Juarez at the house the night of Sunny Hawthorne's death... No alibi. She clicked on another headline that announced an affair between the victim's husband and the missing Margot Cooper, and another that stated, Juarez to Stand Trial.

Several Web sites and articles later, she read, Guilty Verdict in Hawthorne Death. Henry Juarez Gets Life. When she finished reading, her head throbbed.

Why was Parker so focused on finding out about Margot Cooper when this man had already been found guilty? He'd mentioned the money, but something didn't ring true. Two hours of research later, she felt like throwing something at the damned computer. But the PC wasn't the root of her problems. Jack Parker was.

He had an agenda and somehow it involved her mother. Her mother, and the money or the jewels.

She barely knew the man. What did she care? She shouldn't give a flying fig what Jack Parker's agenda was or wasn't.

Yet, as she closed her eyes, she knew she did.

When she opened them again, she saw that a stupid ad had popped up on the screen, its bright lights flashing, advertising new ways to enhance a body part she didn't even have. She deleted it, then clicked on another Web site to read more about the Hawthorne case. Enough with the questions. She needed answers. What was Parker's real purpose in tracking her mother down?

The money and the jewels had never been found...and

Margot Cooper, a potential accomplice, had disappeared. She knew that already. What she didn't know was if Jack wanted to find the stolen property so he could score a big story—or if he had other motives?

Which left her with only one choice.

HENRY JUAREZ HELD on to the black plastic bag with all his worldly possessions as he stood outside the Huntsville Prison doors. He glanced to the right and to the left, looking for the car that was supposed to pick him up. But as far as he was concerned, he could stand there all day just breathing in the fresh Texas air.

Thirty years. The world was a different place now. He'd read about it in the newspapers, seen it on television, but he couldn't really imagine all the changes.

Just then, down the street, he saw a dark car moving slowly toward him. It pulled up across from Henry, then stopped. The door opened. His old friend, Manny Ortega, sat in the driver's seat.

Manny was the only person to keep in touch over the years, and at best it had been sporadic. Manny had immigration troubles, and he'd been in prison himself. Not to mention he had health problems. But he was here today, and Henry was grateful.

Manny, hair graying, got out and with a limp in his walk, crossed the street. When he reached Henry, the two just stood there looking at each other. Finally Manny broke into a big toothy grin and grabbed him in a bear hug.

"You got fat," Henry said, smiling and holding on tightly. Thirty years without being touched—except on rare violent occasions.

"And you look like you've been working out in a gym."

"Not much else to do," he said.

The years apart made conversation difficult and stilted. They were quiet as they got into the car. After a few blocks, Manny said, "My brother has a room you can use until you get on your feet. It's near Denver Harbor Barrio."

Henry nodded. He was grateful to have any place to stay. He had no money and no job.

"And I got this for you." He handed Henry a manila envelope. "It's information on your son."

Henry didn't open it. "There's no point."

"I thought he came to see you?"

"It wasn't a very good meeting." Henry looked out the window but couldn't see much because his vision blurred. He'd signed the adoption papers thirty years ago and never expected to see his son again.

"Why did he come then?"

Henry shrugged. "I guess he wanted to see what a murderer looks like."

"You told him the truth, didn't you?"

"All convicts say they're innocent, my friend. My son is a smart man. He wouldn't believe anything else."

"He'll come around. Just give him time. You'll see."

Henry knew different. His son had been curious to know where he'd come from, but he'd regretted finding out. Henry wanted more than anything to have a relationship with his son, but he knew it was futile.

His heart ached for everything he'd lost, but he'd had a long time to come to grips with the injustice. It was enough to know his son had had a good life, that he'd been loved as he was growing up. He just hoped that one day Jack would find a woman as good as his mother had been, and that he'd have a family of his own. His son's happiness was all he'd ever wanted. He wasn't going to ruin things for him.

Henry sat up straighter in his seat. "Nobody in my family ever got through high school. But my son went to college and now he has an important job at the biggest newspaper in Texas. I might not have been there when he was growing up, but he's a man any father would be proud of."

"MOM SAYS you can drive me to school on your way to work, Uncle Jack."

Ryan looked a lot like his mom, with his blond hair and upturned nose and freckles, Jack thought, as Lana appeared in the kitchen doorway behind her son.

"Can you please take him?" Lana asked.

She looked like a teenager in her low-cut shorts and skimpy top. Too skimpy, he thought.

"Sure. No problem."

"Go get ready then," she told Ryan. "And brush your teeth." Lana picked up the coffeepot and poured Jack another cup. "Hey, what's up with the dress clothes? Tie and everything."

"I have a couple of meetings." He'd worn the same navy dress pants, light blue shirt and red tie when he'd gone to see Juarez last week. Why, he didn't know. It wasn't as if he'd wanted to impress anyone.

"Nice. Blue is definitely your color." She leaned against he counter. "So, Juarez got out early. Anything else?"

Jack shook his head. "That's all I know."

"Are you going to see him again? Do you even know where he went?"

"I can find out, but I honestly don't know if I should. I keep finding out things that make me believe he's telling the truth. And I want to believe him, but then something else comes up that makes me think otherwise. If I could just get some kind of proof...."

"I thought all you wanted was to know more about him."

Jack sat at the table. "That's how it started. But I keep seeing the flaws in the case. And I can see where other people might have had both motive and opportunity." He stopped when he saw the look on his sister's face. "Well, I need to keep looking into it. And no, I won't do anything that's going to hurt Mom and Dad."

"But what if he looks you up? What if he tells everyone you're his son?"

"I don't think he'd want to do that."

"You don't know that. You don't even know him."

"I got a feeling when I was talking to him."

"A feeling." Lana rolled her eyes. "What if he knows where the money is and he finds out you're doing all this so-called investigating?"

Jack didn't want to think about that. He'd started on a mission to learn more about his biological father, and somehow it had become a quest to find out if the man was guilty or innocent. "I think someone else is involved. Someone who believes Margaret Dundee knew where the money is."

"Did you get some new information?" Lana asked.

"No, but when the Dundee house was broken into, nothing was stolen. Nothing destroyed."

"What do you think they were looking for?"

Feeling the humidity in the air, Jack pulled at his tie to loosen it. "That's what I need to find out. Maybe someone thinks the woman was Juarez's accomplice and agreed to put the jewels or some of the money away for Juarez. Or maybe someone other than Juarez committed the crime and thinks Dundee might have incriminating evidence stashed at her house that will surface now that she's dead."

"Or maybe Juarez was going to get his share from Dundee when he got out, but since she died, he sent someone else to do the job beforehand?"

"Yeah. I thought about that, too." He sighed. "Or maybe the break-in really was just a random act."

"What about the daughter?"

"She's back at her job in Scottsdale."

"She's not in any danger, is she?"

"I doubt it. I hope not." The idea made Jack uncomfortable. He should have thought of that. "I'm going back to Arizona next week anyway. I'll see her again."

Lana raised an eyebrow.

"What?"

"Why do you need to see her again?"

He shifted in his seat. He hated when she nailed him. "Because I think she has information that could be helpful."

A big smile said Lana thought he was full of manure.

"I'm ready, Uncle Jack."

"Great." Jack gave Lana the evil eye, then he bent down. "Climb on, tiger."

Ryan hopped onto Jack's back, his hands curled into little tiger claws as he said, "Grrr."

LATER, GRABBING A QUICK SANDWICH at his desk after a meeting ran late, Jack went through his notes about the Hawthorne case. Only it didn't take the notes to make him think about Taylor. He seemed to be doing that a lot—and in ways that he shouldn't. He was actually looking forward to going back to Arizona and seeing her again.

But if the results of his investigation proved his theory correct, she probably wouldn't even talk to him.

He also had to make a decision on whether to talk to Juarez or not. He hated knowing that Juarez had signed him away as if he was a piece of property. But he needed to know more about the man. He needed to know what he was like. Had he loved Jack? Had he loved Jack's mother? What was she like? All he knew was that she'd died not long after Juarez had been convicted. His biological father was the only person who could tell him those things.

Two more appointments and an espresso later, somewhere around three in the afternoon, Jack was back at his desk when the phone rang. He saw by the number it was his sister again.

"Lana, what's up?" he asked as he read the news release in front of him.

"She called here. She wanted to talk to you about Henry Juarez."

"She? Who are you talking about?"

"The daughter. Taylor Dundee."

Jack bolted upright. "She called your house?"

"That's what I said. She asked for you, so I told her if she left her name and number, I'd give you the message."

"And?"

"She gave me her phone number."

Jack rubbed his chin. She couldn't possibly know Juarez was his father. But how had she gotten Lana's number?

"What do you want to do?"

"I don't know. I don't want her talking to anyone." The one time Jack had seen Juarez, he'd asked the man if he was really innocent, why he wasn't trying to find out who really did it. Jack had offered to help, but Juarez had become angry, and said he'd served the time so it didn't matter. He was going to be a free man and that was all he wanted.

Jack wasn't going to make an issue of it. He didn't want to drag his parents or Lana and Ryan into something they had no part of. But he couldn't let it go, either.

"There's been a lot of publicity about his release. She might have heard something."

"In Arizona?"

"Maybe. The television stations are asking what happened to the stolen property. They'll probably be hounding Juarez, and it'll be easy for her to find him."

"So," his sister said. "I still don't know what the big deal is if she does talk to him."

"I ha—" Jack noticed, Wes, his boss, standing outside his cubicle and lowered his voice. "I have my reasons. Just don't give her any information. Okay?"

"Sure. But you're definitely going to have to explain later."

They said goodbye and Jack hung up. He was glad he'd already made arrangements to fly back to Arizona on the weekend.

"Jack." Wesley stopped at the desk next to his and began opening and closing the drawers.

"Yeah, what's up?"

"Do you know where Barney keeps his cigarettes?"

"Usually with him. Why? I thought you quit."

"I'm reconsidering." His boss's expression told Jack the man was desperate.

"Yeah, and you told me to remind you that you don't need another heart attack." In the five years they'd worked together, Jack and Wesley Patchett had developed an easy rapport, a friendship of sorts. But they weren't so close that

Jack could disclose that he'd been using a newspaper story as a cover to get information. That could get him a reprimand, if not fired.

"Bad idea. Eat an apple instead."

Wes ran a hand through his hair. "Right." He started to go then, as if remembering something, said, "Jack, later, if you get a minute, come to my office." Acting like a kid who hadn't gotten his way, Wesley stomped back to his office at the back corner of the room.

The newspaper offices were like every other newsroom Jack had ever seen. Lots of desks, some butted against others, computers, paper everywhere and phones ringing off their hooks. And the incessant buzz of voices talking to whoever was on the other end. There was always something happening, some major story unfolding. Not a day went by without a drama. And every day he went to work, Jack felt buoyed with anticipation.

"Sure. I won't be too long." And like every other newspaper in town, the *Chronicle* had made a big deal about Juarez's release. There were critics on both sides, but most were saying a murderer shouldn't be out walking the streets. And every time he read one of the headlines, he saw the look in Juarez's eyes when the man said whether he was innocent or not didn't matter. If he was, Jack would be the first to write the story.

Until then, he saw no reason to tell anyone anything. Especially since he knew there were those who would hold it against him. Like Levon Maddox, Wes's favorite reporter, who just happened to be a congressman's son. Levon wanted Jack's editor job and had let him know it the day he'd arrived.

Jack had two phone calls and, after finishing the most

pressing work, he headed for his boss's office. Wes may have wanted to talk to Jack, but Jack wanted to put in for some vacation time. As he passed Melanie, one of the new reporters, she stepped in front of him and ran a finger across his chest. "Sherry told me to tell you you've got company downstairs." She smiled suggestively.

Melanie wasn't his type. Pretty, but too young. Preoccupied with things like rock concerts and rap singers.

"Company?"

"Some woman's looking for you. Sherry said she's got an ax to grind. What happened? You get someone pregnant?"

He laughed, even though he didn't find Mel's humor funny. "I'm smarter than that." And he didn't have time for some disgruntled reader who didn't like one of the articles that had run recently. Usually they called or sent an e-mail. They didn't come directly to the office.

"That's what all the guys think."

Jack's phone rang and he took the opportunity to escape, going back to his desk and grabbing the receiver. "Hey, Sherry. What's up?"

"There's a woman here to see you, and I think she's unhappy."

"Tell her I'm in a meeting."

He heard a muffled sound then Sherry relaying the message. After a long pause, Sherry whispered, "She says fine, she'll talk to your boss."

Just what he needed. He glanced at Wes and made a motion to the phone, indicating he'd be tied up. Wes nodded. "Okay, I'll come down. What's her name?"

"She said her name is Taylor Dundee."

CHAPTER SIX

WHAT THE HELL was she doing here! Adrenaline shot through Jack's veins at the thought that she might have come upstairs and said *he* was writing a story on Juarez. "Keep her downstairs until I get there."

"Okay, if I can. She's not very happy."

"Tie her up if you have to. I'll be right there."

Jack rushed out and decided the elevator would take too long. He shouldered open the fire exit door and hit the stairs two at a time going down.

He did a visual check as he went into the lobby and over to the front desk. "Where is she?" he asked Sherry. "She didn't go upstairs, did she?"

The receptionist gave him a skeptical look. "Man, are you uptight. Are you all right?"

"I'm fine, considering I've just run down seven flights of stairs. Where did she go?"

Sherry tipped her head to the right. "Over there."

Taylor, wearing tan pants and a white sleeveless shirt, was standing, arms crossed over her chest, next to the alphabetical listing on the wall by the elevator doors. Apparently he'd caught her in the nick of time. His heart still pumping, he went over, sidled up next to her and said softly from behind, "Can I help you find something, miss?"

She jumped a foot, then swung around. She looked surprised at first, then narrowed her eyes. "Yes, you can. You can tell me why you lied to me."

His nerves were on edge and he didn't have a clue what she was talking about. He glanced at Sherry, who seemed hypnotized by the encounter. He turned sideways so Taylor would have to turn with him and Sherry couldn't see their faces. "I'm confused," he said, palms up. "Lie to you?"

Fire erupted in Taylor's blue eyes. He took her arm to guide her toward the door. "Let's go somewhere private. Somewhere not so public.

She shrugged him off. "I'm fine right here."

He forced a smile. "Well, let's at least sit down," he said, gesturing to the black leather couch half-hidden by the potted palm in the corner. He walked over and she followed, not saying a word until they sat.

"Why didn't you tell me the truth?

"You came to Houston to ask me that? You could have called me," he said to delay while he figured out what she meant. He felt a trickle of sweat run down his side.

"It's easier to tell lies when you don't have to look someone in the eye. But you did pretty well at that, anyway."

He held up a hand. "What exactly are we talking about here?

She pointed to the sign. "It says editor. You told me you're a reporter writing a story. You lied. You tried to get information from me under false pretenses."

Jack chewed his bottom lip. Yes, he'd made up the story so he could get information. It had been a spur-of-the-moment decision and at that very moment, he realized why. He'd left Juarez out of it because he wanted to protect his parents, but mostly it was because he didn't want the

world to know he was the son of a murderer. That's why
he'd lied. And nothing had changed. The only reason Lana
knew about his biological father was because she'd been
there for him after he'd found out. He'd felt like an outsider
all his life, and now that he'd finally achieved the respect
he'd strived for, he wasn't going to give it up.

"I didn't think my job title was important."

"You lied."

Her anger didn't bother him as much as the disappointment he saw in her eyes.

"Are you writing a story or not?"

"No. I'm looking into whether there's a story there to
write."

"You came all the way to Arizona for that."

She didn't believe him and he couldn't blame her. "It's
what I do. I'm sorry." He reached for her hand. "It was a
stupid thing to do."

She pulled her hand away.

O-kay. He stood up and stuffed his hands into his
pockets. There had to be more. "You didn't come to Texas
just for that, did you?"

She looked up at him. "No. I came because I'm going
to do my own investigating."

He nearly choked. "You're…not serious."

She nodded. "I'm totally serious."

Leaning forward, she looked as if she might get up. "I
need answers, Jack. And I intend to get them. That's why
I'm here."

He had to admire her determination. "I wonder," he
said. "Would you be here right now if you didn't think there
was something to it?"

She glanced away. "I think there's some truth somewhere. But I don't believe it's anything like the situation you've described."

"But…you can't just come here and stir things up."

Taylor shrugged, then her gaze bored into him. "What *are* you doing? If a man went to jail for this crime, why are you pursuing it? Why is this story so important to you?"

He went to the window, looked out, then came back and stopped in front of her. "I'm doing it because the money was never found, which means someone else—other than Henry Juarez—was involved and got off scot-free. I'm doing it because it's my job to bring the truth to light. But if too many people are asking questions, no one is going to want to give me any answers and justice can't be served."

He sat beside her again and, keeping his voice low, said, "Look, we both want answers. Maybe we have different reasons for wanting them, but we both have the same goal. It would make sense for us to work together."

Taylor drew back. *Work together?* He had to be joking. "How do I know you won't lie to me again? That you wouldn't get information and keep it to yourself?"

He frowned. "Are you that distrustful? Someone must have really done a number on you to make you so—"

She jumped up, blood pounding through her veins. "The reason I'm distrustful, Mr. Parker—"

"It's Jack."

"The reason I don't trust you, *Jack*, is because you've given me reason not to. Pure and simple."

He looked at his feet and rubbed the inside of his hand with his thumb. "You're right. Absolutely right. And for that, I'm truly sorry."

His apology sounded sincere and she instantly regretted the outburst. She was a calm person, reasonable and in control. Usually. But when she was around him, all her emotions seemed to be on the outside of her skin. "This is important to me, Jack. Personally. I have to have answers. Your interest is different. You can get your story or not and it really won't matter that much."

"So work with me, Taylor. Not against me. That will serve no good purpose." He placed a hand on hers. "Think about it and let me know. I promise you I'm not the kind of person you think I am."

Before she had a chance to respond, he added, "Working together, we can get twice as much done in a shorter period of time. We can share information."

He was smooth. She didn't believe he'd be so eager to share as he sounded. But he had a point. Time was important. She couldn't stay in Houston indefinitely. Roxi was delighted to watch the store and Cara was going to work with her. Taylor Made Boutique was in good hands, but still, the sooner she returned to Phoenix, the better.

He handed her his card. "I think you might have lost my number." He smiled then, a warm, generous smile. "I think we'd make a great team. For a lot of reasons."

It was an obvious come-on, but her heart thudded anyway. She could still feel the warmth of his hand on hers. Only it wasn't warm enough to make her turn into an idiot. A gullible idiot. She was about to give a curt response, but instead, she snatched the card, stood and walked out the door.

Jack found it hard getting through the rest of the day. He'd called Lana a dozen times to make sure Taylor hadn't contacted her again. Later that night, he watched the sunset from his loft condo in Midtown, a trendy area in the heart of Houston, and wondered if Taylor was going to call or not.

He walked into the kitchen for a beer. It had never occurred to him that she'd fly to Houston to do her own investigating. He still couldn't believe it. If she didn't call, he had to have a plan to prevent her from contacting his father…or his boss. He paced the loft like a hungry animal. If she wanted to contact Juarez, she'd probably find a way to do it. Then Juarez would know Jack was investigating. If Juarez *was* somehow involved with the break-in, it could jeopardize Jack's ability to uncover the truth. And if the press discovered Taylor was Margot Cooper's daughter, they'd have a field day with it…and maybe uncover his relationship to Juarez. Jack realized then how much he wanted Juarez to be innocent. He wanted to be able to talk to him, ask him questions, find out what kind of man his father really was. Without answers, he couldn't do that.

As he popped the tab on his Amstel Light, the phone rang. Taylor, he hoped. He reached for his cell before realizing it was the wall phone ringing. He walked over and picked up the receiver. "Jack here."

"Hey, buddy."

"Hey, Cal."

"Well, I know I'm not as exciting as one of your female friends, but you could be a little happy to hear from me."

Jack grinned. "What's going on?" Jack had been working at the *Sun Times* in Chicago and writing a feature story on rodeos when he met bronc-buster Caleb Carson. With Jack's background growing up on a ranch and his own short-lived attempt at bronc riding as a teen, they'd hit it off immediately. After Jack took the job in Houston, he'd bumped into Cal again and they'd been good friends ever since.

"I'm on my way home from Oklahoma. How's Lana and Ryan?"

"They're both fine. You should be asking her though."

"I'm asking you because all of a sudden she won't talk to me. Did something happen while I was gone?"

"Not that I know of." Except Jack did know. His sister was terrified of getting hurt again. And sooner or later in every relationship, she pulled away. Cal's reputation with women on the rodeo circuit didn't help. After dating for two months, Lana had said getting any more involved was just asking for heartbreak down the road.

Jack understood only too well. In that instance, he and his sister had much in common. "She's got a lot to do."

"I think it's more than that."

"She needs time, that's all."

"Time for what?"

"Look, Cal. I told you when you decided to date Lana that I was out of it. I can't be anyone's go-between." He sighed. "I've got enough on my mind as it is."

"Yeah? You want to catch up at Jericho's? I'm on my way there now."

Jack held up the beer in his hand. "No, I've got things to do. But thanks."

"You still on for the party on Saturday?"

The "party" was an annual benefit both men participated in every year. The crowd was always rowdy, the food and drinks great, and the female riders were usually outstanding. "Wouldn't miss it."

"Awesome."

After saying goodbye, Jack went into the bedroom, took out the briefcase w.... ..is file on Margot Cooper, aka Margaret Dundee, and her daughter, Taylor. He set his laptop on the desk and pulled up the spreadsheet detailing events surrounding the murder, from the date Cooper began working at the Hawthornes' to the present.

He typed in the date of Dundee's death, her funeral and the people who'd attended the service. Then he added the date Dundee had purchased her home in Prescott and apparently paid cash for it, since there was no mortgage holder listed, information he'd gleaned from the town's public records. He added a side question: with stolen money? Then he made a note to contact the waitress when he was in Arizona again. The one whose daughter knew Taylor.

As he entered his notes, he remembered the look on Taylor's face when she'd called him a liar. Maybe Lana was right. Maybe he *was* too involved in his job. Too busy being objective to see the real world. Real people.

He'd rather she'd looked at him the way she had in the park in Prescott. She'd given him the once-over, then got all flustered when she realized he'd been watching her.

He liked her. And seeing her today made him like her even more. She had guts. And the courage of her convictions. The fact that she was wrong didn't matter.

AFTER ARRIVING at the Marx Hotel where she'd earlier reserved a room, Taylor paid the cab driver, and on her way inside, made a mental note to rent a car. The past two nights at home, she'd been unable to sleep, tossing and turning, questions spinning in her head. What was the truth and what wasn't? Finally, this morning when she got up, she knew she had to come to Houston for the answers. Whatever they might be.

If her mother had worked for the Hawthornes, then Taylor needed to talk to Mr. Hawthorne. If the man guilty of the murder had worked for the Hawthornes, too, then she needed to talk to him.

She walked to her room, went inside and got a bottle of water out of the mini-fridge before she dropped into the nearest chair and kicked off her sandals. Damn, it was hot in Houston. She rolled the bottle against her neck. Typical hotel decor: a bed, TV, desk and chair, an easy chair and two nondescript lamps. The nicest feature was the big window with a view of downtown Houston, a larger city than she'd imagined.

She'd been shocked to discover in a newspaper article that Juarez had been released. Finding him would be difficult. She'd already called all the Juarez names in the phone book and asked for Henry…to no avail. A stab in the dark. Jack, she realized, might have that information. So she'd called all the Parkers in the book, too, and got his siser. Pure luck on her part.

Confronting Jack at the newspaper had been a real spur-of-the-moment decision after she'd arrived. Remembering the look on his face, Taylor grinned. He hadn't been merely surprised to see her, he'd been shocked. Horrified even.

Given her anger when she'd confronted him, she'd been surprised when he suggested working together. But the more she thought about it, the more it made sense. She had nothing except some old newspapers and the information she'd gleaned online. But she had to wonder what was in it for him.

Did he think she knew more than she'd told him? Did he think she knew there was a stash of unspent money and jewels somewhere? He'd said someone else was looking for something at her mother's. Maybe he thought whoever that was had been involved in the theft, too.

He'd also said he didn't want her to get hurt. But every accusation he made against her mother hurt. It hurt a lot. Realistically, everything she was doing had the potential for hurt—and disappointment. Yet she felt compelled to know whether her mother had lied to her. If her mother had lived a double life.

She needed to know if her whole life had been a lie.

So…she'd work with Jack. For now.

JACK FINISHED brushing his teeth, then glanced at his watch. It was close to seven and he was usually at work by this time. Last night he'd spent too much time calling hotels, trying to find out where Taylor was registered, only to come up empty.

He'd lain awake the whole damned night waiting for her call, but it hadn't come. He'd obviously read her wrong.

He went to the closet and took out a pair of black dress pants, a white polo shirt and his signature boots. His uniform, except the shirts changed color. He kept a sport jacket at the office in case he needed it for a meeting or a business lunch.

He was just shoving a foot into the leg of his pants when his cell rang. Probably the secretary reminding him of his first meeting. He picked up while still working on the pant leg. "Yeah. What is it, Sherry?"

"Is this Jack Parker?"

The sultry voice was unmistakable. His heart raced. "It is. Good morning."

"I've been thinking about your suggestion, and I believe it would be more efficient to work together."

Which meant he needed a plan of action. "Terrific," he said. "If you give me your number, I'll give you a call later today."

She cleared her throat. "I'd like to get started now."

"Okay. I have an early meeting, but when I'm finished I'll call you."

"I don't think you understand."

Holding the phone between his ear and shoulder, he zipped up and then went to the closet for a belt. "Yes, I do. You want to get started and I do, too, Taylor. But I have a couple of things to take care of first. I have a job."

"Fine. When can I come by your office?"

"No," he said quickly. "I won't be there. How about we meet somewhere around ten or ten-thirty? Where are you staying? I can come there and save you a trip."

"I'm at the Marx. Not far from your office."

Jack's muscles tensed. Too close for comfort. "I'll call from the lobby when I arrive."

"Okay. You said you'd share information."

Information. Yeah, he'd said that, hadn't he? "I did."

"So, you'll bring it with you?"

"Right."

"Fine. See you then."

After he hung up, Jack just stood there, bewildered. He had the strangest feeling that instead of getting what he'd wanted, it was the other way around.

CHAPTER SEVEN

SANDWICHED IN THE MIDDLE of a half-dozen overly fragrant women at the concierge desk, Jack wondered briefly if someone from the *Chronicle* was covering the lingerie convention for the local section of the newspaper.

Unable to breathe, he stepped to the end of the desk, where fewer women were gathered. When it was his turn, he asked the clerk to let Taylor know he was there. "Or you can give me her room number and I'll call myself." He'd finished his meeting early and hoped he'd cut her off at the pass if she had any ideas of talking to people without him. People like his dad.

"We don't give out room numbers. I'm sorry."

Jack scanned the lobby for a quiet spot to wait. "Fine, just let her know I'm waiting."

"Not necessary, Mr. Parker," the clerk said.

Jack looked at the man, dressed in his navy and gold uniform with gold buttons on the shoulders.

"She left a note." He handed Jack a folded piece of paper.

Dammit. If she was canceling, or had gone out on her own... He stopped mid-thought when he saw she'd jotted down the room number below an invitation to come up.

"Thanks," Jack told the clerk. He'd expected she'd meet him in the café, or in the bar, somewhere public.

But, what the hey. He'd go to a pretty woman's hotel room anytime.

Inside the elevator, he found himself trapped with more perfumed women. He almost felt compelled to let them know natural was better, but the car made a rocket ascent and the doors swooshed open on the tenth floor. He couldn't get off fast enough.

Holding on to his briefcase, which contained most of the information he'd gathered on the case, with the exception of a few items that might give away his own past, he found Taylor's room and knocked.

First he heard the chain, and then the door opened. She stood there in short white shorts and a skimpy top with spaghetti straps. The baby-blue shirt matched her eyes. "I finished early," he said.

She reached up to her unruly hair, then stopped. "I was expecting you later. I thought it was room service bringing the coffee."

He smiled. "Good. I can use another jolt of caffeine." He stood in the doorway waiting for her to let him in. When she didn't, he motioned. "Can I come in?"

"Oh, sorry." She stepped back. "Of course."

Inside, behind her, Jack saw movement, then a man appeared. *Not alone.* "Ah, I see you have company. Do you want me to come back later?" His gut tightened.

"Are you okay, Taylor?" the man asked.

She turned. "I'm fine, Alex. This is Jack Parker, the *reporter* I told you about."

The man's brows formed a V, as if he were trying to remember something. Taylor's visitor was much younger. Younger than Jack's thirty-five years anyway. "It's no problem for me to come back later," Jack said, even though he didn't want to. He had a sudden urge to punch the guy. Why, he didn't know.

"No, stay. Alex was just leaving."

With that, the younger man picked up a briefcase from the table in the entry and gave Taylor a kiss on the cheek. "I'll call you later." He nodded at Jack. "Nice meeting you."

Just like that, the guy was gone.

Jack's skin prickled. He felt antsy and uncomfortable, as if he'd interrupted some kind of lovers' rendezvous. "For someone who doesn't know anyone in Houston, you make friends fast."

"I try."

No explanation. Fine with him.

"Would you like something other than coffee to drink? There's a minibar that has soda and things."

He shoved his hands in his front pockets. "No thanks. I'll wait for the coffee."

There was a knock at the door. "And that would be it." She smiled, all happy and perky and he didn't know what was ticking him off so much.

The bellman carried in a tray with coffee, a covered platter and a bowl of fruit. Taylor signed the bill, gave the man a tip, then lifted the cover to reveal Danish rolls and bagels, jams and jellies.

She poured two cups of coffee. "Cream?"

He shook his head as he sat on the couch. "No, just black."

When she finished the coffee ritual, she sat in a chair opposite him and took a sip from her cup, savoring the coffee as if it was a steak dinner.

"That tastes so good," she said. "I went out jogging and didn't have time for anything beforehand."

She could have fooled him. No one had a right to be so

perky in the morning. Especially without caffeine. "I was wondering what wound you up. I had a breakfast meeting and I still feel like a slug."

"Maybe you need exercise," she said, studying him.

"I get plenty of exercise," he countered. "I'm a gym person. One hour a day."

"But not in the morning."

"Nope. I'm at work in the morning. Early."

She picked up a Danish and bit off a piece. When she finished chewing, she licked the tip of her index finger, then used the napkin to blot around her lips. "Right. I didn't think about the newspaper thing," she said, then raised her cup. "So, what did you bring for me?"

After taking a sip, she tossed her napkin on the table. "Okay. So, now what? What's the plan?"

He didn't realize he was staring, until she cleared her throat and said, "I want to start as soon as possible."

"Oh…sure. Basically, I thought we'd do what I'd intended to do before." Before she'd showed up unannounced and unwanted. Only he wasn't so sure about the unwanted part anymore. Right now he seemed to want her there very much. Or at least he wanted *her*.

"And what was that?"

"Pool our knowledge and interview people."

"Good." She got up and went to a table by the window, where she opened a briefcase and sifted through the papers. "If we're working together, we can combine lists and divvy up the names."

As he watched her standing there in her white shorts, talking and reading from a paper, her words faded away like a faraway conversation he couldn't quite hear. After a moment, she stopped and stared at him.

He realized she'd asked a question. One he hadn't heard because he'd been so busy looking at her legs.

"In fact, I think we should interview Henry Juarez as soon as possible. What do you think?"

The name jolted him to attention. He pulled himself together.

"And his fam—"

"Let me see that." He held out his hand. Instead, she walked over and sat beside him. She held the paper between them where they could both see, but she didn't let go. She leaned in to point at something, and her shoulder brushed his. Warm. Hot.

Jack reached for the sheet, his hand closing over hers. "I'm sure we have the same people pegged as possible witnesses, but I'm not in favor of divvying up anything."

His hand still holding hers, they turned to each other, which positioned her mouth less than an inch from his. From the expectant look in her eyes, he guessed they'd had the same idea. But as he moved slightly forward, she turned away.

"I—it would be faster to separate. More efficient."

Yeah. Okay. He should be grateful she'd kept him from acting like an idiot. Except he felt disappointed. He'd probably never have a better chance to test the softness of her lips.

And…it would be foolish just to satisfy his ego—or his hormones.

"Maybe," he agreed. "But I'm thinking it's better to have backup at an interview. You may have questions I hadn't thought of and vice versa. We can't count on anyone being willing to talk to us a second time. Especially if they don't want to talk to us in the first place."

She thought about that for a moment. "Why wouldn't someone want to talk to us?"

"You didn't want to talk to me. The others might feel the same."

She thought for another moment. "Except no one else would be as close to this—with as much to lose—as I am. Right?"

Yeah. "Right. But not everyone thinks alike, and who knows what kinds of reasons someone might have for refusing to talk to us? Victims usually have an emotional investment, which means logic and reason don't always prevail."

"Okay. But I also have more time than you, and I don't want to sit around a hotel room waiting for you."

He shrugged. "I'm ready. I've already set up a couple of appointments for today." He arched a brow. "And... most importantly, I have transportation and I know the city."

Thoughtful, she leaned back, drumming her fingers against the pillow. "Transportation, huh?"

He smiled. "Your very own chauffeur."

She tossed the pillow at him. "Okay then. I'm convinced."

He liked the sparkle in her eyes...and the sprinkle of freckles across her nose and cheeks. He was a sucker for freckles. "Hey, that hurts. I thought my irresistible charm might win you over, but I've been beaten out by a car."

She laughed. "You should be grateful. Besides, if we're working together, you'll have plenty of opportunity to work on your charm."

Jack felt as if a barrier had fallen. They'd connected—in a good way. He liked her, he realized. A lot. He just wished there was some way to do this without causing her pain. Pain she'd surely feel when she found out her mother wasn't just an imposter or a thief—but possibly a murderer.

WITHIN THE HOUR, Taylor was changed and sat waiting in Jack's car while he finished at the gas pump. Remembering something she'd forgotten to tell Roxi, she pulled out her cell and called the boutique. "Hey, Rox. It's me."

"Taylor, gosh, it's been so long since I've heard from you," Roxi said. "At least a couple of hours."

"I just thought of something that needed—"

"Maybe you should make a list and then call just once."

"If you hadn't been hustling me out of town so quickly, I might have had time to do that before I left." Roxi had been champing at the bit to run the shop herself, and Taylor's trip to Texas gave her the perfect opportunity.

"The shop is fine. Quit worrying about us and take care of yourself for a change. Cara and I can handle things."

"I know you can handle things, Roxi. I didn't mean you couldn't. I wouldn't have left TMB in your hands if I didn't have the utmost confidence in your management skills."

Roxi snorted. "Okay, now we're getting to the part where I have to roll up my pants. Just forget about the shop and do what you need to do, okay?"

Laughing, Taylor agreed.

"So, how are you and hot guy getting along?"

"The hot guy's name is Jack and, aside from our difference of opinion regarding my mother, we're getting along just fine."

"And did you find out anything about your mother?"

"Not yet. We're on our way to interview two people we hope might give us insights into Margot Cooper's identity."

"You're working together? Cool."

"I haven't told him about the tattoo guy or the other thing yet."

"The other thing?"

"Someone being in my town home."

"Y'know, kiddo, you might want to skip that one."

"I'm not imagining that. If you did things in a particular way and they weren't that way when you came back, you'd be suspicious, too."

"No. I'd think I forgot to do what I usually do."

"Well, that's the difference between us. I don't forget and I know there was someone in the house."

Taylor saw Jack on his way back to the SUV. "I've gotta go, but I'll talk to you later."

"Taylor…" Roxi paused. "Can you please make that a lot later? Like next week, maybe."

Taylor laughed. "Whatever." She disconnected as Jack slid into the driver's seat and handed her a cup of coffee. She was closing the phone and bumped his hand, spilling the coffee. She jerked back, spilling more.

"Oh, for crying out loud," she said, annoyed more at her clumsiness than the sting of the hot black liquid, which was now staining her white pants.

Jack grabbed a couple of napkins and blotted the spill on her upper leg. Her thigh.

"Oh, man. I'm sorry," he said, pressing with the napkins. "I wasn't paying attention. Are you okay?"

She nodded. Her leg wasn't nearly as hot as some of her other body parts right now.

She yanked the napkins from him. "I can do that. It was my fault. I was on the phone and not paying attention."

He pulled back, his expression amused. "Okay."

She dabbed at the stain. "I can't believe so much coffee

can come out of one tiny hole." She dabbed again. "And now it's spreading."

"Do you want to go back to the hotel?" He glanced at his watch. "I've only got a couple hours before I have to be at the office, so we need to hustle."

"No, I don't want to waste time."

"Okay. Your choice." Then he asked, "Everything okay at Taylor Made Boutique?"

It surprised her that he'd guessed who she called. "Fine. Roxi has everything under control." She just wished to hell *she* did. What was it about Jack Parker that got her so flustered?

"That bothers you, doesn't it?"

She turned. "Excuse me?"

"It bothers you that Roxi can manage without you."

She pulled herself up, her back straight. "It doesn't bother me at all. Roxi's very competent. I wouldn't have left the place in her charge if I didn't think she could do the job."

He shrugged. "Then why are you trying to micromanage?"

Taylor crossed her arms. "I—I'm not micromanaging. I'm…being supportive. I want Roxi to know I'm here if she needs me. And I want to be sure things I didn't have time to take care of before I left are getting done. There's a lot to running the boutique. Lots of little things that someone else wouldn't know. It's not just a shop that sells trinkets and doodads—" She stopped when he turned to look at her.

"Are you trying to convince me, or yourself?"

She bit the inside of her cheek. "Don't need to convince anyone of anything. Especially someone I barely know."

He gave her an indulgent look. "Just an observation."

One she didn't want or need. "How about we stick to the business at hand. Who are we meeting first?"

He kept his eyes on the road. "The person who was the most involved. Seymour Hawthorne."

Taylor's pulse raced. Seymour Hawthorne—the man her mother was supposed to have worked for—and, according to the newspapers, had an affair with. She felt sick.

Jack saw the look on Taylor's face and felt a twinge of pity. "Are you up for this? We're almost there." The Hawthorne estate was in Sugarland, the high-rent district in Houston where old money congregated.

She brushed her shiny hair away from her face with one hand. "Up for it? Of course. Shouldn't I be?"

"Just asking."

After a moment of silence, she asked, "Did you grow up around here?"

The personal question came so totally out of the blue, it put him off point for a second. "No, not even close." But he had been here before, poking around the building where all the tools were kept.

"But you did grow up in Texas. Right?"

"I did." Had he told her that before? "How did you know that?"

"When I first met you, I thought you sounded like a friend, who's also from Texas." She grinned. "And you were wearing an Astros T-shirt."

"You're observant."

"Not really." In his peripheral vision he could see her shifting in her seat, apparently noticing that the homes were getting larger and larger and more spread out, some of them with iron fences and shrubbery ten feet high.

"So, where in Texas *did* you grow up?"

"I grew up on a small ranch about thirty-five miles from town. It seemed a long way out back then. I moved to Chicago later and went to the University of Illinois. After graduation I worked at the *Chicago Sun-Times* before coming back here five years ago."

"Really? I'm surprised you didn't lose the accent being gone that long."

He shrugged. He liked talking with her, pretending there was nothing personally at stake in what they were doing together and they were just two singles talking. "How about you? Where did you live before Arizona?"

She looked as if he'd struck her with a club. "I thought you got all that *intel* before you looked me up."

Reality check. "Not all. And back then, I was after facts. Now I'm…interested in you."

She gave him a funny look.

"But I guess it's all one and the same, isn't it?"

She compressed her lips into a tight line. "One and the same."

He stopped at the next light and Taylor said, "This is the street, isn't it?"

"Yep. It's just around the corner." He turned, then drove a half block to the driveway while Taylor peered out the window, her eyes wide. Pulling up to the iron gate, he said, "You ready?"

She nodded. "Wow. Some digs."

Jack opened the window and pressed a button on the intercom on his left. "Jack Parker here to see Mr. Hawthorne," he said when someone answered.

The gates slowly swung open.

"This is amazing," Taylor said. "I can't even see the house."

"It's to the right. On the left are garages and a guest house."

She looked at him. "You've been here before?"

"Correct. I spoke with Hawthorne once before. But I have new questions. And I imagine you do, too."

He drove in low gear around the circular driveway.

"I do," she practically whispered.

Before he finished parking, a valet opened the passenger door for Taylor. Once out of the car, Jack looked around. Everything was green and lush and tropical. And like the first time he was here, he felt a sense of déjà vu. But he'd been under three when his father had worked here.

With a hand at Taylor's back, he directed her up the stairs to the massive double doors with leaded glass windows. The opulence was overwhelming. "I feel like I'm on a movie set," he said in her ear.

"Like the estate in *The Great Gatsby*." She stayed close by his side. Close enough to make his blood rush. Taylor stopped on the step above him.

"He doesn't know about me, does he?" she asked.

"Know what?"

"Why I'm here. That there's a possibility my mother is this Cooper woman."

"He doesn't even know anyone is coming with me."

"It's probably best he doesn't know who I am."

Jack didn't know why she thought that, but there wasn't time to discuss it, since they were already there and the valet was parking their car. "Okay," he said. "And please don't mention the newspaper, either."

The door swung open. A silver-haired gentleman who definitely wasn't the butler stood in the doorway. If Jack hadn't met Seymour Hawthorne before, he would have known him from the hundreds of photographs in the

Chronicle over the years. The man was one of the most important people in Houston. Even now when he must be close to eighty years old.

"Good afternoon," Hawthorne greeted them.

"Hello, Mr. Hawthorne. I'm Jack Parker. We met before."

The man nodded. "Yes, of course."

"And this is Taylor Dundee. I didn't know she was coming along when I spoke with your assistant."

Hawthorne smiled, then held out his hand. "Nice to meet you. Please come in."

They followed him into a room with mahogany bookshelves lining all four walls—the very room where Jack's father was supposed to have killed Sunny Hawthorne. Anger made his chest tight. A rush of adrenaline echoed in his ears.

"Please have a seat." Hawthorne gestured to a leather couch and two upholstered chairs grouped in front of the fireplace.

They got settled, Jack and Taylor on the couch and Hawthorne in one of the chairs. "Thank you for taking the time to meet with us, Mr. Hawthorne," Jack said.

"My secretary said this was about one of my employees, but she didn't say what your interest was, and I'm sure you know employee records are confidential."

Jack's previous interview had been about Juarez being released from jail and a recap of the events on the night of the murder. Hawthorne was forgetful and hadn't remembered much detail. He hoped the man was sharper today.

Jack nodded. "My interest is in a former employee, not a current one."

Hawthorne smiled. "Then you really should talk with my business assistant. She's the go-to person on this kind of thing. No one is in trouble, I hope."

Jack rubbed his hands together. "I don't think your assistant has the answers I'm looking for. This is about an employee who worked for you thirty years ago."

Hawthorne's mouth opened; he was clearly taken aback.

"I told you before that thirty years is too long ago to remember anything," Hawthorne barked, then placed both hands on the arms of his chair, as if to get up.

Jack noticed faint tremors in the man's hands. "I'm sorry to dredge up the past," Jack said. "Bu—"

"I'm sorry, too," Hawthorne snapped, then got shakily to his feet. "I believe we're done here."

CHAPTER EIGHT

TAYLOR COULDN'T let the interview go down the tubes without getting even one question answered. "If I could say just one thing…"

Hawthorne turned sharply to look at her.

"Please," she said. "This is extremely important to me and it has to do with my…aunt who passed away a few months ago."

His expression softened. "I'm sorry your aunt passed away, Miss Dundee."

She pulled out a photo of her mother, then handed it to Hawthorne. "Do you know who that is?"

Grudgingly, he looked and, as he did, his expression ran the gamut from surprise to anger. Then resignation. "Yes…I do," he said, his voice husky. "It's Margot Cooper." Hawthorne's hand trembled as he took the photo. "I was very fond of her."

"Did you know her son?" Jack quickly held up the photo of the boy.

The older man nodded. He seemed to have forgotten his earlier anger. "Yes, but not very well. He was killed in a tragic accident while Margot was working for me. She was devastated. We all were." He stared blankly for a moment. "I didn't know Margot had a niece. She said she had no family except for Matthew."

Hawthorne might cut her off, but she had to ask. "The family wasn't close," Taylor lied. "That's why I want to know about her and her son. It's really important to me."

Hawthorne looked at her, thoughtful. Or maybe bewildered was more apt.

"Can you tell us about the accident, Mr. Hawthorne?"

His mouth turned down, and he rubbed one hand against his thigh. "It was a motorcycle accident. Back then, I had business to attend to, and I wasn't around much. But he was a good boy." He paused, then said, "My daughter, Emily, knew him better than I did, but Emily's mother—God rest her soul—wasn't in favor of the friendship."

Jack gave her a slight wave, which Taylor took as her cue to continue.

"Do you remember when the accident occurred?"

"Of course. I may be old, but there are things you don't ever forget. It was three months before Margot left my employ, and that was in May 1977."

Taylor quickly did the calculations. Her mother must have been hugely pregnant when she left Texas because Taylor was born only a month later in June 1977. Taylor's father had died before she was born, but she couldn't imagine her mother being involved with Hawthorne when she was pregnant with another man's child. Unless that was a lie, too. Unless Hawthorne was...

Oh, man. Taylor *didn't* want to go there.

"That had to be very hard for Margot."

"Of course it was. It was hard for everyone. They were like family."

He cared about Margot and her son. That was obvious. "I read some old newspapers about what happened and I keep wondering why the police were looking for her."

"The police were idiots. The $500,000 was missing and because she'd left, they thought she knew something, or possibly that she might've taken it."

"You don't believe Margot Cooper was...involved in what happened?"

Hawthorne sat up. "Never. I...knew Margot...very well. She was honest, and I told the police they were wrong. She left because my wife fired her, and I was happy when they finally found who did it, even though it turned out to be Henry. I liked Henry. He was a good worker. I thought he was honest, too."

"So, even though you thought Henry was honest, you believed he was guilty?" Jack asked.

The elderly man frowned. "It doesn't matter what I believed. The jury decided based on the evidence." He grimaced. "Frankly, I felt a bit of a fool. I always imagined I was a good judge of character, but apparently I wasn't."

Taylor wondered if Hawthorne realized he may have misjudged Juarez, why didn't he have the same doubts about Cooper? Unless it wasn't just an affair...and he'd actually been in love with her.

"Then you believe the jury made the right decision?" Jack asked.

Hawthorne thought for a moment. "I've always had doubts, I'd be a fool not to. But..." His voice trailed off. He steepled his fingers, then looked from Taylor to Jack and back again. "Miss Dundee, you said earlier that Margot was your aunt. Did you have the opportunity to see her after she left here?"

Taylor straightened her shoulders. Her heart thudded. "I did."

The man's eyes seemed to brighten. "Was she well? Was she happy?"

It wrenched her heart. He still cared about Margot. Thirty years later and he still cared.

Taylor's hand shook as she pulled a photo from her purse, one of Taylor and her mom at the Grand Canyon. She held it out. "This is a photo of me and my aunt fifteen years ago. She never married, but she was very happy."

Hawthorne stared at the photo for the longest time, then finally pointed to it. "That's the locket I gave her for her birthday." He looked at Taylor and smiled. "She kept it."

Taylor's stomach dropped.

"Did you say your aunt passed away?" he whispered.

"Yes," she said simply.

His shoulders slumped, the tremors more pronounced.

Taylor couldn't help thinking that if he cared so much, how could he have sent her away? Where was he when Margot was alone and pregnant? The room suddenly felt cold.

But even worse, now she knew the truth. Her mother's life, Taylor's life, had been a lie.

She'd braced herself for the truth. But thinking it *could* be true and knowing it was were two very different things.

Taylor's hand went to her neck to the locket her mother had treasured. A gift. From Seymour Hawthorne.

Taylor's head spun. Her mother had lied to her about who she was. She hadn't trusted her own daughter. And Taylor had trusted her mother implicitly.

Taylor felt a knifelike pain in her chest. She didn't know who she was anymore.

"Taylor?"

Jack's voice. "Uh…yes. Six, no, seven months ago."

Hawthorne stared at her, as if waiting for something else.

"She…was a talented woman. But, there were a lot of things I didn't know about her—a lot of things I'm trying to understand."

Just then Taylor noticed movement in her peripheral vision. She turned. A woman who looked to be in her late forties stood in the doorway, one hand on the door.

"I'm sorry, Father. I didn't know you had visitors." She turned to go.

"Don't leave, Emily," Hawthorne said, his voice shaky. "This young lady has some questions you might be able to answer."

Emily. Hawthorne's daughter. The one Margot used to take care of.

The woman came forward, carrying herself with the grace of someone who'd been taught the proper way to walk, shoulders straight and chin raised just a hair. She wore a cream silk shirt and black tailored slacks with flat black slip-ons. Her honey hair, cut à la Martha Stewart, completed the high-society look. It was hard to imagine her mother ever taking care of this woman.

"I'd like to introduce my daughter, Emily Hawthorne Kittridge," Hawthorne said. "Emily, this is Jack Parker and Taylor Dundee."

Emily Hawthorne Kittridge reached out to shake their hands.

"They're here to ask some questions about Margot Cooper."

Kittridge's hand dropped, her eyes riveted on her father. "I thought we agreed this was a closed subject."

"It is." The man smiled. "But this is different. It's not

about what happened. Margot was this young woman's aunt."

Kittridge turned to Taylor and Jack.

"Just a few questions," Taylor said. "It won't take long."

"Please sit down, Emily," Hawthorne instructed.

Stiffly, she did as she was told.

Kittridge acted as if she were going before the Spanish Inquisition, so Taylor knew she had to cut to the chase. "Do you know anything about Matthew Cooper?"

"Matt?" The question was barely audible. Emily raised a hand to her mouth and shook her head. After a silent moment, she cleared her throat. "No. No, I don't. He was killed riding a motorcycle. That's all I know."

"Emily?" Hawthorne's expression was puzzled.

The woman looked at her father, warning signs flashing in her eyes.

"But you did know him, right?" Taylor asked.

Kittridge didn't answer, so Taylor continued. "I understand he was your age and that he lived here with...his mother."

The other woman clutched at the pearl buttons on her shirt. She looked everywhere but at Taylor. Finally she said, "He did, but my mother didn't want me being friendly with the help."

Jack had been unusually quiet, letting Taylor take over, which had surprised her, but she saw him stiffen at the last remark. "Well, then," Taylor said, "did Matthew's mother ever talk to you about him?"

"No," she said almost before the question left Taylor's lips.

To say the woman was resistant would be an understatement. On the other hand, Emily would have only been a teenager when her mother was murdered and talking about anything that happened during that time had to remind her of her mother's death.

"I'm sorry," Taylor said. "My mother passed away within the year, so I know what that loss feels like."

Emily looked at Taylor. "I'm sorry for you, dear. I lost my mother years ago, so it should be easier, but somehow it never is."

Taylor saw beads of perspiration form on Jack's forehead, his fingers kneading the blue brocade fabric on the cushion. He looked ready to jump out of his skin. She decided to forge ahead. "Can you tell me about Margot? Do you know if she had any friends or what her social life was like?"

She saw Hawthorne tense at the question, and *stunned* was the only word Taylor could use to describe the look on Emily's face. "I—I don't know anything about her." Emily's hand went to the buttons again. "Why do you want to know all this anyway?" And before Taylor could answer, Emily turned to her father. "I thought you said this was different. It's the same as always. Won't this thing ever die?"

Hawthorne frowned. "Margot took care of you for five years. If the girl wants to know about her aunt, then you should tell her."

Emily's lips thinned. "I don't remember, Father. And I don't have time for this right now. I have to—I have an appointment." She bolted to her feet and hurried to the door.

Taylor said quickly, to catch her, "I really need some answers that I think only you might have. Can we please set up another time, then?" But Emily wasn't listening and before Taylor even finished the sentence, the woman was gone.

Hawthorne seemed in a daze. "I don't know what to say."

Not wanting to leave things as they were, Taylor asked. "And what about you? Can you answer some other questions about Margot Cooper now?"

His expression softened, but he shook his head. "Right now I'm very tired. But if you don't mind, I'd like to know where your aunt is buried."

ON THEIR WAY OUT, Jack thanked Hawthorne for his time. But Taylor was his main concern. He could tell by the slump in her shoulders that she was hurting. He stepped closer and put an arm around her. "It's okay," he said, squeezing her tighter as they waited for the valet to bring his car. "There'll be another opportunity."

She didn't answer, but she didn't pull away, either. And he didn't want her to. He liked the way she felt in his arms.

But his feelings for her right now were more than hormones. He felt protective and, alternately, guilty. He'd brought her into this. He wished he'd handled things differently, but wishing wasn't going to change anything, either.

The valet opened the passenger door for Taylor and Jack went around and got in behind the wheel. The interview had given him insights he hadn't had before. There was tension between father and daughter, tension that was more pronounced when even a question was asked about Margot that Emily didn't want to answer. He wondered if Emily knew about the affair, if she hated her father for it, held it over him. He didn't know if Taylor thought the same, but she needed support and he found himself wanting more than anything to be the one to give it to her.

When they were on the road again, Taylor said, "Did you get the same feeling I did?"

He glanced over. "That Miss Emily is hiding something?"

"Something like that. She wasn't just evasive, she actually lied. Hawthorne said she knew Matt and she claims not to. And…Margot had been Emily's nanny too long for Emily not to know anything about…her life."

Jack heard the hesitation in Taylor's voice every time she said Margot's name. As if she was talking about a stranger. "What did you think she'd tell you?"

"I—I don't know. I guess I thought if she said anything it would help me in some way to understand. I still can't think of my mother as Margot Cooper. I know you don't think there's a reasonable explanation, and maybe there isn't, but I still have to keep looking for one. Whatever name she went by, no matter what events happened in her life, I'll never believe she was a criminal."

He wasn't going to get into that one. Jack couldn't think of any other explanation for the woman to run away and take an alias. Margot Cooper had both opportunity and motive to kill Sunny Hawthorne. There were others, too, but none so compelling as a woman scorned.

"But," Taylor said, "I do understand it had to be tough on Emily to be reminded of her mother's death."

"Maybe. But to me, her behavior seemed defensive."

Taylor readjusted the vent on the dash in front of her. "People react to stress in different ways. Sometimes they do just the opposite of what you'd expect."

"True. I learned early in my reporting career that I had to expect the unexpected."

"So what now?"

He checked the time. "I have some things to do at work. I'll take you to the hotel and come back in a couple of hours."

"That works. I have to call Rox—" She stopped herself.

"What?" he said. "I didn't say anything."

"No, but you were thinking it."

He grinned. "You're a mind reader now?"

"No, I'm a business owner who likes to make sure things are going as they should. What's wrong with that?"

"Nothing. Absolutely nothing."

"Okay, then." She crossed her arms.

He looked over and smiled. Big.

As they neared the hotel, she said, "I do have other people I'd like to talk to. Maybe I'll do that while you're gone."

Jack tightened his grip on the wheel. "I may have already met with some of them. No point duplicating processes." He paused. "We can discuss it over dinner."

When she didn't answer immediately, he added, "It'll be more efficient."

Out of the corner of his eye, he saw her smiling, but he didn't know if that was good or bad. For all he knew, she saw right through him. Hell, now that he thought about it, he knew she did. She was a smart woman.

"Okay. What time?"

"I should be here by six. Does that work?" He pulled up to the hotel and one of the doormen opened the car door for Taylor.

She looked at her watch. "Three hours. Sure, that works fine."

Yeah, fine. If she didn't go off on a tangent in the meantime. And there was no way to guarantee she wouldn't.

HE MIGHT BE AN OLD MAN, but he wasn't senile. Not yet. "Bernice, please bring tea for two and tell my daughter I'd like to talk to her."

"Certainly, Mr. Hawthorne. Is there anything else?"

"No, that's it. Thank you." He opened his desk drawer and pulled out a small teakwood box. He tapped a finger against the side before he undid the latch and opened the top. He pulled out a letter, the last one he'd received from Margot. It had been a long time since he'd looked at it, and he didn't recall anything revealing in it. He'd never understood why she'd written it, because she had to know that he'd never believe she'd been involved in Sunny's death.

What he didn't know was why she'd never contacted him after Henry had been arrested. He'd spent years waiting for a call, a letter—anything to tell him she was okay. That she was happy. He'd messed up both of their lives. But he'd never stopped loving her.

He took a deep breath. He'd offered to leave his family for her, but she wouldn't have it. She'd told him that a relationship built on the broken hearts of others would never survive. No matter how much she loved him or he loved her.

He should have asked more questions. He should have asked Taylor if Margot had been able to do her artwork, or if she'd bought the little house she'd wanted. The money he'd given her couldn't make up for the heartache, but it had given him some peace. He'd prayed many times that Margot was having a happy and fulfilling life. He'd wanted that for her. More than anything.

"Here's your tea, Mr. Hawthorne."

As Bernice left the room, Emily entered.

"Ah, Emily. You're just in time for tea," he said.

"I don't have time, Daddy. I'm getting ready to go out."

"Then we'll talk tomorrow."

"It's about that girl, isn't it? Taylor Dun…whatever." She waved a hand. "I can't believe you let her in here to put us through that again."

He took a sip of tea. "I can't believe you said you didn't know Matthew. Or that you didn't know anything about Margot."

"It was thirty years ago, Father. You promised we'd never talk about it again. It's over and done. What's the point?"

"It's not over and done for the young woman who was here." As he said it, Seymour remembered that though Emily had been close to Margot, his daughter had felt betrayed when she'd heard about the affair. So, they'd never talked about Margot's guilt or innocence and, for all he knew, Emily believed what the police did.

"How do you know she isn't just another would-be novelist looking for a story to make herself rich?"

"She showed me a photograph of her aunt. The woman was Margot."

Emily clutched at the buttons on her shirt. "Well…just because someone looks like her—" she ran a hand through her hair "—it doesn't mean—"

"No, it doesn't. But I saw the photograph…and there was a striking resemblance."

"You're forgetting that other woman who claimed to be Margot's sister and wanted money."

"I didn't forget. But I did see the photograph."

"There are programs that can alter photos with one click of the mouse. Even if it were true, why would she come here?"

He shook his head. "I don't know that, either. She didn't explain. But I got the impression this was something she's just learned and she's trying to find her roots."

"And what if her aunt was Margot? I don't feel any obligation to talk to anyone about her."

Hawthorne got up and went to the window, where light

streamed through the wood blinds, casting prison stripes across the floor below. "Matthew would've been her cousin. You can't blame her for wanting to know about her own family."

Emily paced, alternately fiddling with her necklace and running her hands through her hair.

"Why are you so upset about a few questions?"

His daughter dropped into an overstuffed leather chair.

"Because she might get the police involved again. The press. You know how they are at the hint of scandal. And what about Sienna? Your granddaughter knows very little of what happened back then. If this gets splashed all over the news again, how will it affect her?"

All Seymour knew was that Margot was gone forever, and he felt as if something inside him had died, too. All these years he'd had hope. Hope that someday he and Margot would find each other again. "Sienna's in Europe, so it wouldn't affect her at all," he said. "And if the police got involved again, maybe they'd discover Margot had nothing to do with any of it."

Emily dropped her head into her hands. "Some things can't be changed, Daddy. No matter how much we want it."

"Does that mean you believe Margot was involved?" Seymour said sadly.

She raised her head and looked at him in surprise. "No. Of course not. I never believed that."

He smiled. He didn't know why Emily's opinion about Margot meant so much, but it did. "Good. I'm happy to hear that." After a moment, he said, "So, if she calls, will you talk to this young lady again?"

Emily rose and walked to the door. "No. I won't. I can't."

CHAPTER NINE

TAYLOR CROSSED a couple of names off her list. The most intriguing seemed to be Sunny Hawthorne's personal assistant, Nancy Belamy. According to the articles Taylor had read, the woman had been Sunny's social director, her go-to person for everything she didn't want to lift a finger to do herself.

Taylor had had a tough time tracking the woman down and had almost given up when she'd found a sidebar in one article that said the woman had been staying at her brother's home in River Oaks. Belamy was most intriguing because she'd been at the Hawthorne home the night of the murder.

Before Taylor left Arizona, she'd done Internet research on everyone on her list, compiling information from the plethora of articles on the murder and that which was available from public information.

She'd unearthed the brother's phone number and, posing as an old school friend, Taylor had managed to get his sister's phone number. Fortunately, after years living elsewhere, Nancy Belamy was back in Houston again.

Now Taylor had to decide the best way to get in touch with her, and whether she should candy coat her mission or just lay it out there. She decided on the former since she'd discovered Jack had been right that people were reluctant to talk, much less meet with her. She'd had two former Hawthorne employees hang up on her, saying they'd signed contracts not to divulge anything related to the Hawthorne family.

She steeled herself for another rejection and punched in the number the woman's brother had given her. After four rings, she was about to hang up when a woman answered.

"Hello," Taylor said. "Is this Nancy Belamy?"

"Yes. But I'm not interested in buying anything." Click.

Taylor held out the phone. Now she knew how telephone solicitors felt. Now she also knew the woman was at home. She checked the time. Four o'clock. She had two hours before Jack would be back, so she quickly changed into something more businesslike, a lightweight cream pantsuit, black sleeveless tank top and sandals. She grabbed her briefcase, her TMB purse and, within ten minutes, she was in a cab on her way to Belaire.

As she watched the buildings fly by and the scenery turn suburban, she thought of how concerned Jack had been when they left the Hawthorne home. She liked his concern, that he cared enough to be concerned.

But it was the security she felt when he put his strong arms around her that made her realize how alone she really was. How much she needed someone who cared about her in that way.

No question, she was attracted to Jack. She'd felt it from the moment they'd met. More than once, she'd wondered what his lips would feel like on hers, what it would feel like to make love with him. The idea of having dinner with Jack made her smile.

"Is this where you want to go, ma'am?"

Taylor glanced out the window. The homes were plain and simple, a street of track houses that looked the same except for the paint colors. "It is if it's the address I gave you."

"It is. And the fare is six dollars."

She took out a ten. "Give me three back, please." She glanced at the house again. "Can you come back in a half hour?" Although for all she knew, she'd be done in five minutes.

He agreed, but added, "You'll have to be outside waiting."

"Fine." She got out, and as she walked up the sidewalk, her heart pounded like a tom-tom. She was nervous about what she might find out. But she already knew the worst, didn't she? Her purpose now, she told herself, was to prove her mother was still the woman she knew her to be. And if possible, she wanted to know more about the brother she'd just discovered. If she knew what happened, she might be able to understand why her mother had kept her life in Texas a secret.

How hard that must have been. All those years keeping a secret like that. It boggled Taylor's mind.

At the door, she steeled herself and rang the bell. She waited. And waited. She pressed the button again, then knocked for good measure.

She was about to leave when she saw the curtain in the front window move. A few seconds later, the door opened about a foot and a woman with gray hair who looked to be in her mid-sixties peered out. "What do you want?"

Taylor recognized her voice. "Hello, Ms. Belamy. My name is Taylor Dundee. I was with someone you used to work for earlier today and he suggested I talk to you since you kept records of employees."

"Who did you talk to?"

"Your former employer. Seymour Hawthorne."

"That bastard. I never worked for him. I worked for Mrs. Hawthorne. Sunny."

"Yes, that's why I wanted to talk to you."

"Are you with the police?"

Taylor shook her head.

"Some magazine or newspaper?"

"No. I'm a relative, and I'm looking for information on my aunt, Margot Cooper, and her son, Matt. Can I please have a few minutes?"

The woman still looked wary but let Taylor inside anyway. Entering, Taylor felt as if she was walking into a sauna. A small rotating fan in the corner afforded an occasional sweep of cool air. She indicated the couch with a wave of her hand, then sat on a Bentwood chair on the opposite side. "I can give you ten minutes."

Taylor glanced at her watch. "Then I won't beat around the bush. How well did you know Margot and Matt?"

Belamy pursed her lips, her posture as rigid as the back of the wooden chair.

"Not very well. Margot Cooper worked for the Hawthornes at the same time I did, but her job was to take care of the house and Emily, the Hawthornes' daughter. Mine was to take care of Mrs. Hawthorne's personal needs, her social register, charity benefits and the like."

"How did Margot 'take care of the house'?"

"She managed the housekeepers who did the cleaning, and she did some of the lighter work herself." Belamy lifted her chin. "She spent most of her time taking care of Emily. And believe me, that took a great deal of time."

Taylor could imagine. Emily Hawthorne Kittridge was

a woman who knew her rank in the world. Probably milked it for everything it was worth. What Taylor couldn't imagine was how her mother put up with a spoiled debutante. "What took time?"

The woman scoffed while blotting her face with a handkerchief. "What didn't would be more like it. Emily was always in trouble. She caused her poor mother grief every time she turned around. Taking up with the wrong kind of boys, drinking, staying out all night. Margot had to bail her out all the time so her mother wouldn't find out."

Wow. Taylor could imagine a lot of things, but she'd gotten the impression Kittridge was uptight. Not one to run wild. Not even as a teenager. But then Taylor thought of her mother and realized she hadn't imagined her in another light either. "They didn't get along? Emily and Mrs. Hawthorne?"

"I used to be sympathetic to Emily, because Sunny Hawthorne could be a very demanding woman. But later, I saw the two of them were very much alike. Two women with the same demands are never going to get along, are they?"

Taylor smiled. "I suppose you're right." She cleared her throat, relieved the woman wasn't holding back.

"But whether they got along or not, Sunny loved her daughter more than anything."

"What about Margot's son? How did he fit into the family?"

Belamy frowned. "He died, you know."

Taylor nodded. "Do you remember anything about him?"

The woman moistened her lips, thoughtful. "It was a motorcycle crash."

She knew that already. "Where did it happen?"

"Just outside the compound. Hit-and-run. Near the entry gate."

Near the entry gate. "That close. How horrible for my—Margot." It brought tears to Taylor's eyes. She quickly blinked them away. "Did Margot have a funeral for her son?"

"Yes. It was a small service at—" She thought for a moment. "Crystal Lake Cemetery. I remember because I wrote the check. Sunny took care of the costs for Margot."

"Really? That was very nice of her. I thought...I thought Sunny didn't want her daughter being around the help, so why would she do that?"

The woman drew back. "She wasn't heartless. Margot had just lost her son. And everyone knew she didn't have much money."

"That was very nice of her."

Belamy blotted her face again. "Well, yes and no. There was no way Sunny was going to let her husband pay the expenses, and she probably felt guilty because she wouldn't let Emily go to the funeral, either. After that, the strain between them was even greater." Then placing a hand at her chin, she said, "Why do you want to know all this, Ms. Dundee?"

Taylor quickly decided to stick to her earlier plan. "I'm writing up a family history. I also need information for medical purposes."

"I see. You'd be better off getting medical records if that's what you're after."

"You're right, of course. Only I've found that the more I know, even if it doesn't seem related, the easier it is to track down missing information."

"What specifically are you looking for? I'm afraid I can't give you any insight on Margot Cooper's life outside of her work with the Hawthornes. We didn't interact on a social level."

No, Taylor didn't imagine they did. Her mother was warm and giving and Nancy Belamy was one degree away from frostbite. "You were there the night of the murder?"

She stiffened. Sat even straighter if that was possible. "I discovered the body and called the police. That's well-known if you've read anything about it."

"I have," Taylor said. "You were very fond of Sunny Hawthorne, then."

Tears filled the woman's eyes. "She was like a sister to me. I would have done anything for her, but it all end—"

Ended when she died. "Then I guess you saw Margot there that night, too?"

Belamy abruptly rose from her chair. "No, I didn't. Emily told me she was there and that's what I told the police."

Odd, how everyone thought Margot was a thief and yet nothing she'd read said anyone had actually seen her there the night of the crime. "Why do you think the police believed she was involved?"

Taylor saw the muscles around Belamy's mouth twitch.

"I guess it was the affair," she said softly. "Did you read about that, too?"

Nodding, Taylor stood. The memory obviously brought with it some pain. Taylor had no clue why, but she felt sympathy for Belamy. Whatever had happened that night had changed a lot of lives.

A light flashed outside, and Belamy glanced out the front window. "It's a cab."

"Oh, that would be for me." She didn't want to go yet. But she had to or she wouldn't be back in time when Jack arrived. "I have to go, but would you mind if I contacted you again?"

"I'm sorry. I'm going in for surgery soon, and then I'll be out of town."

"When you're back then. Can you please give me a call?" She scribbled down her cell phone number on a notepad and tore it off the page.

Belamy smiled, but it was more of a grimace. "You'd better go."

"So, WHAT ARE YOU going to do now?" Cal asked Jack.

"Hell if I know. It's not like I planned it this way. Things just happened." Jack had finished work earlier than Taylor expected him so he'd met Cal at O'Malley's Pub, a regular meeting place for them since Jack had moved to Houston.

"For a guy who likes all his ducks in a row, that's pretty funny. I think Miss Arizona has you comin' and goin'."

"Look who's talking. Lana's got you opening doors and pulling out chairs and who knows what all."

Cal waggled his eyebrows. "Yeah, and it's worth it. She says jump and I say how high."

Jack laughed. "That's a first." His buddy was a guy's guy and the rodeo had been his first and only love. Until Lana. Jack found it strange that he'd fallen so hard for her when he could have any number of women who fell all over him when he was on the road. Maybe Lana's remoteness turned him on. A challenge so to speak.

"Once I decided Lana was the one for me, my life changed. That's the trick, you know. Deciding."

"Trick to what?"

"The trick to making life easier. Getting what you want. You just decide how you want it to go and you do it. That's all it takes."

"And what if the deciding isn't up to you?"

Cal raised his beer. His sandy hair looked as if he'd used an eggbeater instead of a comb. His battered Stetson covered the seat on the bar stool next to him. "That's the other trick. You have to know what she wants you to decide." Cal laughed loud enough for everyone in the place to look over.

"Yeah. That ain't gonna happen," Jack said.

"Does she know what you're thinkin'?"

Jack took a swig. "Hell, I don't even know what I'm thinking. A few days ago she was in Arizona. Today, she's here and in my head, twenty-four seven."

"I can see we've got a problem, Houston."

"My only problem is having a drunk for a friend. Are you okay to drive? I've got to be at the hotel in ten minutes."

"If I'm not, I'll take a cab."

"That's the problem. You don't know when to take a cab."

"You're acting like I've got a drinking problem."

Jack looked at his buddy. Why did he even bother? Cal was Lana's problem. Lana was Cal's problem. Or not, if that's what they wanted. "I'm acting like a jerk. Ignore me."

Cal suddenly stopped joking, his expression serious. "If I knew it would help, I'd stop drinking in a nanosecond. But it isn't the drinking."

"I know," Jack said. His sister had scars. Emotional scars that made her wary of men. While he understood that about her and didn't want to see her get hurt ever again, he didn't want to see his buddy hurt, either. Cal was one of the nicest guys he knew. Someone who'd give you the shoes off his feet if you had holes in yours. But if he ever hurt Lana, Jack would never forgive himself. "I told you it wasn't a good idea. You should've listened to me."

"I didn't mean it wasn't worth it. It is. If I end up with Lana, it'll all be worth it."

"Then what's the problem?"

"The problem is that it's not working fast enough for

me. Lana is always wanting more space. If I give her any more, we might as well be living across the continent from each other." He sighed. "I know I need to be more patient but…"

"But what?"

"But I need to know it's gonna happen."

"Then talk to her." Jack got up to leave. "Ask her if she wants the same thing you do. Then you can do all that deciding you're so hot on."

Cal looked at him as if he'd just blasphemed his favorite team. "I can't ask her."

"Why not?"

"I might hear something I don't want to hear."

"Ah, I see." Jack understood all too well. It was called hiding your head in the sand. "Gotta go. I'll catch you later."

Cal waved. "Tomorrow night. Bring the missus."

Jack laughed. Somehow he couldn't picture Taylor cheering on the bull riders. But maybe he'd ask.

Ten minutes later he was pushing the elevator button at the hotel. Waiting for the door to open, he popped a piece of gum into his mouth. Just then he felt a presence behind him.

"Got another one of those?"

The voice caught him off guard. He turned. "Taylor." He handed her his pack of Wrigley's cool mint gum. "What's up?"

A couple of women came up to stand next to them at the elevator.

"Not much," she said, then looked up at the numbers above the door.

So where had she been? Her mouth tilted in a smirk. She bobbed to the music playing throughout the lobby and was even kind of full of herself. "And you?"

The doors opened and the four of them got on. At the same time, a half-dozen teenagers rushed into the elevator before the door closed. They packed in like sardines, leaving Taylor standing in front of him.

The second her body touched him, his body reacted. He tried to move back, but only succeeded in stepping on an older woman's toe. "Sorry," he said. "Crowded in here."

When Taylor turned, her expression said it all. "Sorry," he said, then grinned. "Crowded in here."

She moved slightly away, but he could still feel the heat of her body against his. Man, he hadn't had that happen since he was a teenager. It felt good.

He was almost disappointed when the elevator stopped and the teens piled off. He took a step back, removing himself from temptation. They went up another three floors, then the doors opened and they got off.

Taylor hurried along down the hall to her room. Neither of them said a word, but once inside, she finally broke the silence.

"Well, how was your afternoon? Productive, I hope?"

"Very."

"It smells like it." She flashed a toothy grin.

"I got done early. You weren't here, so I had a beer with a pal." And why was he even explaining? "What did you do?"

Instantly, her cheeks pinked and she turned away. The blush was becoming. After the elevator incident, all he wanted to do was throw her down on the king-sized bed. "I brought my stuff," he said, "but it's in my car. I thought we'd look at it over dinner, and make plans to cover a lot of territory tomorrow and Sunday. If you're free, that is."

"Funny." She went to the window and adjusted the blinds. "I did my own research this afternoon."

"Oh?" His senses went on red alert. Acting casual, he went to the minibar, took out a tiny bottle of wine and held it up. "Yes? No?"

She sat in one of the chairs by the round table in the corner near the window.

"Sure. Why not?"

He took two water glasses and a couple of the mini-bottles of wine to the table, sat and poured them each a glass. He handed one to her. "Anything helpful?"

She lifted her chin, that smug look again. "I think so. At least it's information I didn't know before."

He waited. Finally she said, "I talked to Sunny Hawthorne's former assistant."

His mouth fell open. "Yeah? How'd you manage that?"

"I had the address and looked it up on my laptop. It wasn't too far away, so I took a cab. Her name is Nancy Belamy."

"Yes, I know. I had her on my list. I thought we were going to do this together."

She pulled back, clearly astonished. "Are you repri-manding me?"

"No," he said calmly. "But we had an agreement."

"That was your understanding. Not mine."

He didn't know what part of "working together" she didn't get, but he could tell this was not the time to discuss it. "Okay. I guess I was wrong. What happened when you talked with her?"

Taylor sighed. "She wasn't particularly welcoming, but she did talk to me. And a lot more than Emily Haw-thorne had."

He didn't know whether to be mad or glad that she'd got somewhere. At least she hadn't tried to contact Juarez, or Lana again. Not that he knew of anyway. "Well, let's hear it."

She filled him in as he took notes. When she'd finished he stared at his notepad. "You're good. You should be a reporter."

She looked away, obviously self-conscious.

"Or maybe it's the freckles."

"The freckles?"

"Yeah, they make you look sweet and innocent. Makes people trust you."

She grinned. "Deceiving, huh?"

"That remains to be seen." He polished off the wine. "Are you hungry? I know a great place for Texas barbecue, or if you're in the mood, some Cajun cooking."

"I'm starving," she said, then held her arms out. "If I can wear this, I'm good to go."

She was good all right. Her blue eyes and sun-blond hair stood out against the black top. She wore gold hoop earrings and a chain around her neck that looked oddly familiar. Even in pants, she looked dressed up. "You look great."

Taylor's chest swelled at the compliment. She didn't know if he was just saying she looked great or if he actually thought so. And she was reading far too much into a casual comment.

Still, her stomach fluttered at the thought of having dinner with Jack—even if it was a business dinner.

Once in Jack's car, they decided on the Cajun restaurant. But when they arrived, the crowd waiting to be seated was out the door.

"Maybe we should go somewhere else," Taylor said.

"I forgot, it's Friday. I should've made a reservation," Jack said. "I'll check to see how long it'll be."

He came right back. "Just a few minutes."

"You must know the head waiter to get us in so quickly."

"No, but I know the owner." He grinned, then nodded to a man standing in the back of the line, apparently someone else he knew. "And one of the waiters is a football buddy."

She was seeing a different side of Jack tonight. A man comfortable in his surroundings, a man at ease in just about any situation. But then he had to be, she realized. He had to talk to lots of people all the time in order to write stories. People who might be rich or poor, heads of state or waiters. He treated everyone the same. With respect.

She liked the man she was seeing. Just as much as she liked the one she'd seen in Arizona, the mysterious, intriguing man who wouldn't take no for an answer. Where had Jack been when she'd needed him years ago?

Instead, she'd wasted so much time on Reed.

"Okay," the maître d' said. "Come with me."

Seated at a booth in the corner of the room, secluded from the noise of the main area and from the glares of those in line who thought they should be seated first, the waiter took their drink orders as a band started to play. "What's that?" she asked.

"Zydeco. It's Louisiana music," he said. "Most people think it's Cajun, but it's actually Creole."

"I like it. It's fun. I've never been to Louisiana, so I wouldn't know the difference."

"Where have you been?" Jack unfolded his napkin and put it on his lap, waiting for her answer.

"A lot of different places," she replied, taking a sip of water from the glass the waiter had filled. "But we never went anywhere that I thought worth remembering. My mother used to say, 'Life is the adventure.' I never knew what she meant at the time."

"That's a good way to look at it. Especially since most of life is out of our hands anyway."

"Are you a fatalist?"

"No, but I know we don't get to pick and choose a vast majority of things that happen in our lives. I did some traveling, but where I went wasn't my choice, since it was with the military. Since then, I've been too busy working to travel."

That he'd been in the military surprised her. "What branch?"

"Marines. Right out of high school. Mainly because I didn't know what else to do, and it was a way to get training."

"Then college and the job in Chicago," she said, remembering what he'd told her before.

"Correct." He leaned forward as if to tell her a secret. "My first reporting job was writing obituaries."

She laughed. "We all start somewhere, don't we? How about your family? How did they feel about you enlisting?"

Frowning, he pulled back. "It was my choice."

Funny how that made her want to know more about him. Much more. Had he not had a happy childhood? Had he played sports as a kid? Had he eaten all his vegetables? "Do you have any brothers and sisters?" She pictured him with a big, happy family.

"I have an older sister and a nephew who's the greatest kid ever." His tone softened at the mention of his nephew. He held out his wrist. "He gave me the watch."

She leaned in for a better look. Reed would never have worn a Mickey Mouse watch, no matter who gave it to him. She felt a pull inside, as if being drawn to him, emotionally as well as physically. "And your mother?"

"She's great. Best mom anyone could want."

"And does everybody live in Houston?"

He shifted uncomfortably. "In and near. Hey, enough about me. I need a turn asking questions."

"Okay, but I think your research probably covered everything about me, didn't it?"

He shook his head. "I want to know the important stuff."

"Like?"

"Like where did you come up with the idea for the boutique? It's very clever what you do with those bags." He pointed to the one she'd hung on the back of the chair.

"Well, like you, I think the idea presented itself more than anything. My major in college was advertising and marketing. I worked for a PR firm and one weekend when I was out antiquing with my mother…" She stopped, glancing at him. When she saw nothing but interest, she went on. "At one place I saw all this old costume jewelry in a box. It looked like it was going to get tossed out and I thought there must be a way to use it. I took the box home and began experimenting with designs. And somewhere along the way, I landed on the handbags. I started selling on the Internet and within two years, it took off like I never could have imagined. That's when I opened the shop."

He was watching her intently. "Well, that's enough of that," she said. "Get me started and I don't quit."

He grinned and leaned back in his chair. "You're quite an entrepreneur, Taylor."

"Not really. Everything just kind of grew and there I was in business."

He tilted his head. "You don't like compliments, do you?"

Heat rose to her cheeks. "It was just…unexpected."

"You don't expect compliments in general, or just not from me?"

"I don't like talking about myself, that's all. But I would love to read one of your articles sometime."

Oddly, that sobered him. "I haven't written any recently.

Too busy editing. And most are about business and they're pretty boring."

"So, the story you're researching now isn't boring?"

"I'm here having dinner with a very talented business owner on the verge of being famous," he said, a little too quickly. "Not boring at all."

Despite being self-conscious, his banter made her feel good. The waiter appeared with their drinks, a Shiner Blonde for both of them, then asked to take their orders.

"They have a great crab platter for two," Jack said. "A half dozen uniquely seasoned blue crab, a bucket of French fries and a hammer. We could share if you want."

She agreed and, after the waiter left, Jack raised his beer. "Here's to success in our joint venture."

Taylor raised her own beer and tapped his glass. "Success. Whatever that might be."

He pressed his lips together, apparently reminded that success for him wasn't the same as it was for her.

"I've wanted to ask you for a while now, why this story is so important to you?" Taylor said. "I mean, if you didn't get any different information than what you already have to write about, what then? Do you just chuck it and write about something else?"

"Jack." A model-type redhead curled up next to Jack for a hug and an air kiss. "Where have you been? I've missed you."

"Katlin. Nice to see you." He motioned to Taylor. "This is Taylor Dundee. Taylor, Katlin Barrington."

"Hi," the woman said with barely a glance at her.

Taylor felt as if she'd just become invisible. She recognized the Barrington name from the society section of the newspapers she'd been using for research. Okay, so she couldn't compete. Nothing new there, but she was angry at herself that she'd bought into it again. She'd spent a long time getting a handle on her self-image, and this was no different from any other. She had to remember who she was. Remember her own value. Jack had said it himself. She was quite the entrepreneur.

The thing was, she hadn't thought about Jack with other women. An incredibly stupid omission on her part. Of course he would be with women. What did she think? That he stayed at home every night writing stories?

"Next week," Jack was saying to the woman. "We'll get together next week."

Taylor pulled herself up. In less than a second she'd reverted to her old self, fading into the background, feeling small and insignificant. What did she care if Jack had friends? Even close friends. She'd been the one having fantasies about him and he obviously wasn't having any about her.

She moved to get up. "Excuse me, I'm going to make a trip to the powder room."

Jack smiled and nodded her off. She was used to that, too.

She stayed in the bathroom long enough to be sure the woman would be gone. When she got back to the table, the food had arrived.

"You got here just in time," Jack said. "Any longer and I couldn't have guaranteed there'd be anything left."

"Well, then I'm glad I got here." Sitting, she said, "I hope you'll show me how to eat those things, too."

"Sorry about the business interruption. That happens sometimes."

She shrugged. "No big deal."

"Okay, here's how you do it," Jack said. He proceeded to break off the legs and then picked up the little wooden mallet.

After his crab demolition demonstration, they dug in and before she knew it the empty crab shells made a small mountain in the bowl. The combination of beer, succulent crab and lively music buoyed her spirits and she completely forgot she was there for anything other than having a good time with Jack.

What was it about being with him that made her forget everything else? Including the fact that they were going to do some planning for interviews the following day. "We haven't even looked at the work we brought along."

He broke one last claw with the nutcracker and dipped the tender meat into the butter, then held it out for her to take a bite. "This is the best part," he said. "I saved it for last."

How could she resist? She took the bite, warm butter dribbling down her chin. He quickly wiped it off with the tip of a napkin.

Her heartbeat quickened. Being with him made her feel…a sense of excitement. When he was talking to her, she felt as if she were the only person in the room.

But then he'd done the same with the other woman. Hell, he probably had Jack Parker groupies beating down his door every night. She wouldn't blame them. Right now, she was one of them.

"We'll have to look at the work later," he said, going back to her earlier comment. "When we get back to the hotel."

Right. Except she had other ideas. Ideas she shouldn't be having.

CHAPTER TEN

JACK SET the hard copy of his notes and the chronological timeline he'd put together on the table. "I did this to get a handle on who did what and when. I figured I could add or change things as I went along."

Taylor picked it up and scanned it. "This is really detailed. Where did you find all this?"

"Old newspaper files, police reports and the Internet. I have access to things that you wouldn't."

"Definitely an advantage to being with a newspaper." She smiled, then continued reading.

Every time she smiled at him, he wanted to kiss her. And he wanted to kiss her when she wasn't smiling. But every time he felt the urge, he also felt like an imposter. What would she think if she knew Juarez was his father? That he was the son of a murderer?

The only way to know that was to tell her the whole story.

Yet if he revealed everything to Taylor, he'd jeopardize his attempt to discover what kind of man his biological father really was. Trying to find proof that Juarez was innocent more than likely meant implicating Taylor's mother. He doubted she'd take that kindly. If that was the end result, then he'd have to accept it, but until then, he'd only be making things more difficult for both of them by telling her. And kissing her.

"This is amazing. Unless there's more to the police investigation than what's here, I don't know how they managed to find Henry Juarez guilty of murder."

"That's what I thought, too. But I guess circumstantial evidence builds a case. That and the fact that the guy was a gardener and unable to pay for top attorneys." A long-fermenting anger tied knots in his gut. "The justice system is a crock. Innocent people who can't afford high-powered attorneys end up in jail and the rich get—" He stopped when he saw Taylor frowning. "Sorry. I see a lot in my business and that subject always hits my hot button. I forget that not everyone shares my feelings."

She scrutinized him, then finally grinned, got up and went to the window, where she kicked off her shoes and then raised her arms in the air and stretched from side to side. "Nothing wrong with having feelings. So, do you have any other theories?"

She meant were there any other suspects besides her mother. "I have questions. It's hard not to when you do the research. You've barely touched the surface and you have questions."

"True. I was a juror once, and I know that a lot of information is suppressed, and it's sometimes more revealing than the evidence provided in court." She came back to the table and picked up the timeline again.

He smiled. "Very good. I was right before in saying you would have made a good investigative reporter."

She tapped him with the paper. "And you're evading my question." She sat back. "But that's okay. I'm going to have my own theories anyway."

"No kidding. I never would have guessed."

"Right now, I'm thinking the police didn't follow up on things. If they had, they might have solved the matter of the missing money early on and the evidence against Juarez wouldn't have been circumstantial."

He wasn't sure what she meant. "What things didn't they follow up on?"

"Well, first of all, the most important people weren't seriously considered. People who knew Margot the best and people who knew Henry Juarez."

"What do you think the police might have found?"

"That Margot didn't have any part in the crime. That there would be more evidence that Juarez actually did it. Not just circumstantial."

"Or maybe the evidence would have showed Juarez couldn't have done it. And that Margot could have."

Taylor's eyes widened. "Is that what you're trying to do? Prove him innocent?"

He couldn't answer.

"You are, aren't you?" She shoved her chair back as she stood and it tipped over. "It's more to you than just writing a story." She walked to the window and ran a hand through her hair. "You think Margot killed Sunny Hawthorne," she said, then laughed. "Oh, man. I had this gut feeling, but I didn't listen to it." Shaking her head, she said, more to herself than to him, "Stupid. Really stupid."

He stood and crossed to her, taking her by the shoulders. "Stop it. I don't think anything. I just want the truth. I have reasons for wanting to prove Juarez innocent—"

"Reasons?"

"—but I have no agenda to prove any one person guilty. Only the guilty party."

She didn't wrench away, but the look in her eyes said he'd disappointed her. Just like he'd disappointed every other person in his life. "I've always thought it was possible your mother was involved. And I told you that." He moved closer. "But now I'm not sure what to think. Except…"

"Except what?" she said softly.

As if his body had a mind of its own, he moved even closer. "Except," he whispered, "that I've wanted to kiss you from the minute we met."

Her lips met his.

Blood roared through his veins, but he kissed her softly, gently. Then feeling her melt against him, he deepened the kiss, exploring her tender mouth with his tongue. If he didn't stop, he'd have her on the bed in seconds.

She pulled back first. Her lips were pink and full and it made him want to kiss her again.

"Oh, my," she said, breathless. She stepped back. "That was probably not a good idea."

"Yeah. Probably not." He smiled. "But it was great."

As they stood there looking at each other, Taylor's chest heaved. *Great* was a puny adverb to describe what she'd just felt. *Fantastic* would be more like it. But it was also fantastically stupid on her part.

Their eyes still locked, he shrugged, then turned and went to pick up the chair.

What had gotten into her? No, the question should be, why had she done that when she knew it was inappropriate and even a bit insane given the circumstances. The second he'd expressed interest, she'd tackled him like a linebacker.

She was losing it, no question.

"Whatever it was, it shouldn't happen again."

Righting the chair he gave her a quizzical look. "*It?* You mean you kissing me, or me kissing you back?"

Heat rushed to her cheeks.

"And here I was thinking *it* should happen again and again. But, probably not a good idea if we want to get any work done."

She went to the table and picked through the papers, but was oblivious to the content. "I don't think it's a good idea *at all*."

He looked at her for a moment, then came back and sat across from her. No words. Nothing. He was studying her. Unnerving her. Making her more than a little uncomfortable.

"I think we ought to plan out the weekend," she said. "Because I have to get back to Phoenix as soon as possible."

His gaze didn't waver, and though she felt he wanted an explanation, she didn't want to give him one. Mainly because it might give the impulsive kiss more importance than it deserved.

"I'd like to interview Henry Juarez," she said.

Jack visibly stiffened. "I think we need to save Juarez for last. The information we get from someone else could change the direction of our questions for him."

"Maybe."

"I also think it's better if I do the Juarez interview." He paused. "Alone."

She looked at him askance. "Why? Do you think it's dangerous?"

His mouth quirked up on one side. "Possibly. I also think a guy has a better chance at getting something from...from someone who's been in prison."

"I think I'd be better because he's been without a woman's company for a long time."

"And that's why it would be dangerous." He squinted at the paper. "Regan. That's the victim's sister?"

He was evading. She could feel it. But she had no clue why.

"Right. I'm surprised your 'superior research' missed her." It almost looked to Taylor as if Jack was blushing. She found it endearing. "I don't know how informative she'll be, but she was never interviewed before. Then again, she may know nothing."

"You know the old saying. You won't know if you don't try it."

Wasn't that the truth. She'd wanted to know what it would be like to kiss him, so she'd tried it and now she knew. It had felt wonderful. She could still feel the imprint of his lips on hers, and she wouldn't be forgetting it anytime soon either.

"So, how do you want to proceed?" she asked. "Call first to make appointments or take our chances and drop in?"

"We don't want to waste time, so let's call and see how many people are willing to meet with us." He paused. "I have to find Juarez before we can even talk to him."

"What about his family?"

He looked at her strangely. "His family?"

"Yes. He must have one."

Jack shook his head. "I read that his wife died."

"No kids?"

He turned away, as if avoiding her gaze, then said, "I don't remember reading about any."

"Okay. That will be a challenge. What about Juarez's parole officer?"

"I'm pretty sure that's not public information."

"It might be for you."

"Maybe, but that's last on the list anyway."

She agreed, noting that it almost seemed as if he didn't want to talk to Juarez. Strange, if he thought the man might be innocent.

"So," he said. "Let's start calling. I'll use my cell. One more thing."

She looked at him.

"I've got a benefit to do tomorrow. A rodeo benefit for children's diabetes."

He fought against injustice and attended benefits for sick *kids*. Jack just rose a notch in her estimation. "Okay. I can work alone."

"Or you could come along."

Come along. After that kiss, she should stay as far away from Jack as she could. Problem was, she didn't want to. When she didn't answer immediately, he added, "It's for a good cause. And I'm paying."

Smiling, she said, "Sure. Anything for a good cause." She sat on the edge of the bed, picked up the phone and dialed the first number. Waiting for Regan to answer, and even without looking, she felt Jack watching her. She turned sideways so she couldn't see him. So much for remaining aloof.

CHAPTER ELEVEN

A TALL MAN wearing a Stetson and a woman with long blond hair were waiting at the entrance to the rodeo grounds when Taylor and Jack arrived. The man, who Taylor guessed was Jack's friend Cal, had one foot on the weathered wooden gate and an arm around the woman, who she figured was Jack's sister, Lana. The man waved them over.

"Cal and Lana, this is Taylor," Jack said. "Taylor, this is my sister, Lana, and her sidekick, the award-winning bronc-buster Caleb Carson." Jack grinned widely, then with a wide sweep of an arm, he added, "And this is Ryan, the tiger."

The boy, who must have been only five or six was bouncing around as if he'd eaten a ten-pound bag of sugar. "I bet you're excited to see the rodeo," Taylor said to him.

"I'm gonna ride when I get bigger," he said proudly. "Just like Uncle Jack and Uncle Cal."

Taylor looked at Jack, who shrugged. "Long time ago. I was too young to know I could break bones and end up in a wheelchair." He ruffled the boy's hair.

"Uncle Cal doesn't break bones."

"That's because he's good. If you're not good, you break bones."

Cal, Jack had explained on the way to the rodeo, was his best friend and happened to be dating Jack's sister—

and Ryan called him uncle because of Jack, not because he was dating Lana.

"We've got seats over here," Lana said, pointing to the bleachers.

"You're gonna ride, too, aren't you, Uncle Jack?"

"Just once," Jack said. "And you've all gotta keep your fingers crossed that I don't crash and burn."

"You won't," Ryan said, excitement shining in his big blue eyes. "You can sit next to me," the boy told Taylor. "Cuz I can tell you what's going on."

Taylor laughed. "Great. It's a deal."

Lana nudged Taylor. "He likes to sit with strangers because they buy him junk food."

"Ah, I got it. And here I was thinking it was my sparkling personality."

Ryan ran off to talk to another child and Jack was pre-occupied with Cal and various people who came by, apparently coordinating last-minute details for the benefit.

Lana led Taylor to their seats in the first row of bleachers, saving spots for Jack, Cal and Ryan. "Up here when you're ready," she called to the others.

As she and Lana sat watching, Taylor was struck by how handsome both men were, each in his own way. Jack with his dark, shiny hair and electric green eyes, Cal with his blond model good looks and dark hazel eyes that made his coloring appear almost bronze. The two men made quite the pair and, watching women's heads turn as they walked by, Taylor suspected the two of them had a great time when they went out together. Double trouble.

Oddly, Cal and Lana looked more like brother and sister than Jack and Lana.

Cal pumped hands with Jack and then the two of them

walked off, apparently toward their rides for the day. The earthy smell of animals, dirt, sweat and leather permeated the air. Excitement hummed through the crowd as they waited for the first rider out of the gate.

Waiting, Taylor suddenly felt anxious. Jack was right. This had to be a dangerous sport and she hoped he didn't get hurt.

"Don't worry. Nothing's going to happen," Lana said. "Jack's a lot better than he lets on. He could've been on the circuit if he'd wanted to."

Taylor hadn't realized she was that transparent, but then noticed her hands were clenched and her fingernails were digging into her palms. "Really. He didn't mention that part."

"The good thing is that Jack only does this once a year. Cal does it all the time. It's his job."

Taylor looked at Lana, such a beautiful girl she could've been a model. She was a single mother, that was obvious, but Jack hadn't said whether she was divorced or what. "That must be hard. Does he ever get hurt?"

She gave Taylor tight smile. "He does. But he's been lucky and hasn't had any major injuries. Nothing disabling anyway."

Lana's tone told Taylor that she wasn't happy with Cal's choice of career.

"But that's all he knows. He says he's going to quit when he has enough money to start his own business."

Taylor smiled. "And you're happy about that?"

She laughed. "He's had enough money for years. It's in his blood. He can't give it up. Just like Jack couldn't give up the newspaper, even though he says he wants to write the great American novel."

Taylor knew the pull of passions that strong. It didn't

matter to her whether her business made money or not. She was driven to design and create. "I can understand." Only too well. Her mother had been the same.

Just then, Jack appeared at Taylor's side. "Here," he said, handing her a cowboy hat. "I rustled this up for you."

She smiled. It looked new. "Thank you," she said as he put it on her head.

"Perfect." His gaze lingered on her lips. And in the next instant, he was gone.

"Oh, boy," Lana said.

Taylor looked at Lana, who shrugged. She didn't know what Lana meant, but she thought the gesture was sweet. He'd bought her a hat. Or commandeered it somewhere. Either way, he'd thought about her.

"They're ready," Ryan said as he bounded up the stairs and then dropped down beside Taylor. "This is the best part."

A couple of clowns came out, did a few antics and then bowed to the crowd. A hush spread through the stands, and tension seemed to mount as they waited. The announcement came, the first rider was on his horse.

"He has to set his hold," Ryan said.

The cowboy nodded, the gate shot open and the horse burst out of the side of the delivery chute, bucking high. The powerful animal did a spin, bucked, jumped and kicked with a vengeance. The rider, holding a thick rein, raised his free hand in the air.

"He's gotta keep his hand up," Ryan said, "without touching anything."

Four seconds later it was over.

"He got disqualified," Ryan explained. "He didn't put his feet above the horse's shoulders before the horse's feet touched the ground."

"That hardly seems fair," Taylor said. "All that time and preparation for a four-second ride and a disqualification."

"And unless you're really good and win all the big prizes," Lana said, "the money isn't worth it."

Okay. Taylor knew why Cal and Lana would never get married. And it was pretty obvious Lana didn't want her son in the business, either. So why was Lana seeing Cal anyway?

Just then Jack appeared on the horse in the chute. A nod, and the gate burst open. Apparently he did everything right since Ryan was whooping and pumping his fist. But his ride seemed awfully short, too. Cal's ride was similar and, afterward, both men joined them in the stands, bringing beer and hot dogs.

After the bronc riders came the bareback riders, then the steer wrestlers, team roping and calf roping, followed by barrel racers, all of whom were women. The grand finale were the bull riders.

By the time Jack had finished talking to people and cleaning up some of his benefit duties, it was late. Taylor was exhausted.

In the car on the way to the hotel, she said, "I don't know why I feel so tired. All I did was sit there."

Jack smiled. "Tension. Expectation. It's a mental exhaustion."

"Not for you though." She smiled. "Ryan said you 'did good.'"

He nodded. "It wasn't too bad. I surprised myself." He turned to look at her. "Maybe I just wanted to show off."

He was flirting with her. And she liked it.

He turned on the radio and found a country station playing a Rascal Flatts song, one she actually recognized. Outside, a fat yellow moon lit their way and, between the music and the hum of the tires on asphalt, Taylor nearly drifted off. She felt content. Something she hadn't felt in a long time.

Jack drove with one hand on the wheel and the other on the seat between them. She hoped that maybe he'd take her hand, and when he didn't, she thought about taking his. She wanted to feel his warm skin against hers. She hadn't realized until this minute how much she missed that. How much she wanted to feel close to someone again. No, not *someone*. She wanted to feel close to Jack.

Despite that, she was relieved he didn't touch her. Because then she would have had to make a decision. Think about consequences, about getting hurt.

When they reached the hotel, he walked her inside. "I'll go up with you," he said.

"It's not necessary. I'm fine."

They stopped at the elevator and he turned her to face him. "I like your hat."

She smiled, then started to remove it. "Here, you may need it again."

He plunked it back on her head. "It's yours. I bought it for you."

"It's a great hat."

"It's great on you. And—" he took both her hands in his "—I had a great time. I hope you did, too."

How could she answer that? She'd felt wonderful and alive and she hadn't wanted it to end. She took a deep breath and, keeping her voice even, she said, "I had a great time, too."

The elevator dinged and the doors opened. She started inside, but he caught her hand and stepped in with her, and before she knew it, he'd pulled her close, his mouth a fraction of an inch away from hers. "It was more than that, Taylor. You know it and I know it."

She stood there looking at him. "More. It was more." And if he thought she was going to push him away, he was crazy. She wanted to kiss him again and she wanted him to kiss her. She wanted to taste his mouth and feel his body against hers and not just for a few elevator minutes.

His lips brushed hers, feather-light and delicious. Testing, tasting. He pressed against her, his body hard and hot. She felt him reach for the buttons and the elevator rose. His hands glided up under her shirt, his fingers touching, caressing, teasing. The doors opened and she turned. Their floor. She pulled down her shirt and headed for the door, keys in hand. She couldn't get there fast enough.

Jack was right behind Taylor all the way. If she wanted him to stop now, she was going to have to tell him right out, because he felt like a speeding train without brakes. But she didn't. She opened the door to her room and then they were in each other's arms.

"Shower," he said. "I've got rodeo dust all over."

"Okay, shower it is." They went into the bathroom, peeling off clothes on the way.

The hotel water was immediately hot and they were both inside, soaping each other, rinsing off with their hands and the washcloth, their lips and bodies entwined. It seemed only seconds before he was inside her moving against her soft, tight ⋯ness and then it hit him. *Condom.* He almost couldn't stop. But he did.

"What?" she said breathlessly. "What's wrong?"

He wheezed, "Protection."

"Oh, shit."

He propped himself against the shower wall. "In my pocket. The wallet."

She didn't flinch. With all the class in the world, she stepped out of the shower, pulled the condom from his wallet, came back in, rolled it on and then stood with her legs apart. He'd never been so turned on in his whole freaking life.

THE PHONE RANG, waking Taylor from a dead man's sleep. Groggy, she glanced around. Jack wasn't there. She reached for the phone.

"Bagels and cream cheese or blueberry muffins?"

"Both. And lots of coffee."

She hung up and rolled back on the bed. She'd never felt more wonderful. She stretched and practically purred, she felt so good. There was no way to know what this meant, but she didn't care. It had been a moment. They'd had a moment. She smiled. She'd have to tell Roxi she'd taken her advice and Roxi was right. Marriage and family were wonderful if they came, but if they didn't, why not enjoy what was there when it was there? She just might have herself a new philosophy.

Well, for a few minutes anyway. She knew herself too well.

The door opened and Jack sauntered in. "Coffee's here."

"Great. I need it desperately. I can't function without my morning cup."

"Sure, but you'll have to come over here to get it," he said, setting the cardboard tray on the table.

She did a double take. "What, you didn't see enough of me naked last night?"

"Actually, I have work to do, and if I bring it to you, I might get sidetracked."

"Did something happen?"

"Something is always happening when you work for a newspaper. I got a call on a breaking story, so I've got to go. I'll call when I'm done to see what we can eke out of the rest of the day. You might want to take it easy for a change. Get a massage. Have your nails done."

She wanted to savor the afterglow and she wanted to savor it with him. But there she was doing it again. Putting meaning into something that might have no meaning at all. If she was going to do Roxi's "be a man" thing, that was a habit she had to break.

"Okay." She got up, grabbing the sheet as she did and wrapping it around herself, and then walked over and took the coffee he offered.

"I'll call." He gave her a quick kiss and then he was gone.

HEAT ROSE from the concrete steps leading up to the Regans' front door. From the moment Taylor had stepped off the plane, she'd felt as if she were in a gargantuan steam room. A person could fry eggs on Arizona sidewalks in the summer, but at least it wasn't hot *and* humid.

Jack wasn't going to like the fact that she'd gone alone, but she'd had no other choice after he'd called and said he had business that would keep him all day and probably the evening. And Regan had said she couldn't fit them in any other time. Taylor was grateful Regan had even agreed to a meeting.

Pushing the hair out of her eyes, she knocked on the door and waited. The place was every bit as opulent as the Hawthorne estate and Taylor couldn't help wondering what it would be like to have so much money you never needed to think about paying the bills. Or anything else for that matter. Thanks to her thriving business, Taylor now had more spendable income, but she was so used to pinching pennies, she rarely splurged on herself.

Her hand shook as she raised it to knock again. She'd slipped up on the phone and told Regan she wanted to talk about her mother, so she was going to have to continue in that vein. Just then the door opened. A young woman about her own age answered. "Hello," Taylor said, then introduced herself and explained she had an appointment.

"Yes, my grandmother is expecting you," the woman said, then led Taylor inside and into a large white-on-white living room. The varying shades of white accented the dark wood floor and what looked to be hand-carved accent tables.

Helena Regan was sitting in an ivory brocade wingback chair next to a small table, a cane at her side. She looked remarkably young for a woman who had to be in her eighties.

"I'll be upstairs if you need me," her granddaughter said, then left the room.

"You wished to talk about my sister," the woman said in a soft, decidedly Southern accent while indicating that Taylor should sit in the other chair. "You said your mother knew her."

"Yes. She died recently and I'm trying to put together something about her life. But I don't know that much about the time she spent in Texas working for the Hawthornes."

"What was your mother's name, dear? Did I know her?"

"Her name was Margaret Dundee. What I really want to know is what working for your sister and her family might have been like."

"The name isn't familiar to me. Why don't you talk to Seymour or Emily about it?"

"My mother worked there during a bad time. It was before I was born, thirty years ago."

She raised a trembling hand to her throat, pausing as if her mind might be elsewhere. "Thirty years ago. That was a very bad time indeed." She continued rubbing her neck and, after a long moment, said, "Nothing was the same after that."

Taylor felt reluctant to go on. She knew what it was like to have your whole world change in an instant. "I can only imagine. Did Mr. Hawthorne or his daughter ever talk to you about what happened that night?"

The woman's shoulders came up sharply. "They didn't have to. The media made everything public."

Taylor moistened her lips. "Yes. I've read the coverage. That had to be so hard on everyone in the family."

"Poor Seymour. Emily made it worse by going away to Europe. She didn't even come back for her own mother's funeral."

That piqued Taylor's interest. "Really? I can't imagine not being at my own mother's—" She stopped. The woman didn't need to hear Taylor's heartbreak.

"I'm sorry, dear. Only those who've lost a loved one know the damage it does. Seymour never got over Sunny's death. He did love her, God only knows why."

Taylor's mouth felt dry. She'd thought Hawthorne a nice man who'd made a mistake. Now she had to wonder. If he'd loved his wife, then what was he doing with her mother?

"And then the newspapers made him out to be a cad and a philanderer. It was terrible."

"Was he?"

"I don't believe so. But Sunny never appreciated him. If he strayed, it was her fault."

So no love was lost between Helena and her sister. "Did you two have a falling-out of some kind?"

Helena laughed. "Oh my, yes. Sunny had a falling-out with everyone. It was so long ago, I don't even remember what it was about. Probably some boy or something." The woman's eyes suddenly misted over. "I felt terrible, of course, when she was murdered. I wished so many times that I could go back and fix things between us, but by the time I realized my mistake, it was too late."

"I can only imagine how terrible that was for everyone. Especially Emily. It must have been hard reading horrible things in the newspapers."

"That girl was always trouble," Helena said. "Running around, staying out all night, getting herself in more situations than any one child should."

"Did Emily know Margot Cooper's son, Matt?"

Helena turned, her small eyes widening. "You really don't know anything, do you?"

"A-about what?"

"Emily and that boy were more than friendly, if you know what I mean."

"Oh." Apparently she didn't know much. "I knew they were friends. Do you mean they had an affair?"

The older woman nodded. "But Sunny wouldn't allow it and sent Emily to visit relatives for the summer." Regan raised her chin. "I didn't believe it. Not for one minute."

"Why? Where do you think she went? And why would your sister lie to you?"

"She didn't want anyone to know Emily had gotten pregnant by that housekeeper's son, but Emily told me her mother was sending her somewhere to get rid of it. Emily asked me to intervene on her behalf." The woman got a faraway look in her eyes. "That's it," she finally said. "That's why Sunny wouldn't speak to me anymore."

"Pregnant?" It took a moment for Taylor to process this. Had Emily had an abortion? Instinctively, Taylor placed a hand on her own stomach. Having a child was a gift. A wonderful event, no matter how it came about.

"Emily wanted to marry that boy. And she was so head-strong, she'd never have done what Sunny wanted her to. Her mother made arrangements for an adoption." Helena looked at Taylor. "What kind of work did your mother do for Sunny?"

A child given up for adoption. A child of Matt's maybe, who could have been Taylor's niece or a nephew. "I don't know exactly. That's why I'm asking questions. She…uh…she and Margot Cooper were very close. So, I thought if I talked to people who knew Margot, I might find out more about my mother."

"Well, if your mother worked for my sister, perhaps she was one of the maids. Whatever the case, I'm sure it wasn't easy for her. As far as I know, Margot took a lot from that woman, but she took it only because she was close to Emily. That's why the police thought Margot might have been involved in my sister's death. Pity. She was a nice person. And even though Emily was a brat, I always felt sorry for her, too. She really couldn't help how she turned out, you know."

"Do you believe Margot…was involved somehow in… the crime?" Taylor couldn't bring herself to say the actual words.

"I was surprised when she disappeared. I thought it had to do with Seymour."

Regan sighed. "I'm sorry I don't remember your mother, dear. I'm afraid I've not been much help."

Taylor gulped some air and waited, letting everything sink in. Now she knew there was a child given up for adoption. Matthew Cooper's child. Possibly. "Oh, you've been very helpful, Mrs. Regan. And I truly appreciate it."

"UNCLE JACK." Ryan's little-boy voice on the other end of the phone brought Jack fully awake.

He glanced at the clock. "What's going on?"

"My mom says you should come and see my program at school."

"Okay, buddy. When is it?"

"Tomorrow at six o'clock. Can you come?"

"Sure. I'll be there," Jack said as he rolled out of bed. He hadn't made it back to meet Taylor last night, but had left a message telling her he'd be at the hotel at ten o'clock. A few seconds later Lana came on the phone.

"Hi, Jack. Mom called and wants us all to come over for dinner tonight."

The family had a standing dinner together once a week, but it had been a while since Jack had made it.

"I'm meeting with Taylor and I don't know when I'll be done."

"Oh, Taylor again. She seems to be taking up most of your time these days."

His felt a quick surge of adrenaline—happened every time he thought about Taylor. "We're working together."

"Uh-huh," she said.

"Don't be a smart-ass."

"Hey, I'd like nothing better than to see you with someone. Maybe spread your protectiveness out a little so I'm not the only beneficiary. But Mom might not feel the same if it keeps you from dinner too often."

"I'll call her," he said. He had to beg off the charity basketball game his dad wanted to go to as well.

Jack's phone beeped. He had another call. "I gotta go, Lanny. I'll call later." He punched flash and picked up the other call. "Yeah, Parker here."

"Hello, Mr. Parker. I'm sorry to call you so early, but I would like to talk to you about Henry Juarez."

Jack shoved off the quilt and bolted upright. "Who are you and what's this about?"

"I'm a friend of Henry's. I think he's in trouble."

Jack gritted his teeth. Why wasn't he surprised?

"He should be taking his medicine and he left it at my brother's and never came back for it. He wouldn't do that because he could die without it. I don't know what to do and I found your number in his things. I knew you when you were a baby."

"You knew me?" Jack asked very slowly.

"Yes, sir. Henry and I have been friends for forty years. We came to Texas together."

For a moment, Jack couldn't draw a full breath.

"What medicine is he supposed to be taking?"

"It's for diabetes. If he goes without it too long, he can go into a coma and it can be fatal. He's been staying in a room at my brother's place in the barrio."

"When did he go missing?"

"Last night."

Jack knew the police didn't count an adult missing until twenty-four hours had passed and even then it was hard to say whether someone was missing or wanted to disappear. But the fact that he'd gone without medicine he needed to live was significant. "Did you report it?"

"I wouldn't do that. He could get in trouble with his parole officer and go back to prison."

Jack felt torn. He had no connection with Juarez—and yet he did. Half the time he wanted to hate the guy and the other half he didn't know how to feel. "Can you give me the address where he's staying? Maybe I can get some clue as to where he might have gone. If you could meet me there, maybe you can help."

Manny Ortega gave Jack the address and they agreed to meet in a half hour.

It was eight now so he had two hours before he had to meet Taylor. Where could a guy without money go? How could he get around without a car?

He hung up and turned on the water in the shower. Calmly, he took out a pair of jeans and a T-shirt, and when the water was lukewarm, Jack stepped inside and stood under the spray, letting it pummel his face.

The one time he'd seen Juarez, it had been at the prison after Jack had learned he was getting out. He'd finally gone to see him to put an end to the questions he'd had for so many years. He'd wanted to look the guy in the face and ask him why he had given his son away.

Juarez hadn't answered, he said he couldn't. Despite that, Jack had felt some kind of obligation to offer Juarez money to help him get on his feet. Juarez refused. Jack had offered to help him find a job. Juarez refused that, too.

The only thing Jack could figure out was that Juarez wanted nothing to do with the son he abandoned. Or… maybe he knew where the missing money was and intended to collect it. For all Jack knew, Juarez was living in another country by now.

And now he felt obligated again. By the time he reached the address Manny had given him, it was later than he'd anticipated, and he couldn't see how he was going to make his meeting with Taylor and called her room. Getting no answer, he left a message.

He parked in front of what had been, once upon a time, a white clapboard house. It should have had a Condemned Building sign on the front. He'd been in the barrio before, in Chicago during his early days as a reporter, but never in Houston. It was enough that he saw it on the TV news every day and in the *Chronicle*.

For all he knew, he'd lived in the barrio when he was born. If he'd ever been able to see his original birth certificate, he would know. But even that information hadn't been available to him.

He sometimes felt that his life, the person he might have been, had been stripped away and he'd been programmed to be someone else. Someone who fit the family who'd adopted him. Not that his parents weren't wonderful. They were. They'd given him love and opportunities he wouldn't have had otherwise.

But they would never understand what it felt like not to have your own identity.

A car pulled in behind him, blaring rap music with the bass so loud it made his car vibrate. He got out and walked up the weed-choked sidewalk, the scent of barbecue and something sweet in the air. He saw a man in the doorway. Manny maybe? Or his brother?

As Jack got closer, a barrel-chested older man stepped out of the shadows and reached to shake Jack's hand.

"Jack."

He nodded.

The man introduced himself, at least that's what Jack gathered since he didn't understand a word except the name.

"I don't speak Spanish," Jack said.

"I'm Manny Ortega. Thank you for coming." Manny motioned for Jack to follow him inside, where another man sat at an old metal kitchen table. The house was tiny, one room with a kitchen off to his right, an old TV on a patio table.

"This is my brother, Richard," Manny said.

Jack shook hands with the other man. Noticed a prison tattoo on his forearm.

"Sit," Manny said, motioning to one of the chairs.

"Why did you call me?" Jack asked.

Manny sat in a green plastic lawn chair on Jack's left. "Because you're his son. You're blood." He shrugged as if it was the most natural conclusion in the world.

"I've seen him once in thirty years. For five minutes. We aren't close."

"But he has no one else. Blood means something, doesn't it?"

How the hell would he know? "You said he was gone and he didn't take his medicine. How long has he had this…what was it?"

"Diabetes. He's had it for years. When we were kids and just got here from Mexico, he had a spell and I took him to the hospital."

Jack hadn't known that. But he knew a lot about childhood diabetes from the benefits he'd supported for years. He knew how dangerous it could be if someone neglected to take their medication. "Do you know where he was going when he left the house and what time it was?"

Manny nodded to his brother, who said, "He goes to day labor every day to pick up whatever work he can. He leaves at about six-thirty in the morning. I didn't see him go, but he was gone when I got up."

"Does he go anywhere else?"

"He's never mentioned any place," Manny said. Richard shrugged.

"How has his mood been?" Jack asked, though it seemed strange asking. Being in jail for thirty years had to be more depressing than being out, no matter how bad the job situation was.

"He was the same every day. He gets up, goes to work. If he gets work, he's gone for the day. If he doesn't, he comes back and collects some cans and things. He doesn't complain."

Jack rubbed his hands together, uncomfortable thinking of anyone having to stand on a corner hoping for work to make minimum wage. Collecting cans. "Can I look at his room? Maybe there's something that will explain where he might have gone."

Manny motioned to a door across the room. Jack crossed and went inside. It wasn't much bigger than a closet and had no window. A tiny cot and a metal lawn table took up most of the room. Some shirts hung on hangers from a nail on one wall. Jack sat on the bed and picked up a folder on the table.

A picture fell out and he reached to pick it up. As he did, he recognized Juarez as a young man, with a woman at his side. They were holding a small boy between them. He tilted the photo to the light.

"You were a pretty boy," Manny said from behind him. "Your mother had to keep telling people you were a boy and not a girl."

Jack dropped the folder on the bed and some other photos fell out. He stood. He couldn't do this. He cleared his throat. "Do you know of any place else he might go?"

Manny shook his head. "No, but Richard said he got a phone call from someone at the jail. Henry told Richard he didn't want to talk to him."

Jack didn't like the sound of that. He scraped a hand across the stubble on his chin. "Maybe you could call some of the local hospitals. The free clinics. Just in case he got sick," Jack said, then realized that probably wouldn't happen. He doubted there was even a phone book around.

"Never mind. I'll call around. Stop at a few places in the area. Give me your phone number and I'll let you know if I get any information."

Manny held out his cell to show his number and Jack put it into his phone's memory list. Ironic that no matter how broke people were, everyone had a cell phone.

"That's all I can do," he said to Manny.

"*Gracias.* You're a good son," Manny said. "I know he's very proud of you."

Jack clenched his teeth. He held up the photo again. "I might need this to show someone when I'm looking."

He couldn't get out of there fast enough and it seemed like a long time before he could get enough air into his lungs to breathe without it hurting.

Looking for Juarez took the rest of the day. He called hospitals and clinics; he went to a couple of bars and homeless shelters. When he finally called Manny back, he was told Henry had returned—he'd been out looking for a job. "If he was looking for a job, why did he leave his medication at home?"

There was a long pause. "I...don't know. I didn't ask."

Jack shoved a hand through his hair. The hesitation in Manny's voice made Jack wonder if that was the truth. Before he hung up, Jack said, "Maybe you should."

He closed the phone, then reached into his pocket and pulled out the tattered black-and-white photo.

His mother had been pretty. They looked like a happy family. A family of strangers.

CHAPTER TWELVE

TAYLOR PACED the hotel room. Two days ago, Jack had
left a message that he couldn't make it, but would call
later. Then he'd left another message that he had business
to take care of and would call when he could. But he
hadn't.

She'd made more searches on the Internet, but found
nothing helpful, and the trip she'd made to the library had
been a bust. A phone call to Kittridge found her out of town
and she wasn't expected back until late today or tomorrow.
Taylor had called two people who'd worked for the Hawthornes but had since moved out of the state. She was at a
standstill.

Unable to sleep, she'd been up since five. She'd gone
jogging, had breakfast in the hotel restaurant, grabbed a
double espresso to take to her room and then went through
all her papers again. Now her nerves felt like snakes
crawling under her skin.

She heard a knock. *Jack.* She rushed to the door.

"Hey." He stood with one hand braced against the door
frame. Not a care in the world.

"Hey."

He stepped inside. "Sorry I've been unavailable. You got
my messages, didn't you?"

"I did. We need to talk to Emily Kittridge again," she said without preamble.

He took off his hat. "Something new come up?"

"A lot new." She explained her meeting with Sunny Hawthorne's sister as she walked over to the bed and sat on the end, then told him the gist of the conversation. "The bottom line is that Emily Kittridge hasn't been telling us the truth. She lied about her relationship with Matt and with Margot. Mrs. Regan believes Emily became pregnant and her mother sent her away to give the child up for adoption."

"Okay. How does that change things?"

"Matt's crash occurred right in front of the Hawthorne estate."

Jack walked over and sat in one of the chairs by the window. "Which means what?"

"I don't know. I'm no detective. But it's strange that none of this came out thirty years ago. I read the court transcripts. There's nothing."

"But I'm still not getting the significance. The only information that has significance in court is information that might affect the case somehow. Apparently no one thought Emily Kittridge's pregnancy was relevant. And I have to say—"

"Well, I think it is. Sunny Hawthorne didn't want her daughter involved with Matt. Matt dies in a hit-and-run right at the gates to the Hawthorne estate, and no one—Kittridge, Hawthorne or Belamy—ever mentioned it was a hit and run. It's certainly worth following up. If nothing else, to show there were other people who had reasons for wanting Sunny Hawthorne dead." She wrung her hands together.

"Other people. You mean like Matthew's mother?"

Her eyes got big. "No, I didn't mean her. But there were

other people besides Margot who disliked Sunny Hawthorne. People she'd mistreated."

Jack watched her go to the window, then come back again. She turned, as if wondering where to go next. "Is something else wrong?"

She swung around. "No. Why?"

"You're pacing like a caged animal."

"I—I'm just anxious to get done with this and go home."

He stood. "We'll go see Kittridge again. Did you call her?"

"I did, but she was gone. They expected her back about now. Come to think of it, I'm not sure she'll even see us if we call ahead. Let's surprise her."

"I'll just use the boys' room and then we'll go."

Taylor didn't know why she was so jumpy. Or maybe she did. She'd barely seen Jack since they'd made love and the only conclusion she could draw was that he'd been avoiding her. She told herself a hundred times that it didn't matter. They'd had a fling. No big deal. They were adults.

"Okay," he said, a couple minutes later. "Let's get this show on the road."

"Great."

Once they were in the car, they drove in silence until Jack finally said, "I'll listen if you want to talk about it."

"Talk about what?"

He shrugged. "Whatever it is that's bothering you." She didn't respond. "All right, we won't talk about it. But don't tell me there's nothing wrong."

"We won't talk because there's nothing to talk about." What would she say? I'm so needy I crave reassurance. Or maybe, hey, that one-night stand was great, can we do it again, like for the rest of our lives? She was more confused than ever. The only thing she knew for sure was that she couldn't play the man game Roxi had suggested. She could no more have casual sex with someone than she could ride bulls in a rodeo competition.

As they rounded the curve to the Hawthorne estate, Taylor was glad to have something else to focus on. "I hope she's here."

"You wanted to surprise her," Jack said.

She had a multitude of questions for Kittridge. "Don't you think it's odd that Emily still lives with her father? I know her husband's dead, but still, it seems strange."

He shrugged. "I hadn't thought about it. Maybe she does it to keep an eye on him. I think he has Parkinson's disease."

"Really? What makes you think that?"

"The tremors in his head and hands."

"You're very observant," she said, giving him back the same thing he'd earlier said about her.

He grinned. "It's the nature of my job."

"Hmm. I'd have to say I'm more of a doer than an observer."

"I noticed that."

"And what else did you notice?" That she might be in love with him?

"That you ask a lot of questions," he answered as he turned into the driveway. Driving toward the gate, another car passed them going out. Jack hit the accelerator and went through before it closed.

He glanced at Taylor. "Saves me from having to make up a story to get in."

No one seemed to be around when they drove to the house and parked. No valet today. It was early, maybe that was why. They got out and went to the door.

A woman wearing a white apron answered.

"We're here to see Emily Kittridge," Taylor said.

"Is she expecting you?"

"No, but it's important that we talk with her," Taylor said.

Stiffening, the woman started to object when Jack cut in. "Please tell her Jack Parker and Taylor Dundee are here to talk to her about the baby."

Frowning, the woman said, "Just a moment, please." She left them standing at the door.

Taylor turned to Jack. *"The baby?"* she whispered.

He shrugged. "If she thinks we know something that she doesn't want to be public—" His gaze shifted from Taylor to over her shoulder. He smiled wide. "Hello, Mrs. Kittridge."

Taylor swung around.

"Valencia said you wished to speak with me."

"Yes, if you can spare a few minutes," Taylor said. Kittridge motioned them inside and to a room on the left. When they were all inside, she shut the door.

Two plush couches, a few assorted side chairs, tables and a grand piano filled the room. The piano top was cluttered with family photographs in silver and gold frames. Taylor stood by the piano, her gaze on a photo of a young blond girl. A girl of about twenty who looked eerily familiar.

Jack nudged Taylor and she came to attention. "We're sorry to disturb you so early, Mrs. Kittridge," she said. "But we've learned some things that we'd like to confirm with you."

Standing with her arms crossed over her chest, Kittridge snapped, "How much do you want?"

Taylor looked at Jack, then at Kittridge again. "Excuse me?"

"Let's not play games. You've dug up some obscure information and now you want money."

"Y-you think that…" Taylor sputtered.

"I don't think. When you come from a wealthy family, you get used to it."

"You're joking, I hope."

Jack took Taylor's hand. He looked at Emily. "That's not why we're here. We're trying to unravel a mystery that involves Margot Cooper. Can we sit for a moment?"

Taylor saw fire in the woman's eyes, but even so, she waved a hand toward the chairs.

"I don't know what mystery you're talking about. As far as I know there is none. Margot disappeared. That's no mystery."

"I knew her," Taylor said. "She never mentioned living in Texas. She never mentioned working for your family."

The woman stiffened. "For obvious reasons. The police were looking for her."

"She was a wonderful person."

Kittridge looked away, her expression softening. Her mouth formed words that seemed difficult for her to get out. "Yes…she was. My father told me she passed away. I'm sorry."

"Me, too," Taylor said. If Emily felt anything about Margot's death, the emotion was fleeting.

"Since she was your aunt, you probably know whether she ever married and had the family she always wanted."

Taylor looked at Jack. "She had a daughter."

Taylor noticed Emily spent a lot of time twisting the wedding ring on her finger.

"Did you know she had a daughter?" Jack asked.

The woman's lips pinched. After a long hesitation, she said, "I'd heard once. I think the police might've mentioned it."

"After my...aunt's death, her home was ransacked. We think it might be someone looking for the money that's never been recovered."

Emily sat up, her shoulders so straight she could have balanced a knife on end. Then she smiled strangely and actually laughed. "Oh, people are so stupid. Margot didn't take the money. I don't know why everyone thought that."

Taylor exchanged glances with Jack.

"Do you know this for sure? Or is it because you believe she'd never do something like that?"

Emily cleared her throat, hesitated. Finally she said, "She'd never have done something like that. As you said, she was a good person."

Relieved, Taylor felt like jumping up and shouting *Yes!* Even if her mother had kept the past from her, she wasn't the person Jack thought she was.

Kittridge fidgeted with the ring again, then smoothed the front of her pants, apparently ready to end the meeting. But Taylor wasn't ready yet. "We've been told that you had a baby."

Emily's hand went to her throat. "Where did you hear that?"

"Your aunt. She said the child was given up for adoption."

Stunned was the only word for Emily's expression. She closed her eyes and her shoulders slumped, as if all the air had left her lungs. "Dear Aunt Helena. She's old, you know. Old and addled."

"But is it true?"

"Talking about this will only open old wounds."

Kittridge's softer tone said her resistance wasn't as strong as it had been, so Taylor decided on another tack. "I know. And I'm sorry about that." Taylor pulled out the list from her bag. "I suppose Nancy Belamy, your mother's assistant, will be able to tell me. Or perhaps—"

Kittridge shot up from her chair "Why can't you just go away and leave us alone? I'll give you money if you'll just go away."

Taylor wished she could just go away. But her life had been turned upside down and she needed to know why. There had to be a reason her mother had changed her name and lied to Taylor about it. If it wasn't the money, then what was it? The only thing Taylor could think was that it had to do with Margot's son. Something about his death.

"The last thing I want is your money, but I'll be happy to go away if you'll just tell me about Matthew Cooper."

Kittridge leaned against the back of her chair. "It's true. I became pregnant, but it wasn't Matt's baby. The father was a boy I liked for a long time, and when he ditched me, I was devastated."

"And your mother wanted no part of the child."

Emily scoffed. "I was sixteen. My mother controlled my life. She never cared about anyone but herself. She wasn't about to have a bastard child in her house. Especially one who had no social standing."

Taylor was amazed at how coldly the woman could talk about her own child. There was no feeling in her voice or in her manner. Was she even telling the truth? "So what happened?"

"She sent me away. I had the baby and that was the last time I saw it."

It? The term set Taylor's teeth on edge. "Was the baby a boy or a girl?"

"A girl," she said softly.

Finally, Taylor saw some emotion.

"Were there other people, the help maybe, who also had…problems with your mother?"

"Yes," she said without a shred of hesitation. "A lot of people. She treated the staff like they were slaves."

Taylor remembered the aunt had said Emily was cut from the same cloth as her mother. But apparently Emily thought differently.

"Was Henry Juarez one of those she treated badly?" Jack piped up.

Kittridge started fidgeting again, her eyes darting, as if searching for an escape route.

"I don't know anything about that man," she said succinctly.

"I understand your mother's assistant was the one who found her," Taylor said.

"Nancy was the only person who could handle my mother. The only person my mother trusted."

Taylor looked at Jack, who shrugged. "Have you kept in touch with her since then?"

"No, I haven't. She's…she's gone. I don't know anything more than that. She could be dead."

A knock at the door made them all turn. The young woman, the blond girl in the pictures whom they'd met briefly the first time they were there, came in and said, "I'm sorry to interrupt. Valencia said you wanted to see me."

Emily's expression hardened. "That was an hour ago, Sienna," she snapped, then raised a hand to her head and rose unsteadily to her feet. "I'm not feeling well. I have to lie down."

She walked toward the door, and the girl helped her out. Before she did, Sienna said, "I'm sorry. Valencia will show you out."

Taylor looked at Jack. He shrugged.

Back in the car, Taylor said, "I wonder if we should talk to Emily's daughter?"

"Sienna was attending school at the Sorbonne in France until a few weeks ago. I doubt she'd be much help. And she may not know about her mother's past."

Rubbing the muscles in her neck, Taylor couldn't believe he'd actually said that. "You didn't care that I didn't know anything about my mother's past when you came to see me."

He chewed on his bottom lip. "I thought you had to know something since you two moved from place to place so often. It wasn't that I didn't care. I am sorry I disrupted your life." He turned to her, then took her hand. "But it hasn't been all bad, has it?"

Taylor's pulse jumped. It was the first real mention of their intimacy—*if* that's what he was talking about. It might be a simple casual remark and have nothing to do with their night together. But it scared her. What she fantasized about and what she needed were two different things. "No. Not all." Her voice caught in her throat. She pulled her hand away. "With all this other stuff happening, I'd have found out anyway. It might have been even worse."

She felt very tired. Dragged down, as if all emotion had been wrung out and there was nothing left to feel.

Her belief that her mother would never have taken the money had been confirmed. She was hurt and disappointed to know that some of the other things were true, that her mother had kept part of her life a secret. But despite all that, she knew her mother was a good person, and she still had an intrinsic belief that there was an explanation for it all, and someday, that explanation would present itself.

"I have to go back to Phoenix," Taylor said. "I don't think learning any more will do me any good. And I have a business to take care of."

Jack turned, his eyes wide as if surprised. "Sure, I can let you know if I come up with anything important."

Taylor smiled. "Thanks, but no thanks. I'm satisfied with the information I have."

He raised his eyebrows. "Okay. But if you change your mind—"

"I won't." She paused. "But…there is one more thing I need to do."

"What's that?"

"Talk to Henry Juarez before I leave."

JACK DROVE them back to the hotel in silence. Taylor seemed fixated on finding Juarez before she went back to Arizona, but he couldn't let that happen. He had no idea what Juarez might tell her, and he didn't want anyone to know his relationship to Juarez—not until he knew if there was going to be one. And for that, he needed answers. If he got them, then he'd tell her—and his parents.

In the elevator on the way up, Taylor got out the key to her room. "I'll try the Internet again. There has to be some way to track him down."

After learning about Juarez's illness and searching for him in places Jack couldn't imagine living, he'd felt badly that he hadn't done something more to help. Anonymously. He could have done that. Maybe given money to his parole officer. He didn't know how Juarez could ever get his life together if he had to live a hand-to-mouth existence.

He fingered the photo in his pocket. They'd looked

happy, Jack and his parents. Juarez had always claimed he was innocent. Jack had seen the taped police interview and not once had Juarez admitted his guilt. He also knew that when a prominent citizen was a victim, someone had to be found guilty, especially in an election year. The evidence was circumstantial, but apparently it had been enough for a jury. Knowing all that, why couldn't he believe it? Where was his faith? Taylor believed in her mother, even when she might be wrong. Why couldn't he do that?

As she opened the door to her room, Taylor was saying something about plane reservations and time schedules and who to talk to before she left, but all Jack could think of was how to keep her from Juarez.

While she was on the phone, he took a beer from the mini-fridge, then noticed the drawers in the television unit next to him were slightly ajar.

"Okay, I have a ticket for Friday evening," she said.

He crossed to her and took her by the arms, stopping her from picking up a paper on the floor. "Don't move."

"Why not? Is there a bug on me or something?"

"No. I want you to look around and tell me what you think." He didn't want to put ideas in her head, either.

She turned, her eyes searching. "Oh, my." She took a step. "Someone was in here."

"How do you know?"

"I'd never leave the light on in the bathroom." She pointed. "The latch on my suitcase in unlocked. I always lock it when I leave."

"The maid, maybe?"

"I was here after they cleaned." Still standing in the same spot, she wrapped her arms around herself. "What now?"

"Check to see if anything is missing."

She quickly rummaged through her things. "Nothing that I can tell."

He went over and put an arm around her. "We'll get you another room."

"You know, this all started before my mother's accident."

He pulled his head back to study her. "What makes you think that?"

"I found a newspaper ad in my mother's safe-deposit box—'Looking for Margot Cooper.' It was from a couple of weeks before the accident. And…my mother's neighbor told me she'd seen a man at my mother's around that same time. A man with a tattoo on his arm, and I know my mother wasn't hanging out with the Hell's Angels."

He dropped his hands.

"What? Does that mean something to you?"

He turned away, stuffing his hands in his pockets. "Uh…no. But it makes me think about some things." Thoughtful, he rubbed a hand against his chin. "I think I should stay with you tonight."

"And not change rooms?"

"No, we'll do that, too."

She appreciated that he wanted to protect her, especially since she was starting to feel a little sick.

Jack went over to her suitcase. "Change clothes if you want, then get together the rest of your things. We'll switch your room and grab a bite to eat."

Taylor changed into a blue tank top and denim pants that came not quite to the ankles. When she was ready, they went to the lobby, but couldn't get another room for a couple of hours. They left her luggage with the bell desk for storage and then they took the elevator down to the parking garage.

"I'm starving," he said. "How about you?"

She seemed preoccupied and took a moment to answer. "A little," she said, then delved into her purse for something.

"I can give you a name and number for Sunny Hawthorne's hairstylist to follow up with," Taylor said as they stepped off the elevator.

"Any particular reason I'd want to talk to the stylist?"

"To get information. You hadn't thought of doing that?"

"Nope." They located his SUV and got inside. He started the engine and pulled out. "I usually only interview people who might have something to do with the focus of my story. In this case, it was the money…who took it and where it might have ended up. I didn't have any reason to interview the hairstylist."

"Well, if you were a woman you'd know that women confide in their hairdressers. What if Sunny told him about someone who hated her or threatened her? Someone who needed money? Any little thing could change the whole picture."

"Great powers of deduction, Watson." And he meant it. She wasn't merely pretty, she was smart.

They were just coming up to the street exit when he heard a screech of tires and saw a car coming at them full speed.

"Watch out," he shouted as he jammed the accelerator to the floor and shot out of the garage. At the same time, he felt a sharp jolt as if hit from behind. The SUV spun around, then came to a stop in the street. Tires screeched. Horns blared as other vehicles stopped to keep from hitting them.

"Are you okay?" His heart thundered in his chest. Taylor was still hunched over. "Are you okay?" he repeated.

She lifted her head slightly before sitting up, her face pale. "Yeah. But I'm scared shitless."

"Me, too," he puffed, and glanced around to see if the other car was still there.

Her mouth opened in surprise and she pointed behind him. "Look," she said, her voice shaky. "That man. That's Juarez, isn't it?"

Jack jerked around. Not more than thirty feet away, Juarez stood at the entry to the parking garage. Their eyes locked. Jack gripped the door handle, shoved it open and turned to get out, only to be jerked back by the seat belt. "Dammit." He twisted around and pressed the release, but when he looked again, Juarez was gone.

"Wait here," he said to Taylor, then took off across the street, but he didn't know which direction to look. He stopped, scanning for Juarez. No sight of him. "Henry!" he shouted. The only response was his own voice echoing back at him.

Heart racing, Jack walked back to the Lexus and as he got inside, a police car pulled up behind them. He didn't know what to say. Did Juarez have anything to do with the car that tried to ram them?

An officer strode up to the SUV and Jack opened the window. "I'll need to see a driver's license and car registration."

"Someone tried to run us down," Taylor injected. "And I know—"

Jack clamped his hand over hers and squeezed. "He wants my license and the car registration, Taylor. Can you get the registration from the glove box please?" Then he said under his breath, "I'll handle this."

The officer took the basic information and Jack told him what had happened.

When the guy left to talk to a few witnesses, Taylor

said, "What was that about? Why didn't you tell him about Juarez?"

"It happened so fast, I can't be sure who it was."

She looked puzzled. "It was Juarez and someone tried to hit us."

"We don't know either for sure. The guy's accelerator might have stuck. And even if it was true, we don't know that Juarez had anything to do with it. If that was, in fact, him."

"He ran away. A car tried to run us down."

"You might be right. But I can't see fingering someone on the basis of flimsy evidence. Besides, nobody would hurt you if they thought you knew where the stolen money was. If it was intentional, and I'm not saying that, it would more likely be because we're getting too close to uncovering a secret."

Her mouth hung open. "Like what? Like the identity of someone else involved in the crime?"

"That's a good guess."

"Shouldn't we tell the police that?"

"Maybe, if we had something to tell."

After the officer came back and told them they could go, Jack assessed the minor damage to his SUV, got inside, started the car and merged into traffic.

"Why didn't you tell them the man you saw might have been Juarez?"

Blood rushed through his veins. "Because I couldn't see clearly. And it was the driver of the car who tried to hit us. Not the man standing there." He chagned lanes. "Even if it was Juarez, he was just standing there. He wasn't doing anything."

"Jack." Her voice rose. "He's a murderer. He spent thirty years in jail for murder. If he was there, it's logical to think he had something to do with it. And if nothing else, he was a witness."

The muscles in Jack's neck knotted. "He paid his debt. He's supposed to get a second chance. It's innocent until proven guilty, not 'convicted once, guilty of other things forever.'"

She was looking at him like he'd lost it. And he wasn't sure he hadn't. He might have as much doubt about Juarez as she did. "I'm sorry. I told you before, that's one of my hot buttons."

She slammed her back against the seat, arms folded across her chest. "I want to go back and talk to the police."

He gritted his teeth. Making a right turn, he headed back to the hotel. "Fine. Then we'll go. But you better be sure."

No response. A wall of silence loomed between them, and even though he didn't want to rat out Juarez, he couldn't help worrying about Taylor's safety. As they neared the building, he said, "I think you should change your plans."

"I don't need you to think for me."

His hands tightened on the wheel. "It was a suggestion."

"I don't need those, either."

"Fine."

After parking, he hit the safety lock so she couldn't get out and turned off the motor. "I'll unlock the door after you listen to what I have to say."

The look she gave him could have cut steel.

"Is there another problem?" she asked

"Yeah. I don't even think you should stay here tonight."

She turned. "I'm not. I'm going to change my flight and go home as soon as possible."

"I don't know if going back to Arizona is the answer, either."

"If I'm gone and I stop asking questions, what reason would anyone have to do anything?"

"I don't know. And that's the problem."

Dammit. If he knew her going home would keep her safe he'd take her to the plane right this minute. But he didn't and if anything happened to her, he'd feel responsible. He started the engine again. "Backing off is a good idea. At least for a few days. I have an idea, but I need you to trust me on this."

"Why can't you tell me?"

He wanted to, but he couldn't. Not until he found out what Henry Juarez had been doing near the hotel. He searched her eyes. "That's where the trust comes in."

It took a while before she said, "Okay. What do I have to do?"

"I'm going to take you to a safe place until it's time for you to go, and I'm going to take care of something else. I'll be in touch and you can call if you need to."

"Where will I go?"

"I'll tell you in a minute." He got out his phone and hit the auto dial. It rang three times before she picked up.

"Hey," he said. "How are ya?"

"I'm fine," his mother said. "I'm sorry you couldn't make it for dinner. We missed you."

"I'm sorry, too. Listen, I need a favor."

"Sure."

"Do you have a room available?" Jack explained he had a friend who needed a place for one night and his mother was excited to help. Mostly because Jack's friend was a woman.

"It's done," he said, hanging up.

"Where am I going?"

"To my parents' home."

She turned to face him, her eyes wide. "Your parents will take in a stranger just like that? No questions asked?"

"My folks have a couple of rooms they rent out like a bed-and-breakfast. They do it mostly because they like meeting people. And since you're a friend of mine, they won't charge. We'll get your suitcase, then cancel the room and it will look like you've gone home or someplace else."

She didn't answer right away, so he added, "And if you still want to leave, I'll come back and take you to the airport before your flight."

Pondering, she finally said, "All right then. Let's do it."

They went back, retrieved her luggage and, as they were getting into his SUV, she said, "Where do your parents live?"

"About sixty miles out. It's a ranch. A very small ranch that used to be in the boonies. Now it's part of the ever-expanding suburbia."

They got inside and Jack started the vehicle. Buckling her seat belt, Taylor said, smiling, "You grew up on a ranch? How about that." She turned to look at him. "Yes, I can see the cowboy in you. The boots, the hat."

"My friends would disagree. And after living in Chicago and Houston for the past ten years, I feel pretty citified."

She got quiet all of a sudden. "I'd still like to talk to Juarez."

He looked over, and lifted his fingers from the wheel. "Not Nancy Belamy?"

"Well, yes. She was there. She knew my mother and my brother. Being around someone who actually knew him... You'd want to know, wouldn't you?"

"I suppose." He'd wanted more than anything to know his biological father. But he hadn't anticipated the outcome.

"Do you have any other siblings besides Lana?"

"That's it. Just the two of us."

"Even so, you're lucky. I always wanted a brother or sister. Someone to confide in. To be close to."

"To fight with."

She laughed. "That, too. I think it's better to have siblings. A kid learns to share and interact with others. From what I've seen, you and your sister are close."

"We are. She's four years older than me, so she took care of me, helped me fight all those kid battles. I looked up to her." He shrugged. "It's hard being a single mom, so I help with Ryan."

"Isn't Ryan's dad around?"

"He died when Ryan was a baby. Rodeo accident."

"Ah, I see."

"See what?"

"Why she'll never marry Cal."

"Not unless he quits the circuit."

"It's too bad, because she loves him."

He turned. "She said that?"

"No, but I could tell. And he adores her." She crossed her arms and leaned back in her seat. "It's too bad people can't take the good parts of someone and forget the rest of it. Life would be so much easier."

"Yeah," Jack said. "But it's hard to forget."

"Maybe *accept* would be a better word. We should take the good and accept the rest."

"Is that what you do?"

"Sometimes to my own detriment. I don't seem to know where to draw the line."

"Well, I'm glad you didn't draw the line with me." He looked over and saw a faint blush on her cheeks.

"That, I'm thinking, was a mistake."

"Really?" He grinned.

"Really."

He liked her ability to joke about things. He liked most everything about her, he admitted. In fact, if he was ever to fall in love, he imagined it would be with someone like Taylor. If he ever fell in love.

They rode for a long time in silence, with only Tim Hall's music in the background. Then, out of the blue, she said, "Maybe I'll wait for a few months and then come back and talk to Juarez and Belamy. What do you think about that?"

What he thought was that it wasn't a good idea for her to leave at all.

Jack tightened his grip on the wheel. If someone hurt her, he couldn't guarantee what he might do. "I think right now…you'll have to put up with my parents." He pointed ahead to a sign that read, Parker Ranch.

CHAPTER THIRTEEN

TAYLOR HADN'T KNOWN what to expect, but she was greeted at the door by two middle-aged people who could have come right out of a television commercial for toothpaste. Her first impression was big smiles and unassuming clothes.

"My dad, Bill," Jack said. Bill was much shorter than Jack and had light brown hair with some gray sprinkled in.

"And my mother Diana."

Taylor shook hands. Jack's mother had no gray and actually looked quite young, with short golden brown hair, wholesome features and a soft Texas accent.

Jack didn't resemble either of his parents and Taylor decided he must take after an uncle or grandfather.

Diana clasped Taylor's hand and led her to a bedroom that was all peach and white with frills and flowers. Totally different than Taylor's more contemporary furnishings in her town house. But the room was welcoming and even had fresh daisies on the table.

"We have a list on the table that explains breakfast and all that, but since you're a friend of Jack's none of that applies," she said, her eagerness to please bubbling over.

"Thank you. I—"

"You can just make yourself at home, sweetheart. *Mi*

casa, su casa, as they say. Dinner will be ready in a few minutes." With that, the woman turned and went in another direction, leaving Taylor standing at the door to the bedroom.

Jack was talking with his father, but Taylor couldn't hear the conversation, just the low hum of male voices. She wondered if Jack was telling him that someone hit his car.

She sat on the edge of the bed. Comfy. But being there felt odd.

When they finished, Jack came back and took her by the hand. "My mother says dinner's ready." The warmth of his touch seemed so natural and welcome.

The dinner was a beef brisket with some kind of barbecue sauce and heaps of potatoes and gravy and corn, with apple crisp for dessert. Taylor ate too much, to the point that she even felt a little nauseous. She almost nodded off during the tales of Jack and Lana's antics as kids. Mostly Lana. Oldest child syndrome. She wondered if Jack noticed that, too.

She excused herself before Jack left, but she heard his parents talking about some arrangements to go somewhere the next day. They were nice, friendly people, but she was glad to escape to her bedroom.

She'd felt an overarching tension of some kind, but couldn't pinpoint where it was coming from. Jack maybe. It was almost as if Jack was there in person but not in spirit. Or maybe it was her, maybe she was projecting her own feelings. She longed for the comfort of her own bed and the ease of being with good friends. She missed having her own things around her. She was glad to be going home.

After a quick shower, Taylor climbed into bed, so tired she expected to fall immediately to sleep. Instead her thoughts ping-ponged from one idea to another, trying to make some sense of it all. But the thought of home kept coming back to her. That's when she realized she'd accomplished what she'd come here to do—find out if her mother was the person Taylor believed she was. Holding on to that, she felt as if a shade had suddenly been lifted.

Her mother *was* the person Taylor believed she was. She didn't need to make sense of anything. She knew her mother's character, regardless of a past life. That's all that mattered. She still wanted to know more about the brother she'd never known, but she had a strange sense of peace about it. If that's all she ever knew, she could be happy with that, couldn't she?

Except that wasn't all. There was Jack.

IT WAS LATE when Jack got back to town and, instead of driving home, he went directly to the barrio. Juarez had some explaining to do.

The neighborhood was alive with music and girls and guys hanging out on the corners, kissing and playing around, music blaring from cars nearby. The energy was electric and he realized, if circumstances had been different, he might have grown up here or somewhere like it. He wondered what kind of person he'd have been if he had.

His parents had given him a good life, taught him solid values and impressed on him that family is the most important thing. No matter what, family comes first. He wondered if that included Henry Juarez. He thought not. Why else would they have been so set against him searching for his biological father when he was young?

He would have liked to be able to share it with them. But he couldn't. Not yet. The only person who knew was Lana. She'd told Cal, but Jack wasn't comfortable talking even to him about it.

Reaching the door, he saw it was open a crack and he heard what sounded like a television program. He knocked, and the door shot open. Manny's brother Richard stood in the opening.

"I need to talk to Henry," Jack said.

Richard stepped to the side and Jack saw Henry Juarez at the table in the kitchen, a can of soda in front of him and a cigarette in his hand. He didn't look surprised to see Jack and, after a few seconds, he motioned Jack to sit across from him.

Jack stalked over to the table, too agitated to sit. "What were you doing at the hotel?"

Juarez tipped his head, as if not quite understanding, or not wanting to. He took a drag from the cigarette. "I went to meet someone."

"Someone who tried to ram my car. You don't keep very good company."

Juarez narrowed his eyes. "You think the worst of me, and I can't blame you."

Jack leaned forward, hands flat on the table, his jaws clenched. "This isn't about what I think of you. I want to know what you were doing at the hotel."

Juarez stood, facing Jack directly. "I told you why I was there. I went to meet someone."

"You just happened to meet someone at the same hotel where Taylor is staying?"

"Taylor? Who is Taylor?"

"Taylor Dundee. Margot Cooper's daughter."

"Margot Cooper?" Juarez said. "Did someone find her?" His expression brightened as he said it.

Juarez didn't know about Taylor or Margaret Dundee. Of course, he knew Margot Cooper, but he'd have no way of knowing Jack had located the woman. It had taken Jack the better part of a year to find out what he had. "Yeah. Someone did. She was living in Arizona under an assumed name and she passed away six months ago. An *accident*."

The man's eyebrows knit together, and Jack saw his disappointment. "I had no idea. Who did you say was at the hotel?"

"Her daughter, Taylor. She came to Houston to learn more about her mother."

"I'm sorry Margot is gone. If she hadn't disappeared, things might have been different."

Jack wasn't sure what he meant. "You wanted her found?"

Henry nodded. "She was the one person whose testimony might have helped. She knew when I left that night, because we both left at the same time."

This wasn't why he'd come here. He didn't need to get any more confused. He was here about Taylor.

"What were you doing at the hotel?"

Juarez hooked his hands over the back of the chair, his gaze lingering on Jack's face. "I was there to meet someone."

Jack heard the sincerity in Juarez's voice. Concern. But there was no way Jack was leaving without a full explanation. "I get it. *Who* were you meeting and why?"

"If I tell you and it gets out," Juarez said, "it could be bad for me."

"Would it be bad if I told the police you were there?"

He looked surprised. "You didn't tell them?"

"Not yet."

Juarez rubbed a hand over his forehead so Jack couldn't see his eyes. "A former cell mate called and asked me to meet him, but he didn't say why. When I got there, he demanded that I tell him where the money from the robbery was hidden. He had a gun and said someone was going to get hurt if I didn't tell him. Then you and the woman came into the garage. I caught him off guard and took the gun. I think he was trying to get away from me when he hit your car."

A cell mate. Jack was reminded of what Taylor had said. The man at her mother's. "What's his name? When did he get out of prison?"

"Kevin Darnell. It was seven or eight months ago. I don't remember exactly."

"So you told him about the missing money?"

"We talked a lot over the years. I told him the police were looking for Margot because they suspected she had it. But I never thought she did."

The person Juarez told about the money could be the same person who ransacked Taylor's mother's house.

"Is the guy dangerous?"

"Anyone can be dangerous."

"What did you do with his gun?"

"I threw it away."

Jack looked up and saw Richard taking in the whole conversation. When he saw Jack, he averted his gaze and then stepped outside.

"Then," Jack said loud and clear to be sure Richard heard, too, "You tell this creep that Taylor has no idea where that money is."

IT WAS NEARLY NOON on Friday before Jack returned to pick Taylor up. After some discussion about how relaxing Taylor's stay had been, Jack waited while Taylor thanked his parents, then they said their goodbyes and were on the road again. Last night he'd talked to Bobby Smith, a former cop-turned-private-detective he knew well and asked him to run a search on Juarez's former cell mate, find him and tell him to back off. His friend promised to get back to him as soon as he knew something. Jack had gone to the office for a few hours and now he had to keep Taylor from getting on her flight home.

Every time he thought about her leaving, he got that same empty feeling.

He reached over and touched her hand. "I received some information last night that might end all of this, and I have someone working on it right now." Getting no response, he put both hands on the wheel again.

After a long moment, she managed, "What's the information?"

"I can't say. This is part of the 'trust me' thing."

"Okay," she said, but he wasn't sure she meant it.

"So where are we going now?"

He looked over and smiled. "I thought you should see a little of the real Texas and not just the inside of a hotel. We'll be there soon."

"And where exactly is *there?*"

"Lake Conroe."

"A lake in Texas. And here I thought it was all cattle ranches and oil wells."

"That's the movie version, though there are a lot of ranches and wells."

She frowned. "Is it far? I have a plane to catch later tonight."

"Not too far. Less than an hour. Don't worry. I'll get you to your flight."

He felt better about her leaving now that he knew Bobby would find the man Juarez told him about. Assuming his theory was correct.

"You don't have to take me sightseeing, you know."

He glanced over. "Do you have a hot date or something?"

She made a face. "I don't even know anyone in Houston except you."

His gaze back on the road, he said, "What about my parents and the guy I met in your room?"

"Alex?" She laughed. "Alex is Roxi's brother who happened to be in Texas on business and stopped in to say hello." Taylor was surprised he remembered, and even more surprised that her explanation made his eyes light up. "But he is kinda cute."

He frowned. "If you like teenagers."

She looked at him, unable to figure him out. He almost sounded jealous. "Your parents are wonderful," she said. And she was being stupid.

"They are. I'm glad you liked them. So, are you hungry?"

"A little." Actually, she was starving, despite the breakfast she'd had. She seemed to be hungry all the time.

"Good. I know a perfect place to eat."

Studying him, she realized he'd actually planned this. It wasn't a spur-of-the-moment thing.

"You can't be in Houston and not go to Reno's place. I guarantee you'll like it."

She smiled to herself. What she liked was the idea that he'd considered her and that he wanted her to see a place he thought was special. In the short time they'd spent together, she'd gotten to know him better than a lot of people she'd known much longer. He cared about people and he was honest. She hadn't thought she'd ever trust another man, yet she found herself trusting him. But it was more than that. She cared about him. And that was precisely why she had to leave.

When she cared about someone, she ignored all the red alerts that told her to run in the opposite direction. Instead, she'd find things about the person that fit her fantasy. Which was probably why love had always been disappointing. She knew that about herself, but what she didn't know was how to stop doing it.

She leaned back and watched flatlands and freeway turn into rolling hills and small back roads with trees dotting the landscape. She couldn't identify most of the foliage, except for the giant oak trees and some swamp cypress, which meant there had to be water nearby.

Ten minutes later, Jack pulled into a parking lot, stopped the car and looked over at her. "This okay?"

A ramshackle building that looked as if it was made from old gray barn planks hunkered in a copse of bushes and trees. The Crazy Crab. It looked like a dive. "Sure. It's fine. Whatever."

Just as she was opening the car door, Jack appeared and offered his hand.

"What's with the sudden attention?"

He smiled wide. "Just being helpful."

With that one smile, all her fantasies were reborn.

The place might've looked like a dive outside, but inside it was quaint and cozy, smelling of cedar and pine along with baked bread and something spicy. It was relatively empty, with just a few patrons sitting at a bar on one side. Empty tables with checkered cloths filled the rest of the room.

A chubby bald man wearing an apron hurried over. "Jack, my boy. How are you?"

Taylor heard a Cajun accent, the kind she'd heard on a cooking show.

"I'm perfect, Reno. How are you?'

"Couldn't be better. And who's your lovely lady?" the man asked as he winked at Jack.

Taylor felt a blush coming on.

"Taylor Dundee, meet Reno Yates. He's the owner of this fine establishment."

The man bent to kiss Taylor's hand. "A pleasure, madam," he said, then turned to Jack. "Your lady is lovelier than sunshine. Now come with me. I'll give you the finest table with a view. Then I'll prepare a special meal for you. No need to order."

Your lady. It had a nice ring.

They followed him to a table with a view of the large lake.

"This is a small branch of Lake Conroe," Jack said.

Taylor stared out at it. "Too bad it's so muggy. It would be nice to sit outside."

"You'll just have to come back when it's cooler," Jack said.

Taylor's pulse quickened even though it was a casual remark. "Maybe I will," she said. "It's been a long time since I've actually taken a vacation."

A waiter came over with water for both of them and a beer for Jack. "And you, ma'am?"

"The beer's great," Jack said. "It's local. Brewed in Houston."

And apparently Jack came here a lot to get service without asking. "I think I'll have iced tea," she said, hoping the nausea she'd felt last night didn't return, hoping she wasn't getting the flu or something.

"Not a beer person, huh?"

"Oh, no. I like beer. But…it makes me tired if I have it in the middle of the day."

He was looking at her. Studying her.

"So, I gather you come here often."

"I do...when I'm in the area."

"And what else do you *do* when you're in the area?"

"I go fishing. Lake Conroe is great for largemouth bass. I believe the record was over fourteen pounds."

"Really? I never pictured you as a fisherman type."

He leaned forward, resting one arm on the table. "Why not?"

"I don't know. You don't seem like you'd be able to sit in a boat for hours waiting for a fish to bite. And that's what fishermen do, isn't it?"

"Some. I prefer fly fishing. More action, more moving around." He smiled. "And I like to make my own lures."

This was a side of Jack she never imagined. As he'd said before, he seemed more city than country.

"And what do *you* do when you're not creating high fashion purses and running your boutique?"

"You don't know?" she said coyly. "I thought you had me checked out before you ever got to Arizona."

He grinned. "Actually I was too focused on one area to pay much attention to anything else."

She looked away. What he probably meant was that there wasn't much else in her life to notice except work and more work. "My work *is* my pleasure," she said. "I guess I'm fortunate that way."

"Still, you must enjoy doing other things."

"Well...sure. I jog. As you know. I go to movies with friends once in a while. I like to travel, but I've been too busy with work to have much time for—" She stopped, realizing how pathetic she sounded. Too bad it was true.

He shook his head. "I don't get it."

"Get what?"

Just then the waiter brought her iced tea and said, "Your meal will be right out."

Almost at the same time, Reno, the owner and chef, came out wheeling a cart filled with steaming food. He lifted the silver lid from a large skillet. "Reno's Jambalaya, with mussels, chicken, shrimp and New Orleans andouille sausage." He kissed his fingertips. "Mmm-wah."

Taylor's mouth was watering already.

"It's perfect, my friend," Jack said.

"To top it off, I have Reno's bread pudding with whiskey sauce and chicory coffee."

Jack looked at Taylor. "Don't worry, the alcohol burns off during cooking. You won't get tired."

Reno dished up two platters. "Please enjoy," he said, then he left them alone again.

"How did you get to be such close friends with the owner?" Taylor asked.

Jack shrugged. "Reno's a friendly guy. Once he takes a shine to you, that's it. You're a friend forever."

"You're very lucky." Taylor meant it. Aside from Roxi and Cara, she led a solitary life, her business notwithstanding. But just because she sometimes wished for more didn't mean she wasn't happy. Solitary or not. Not everyone was meant to be a social butterfly.

An hour later, and after many stories between them, they'd finished the bread pudding and were ready to leave. Taylor felt sated. It had been great just to sit and talk and not feel as if she had to rush to do something. The drawback was that talking with Jack for so long made her hormones hum.

Jack's every gesture, his every word seemed sexy and sensuous. His voice, his eyes, every part of him screamed hot. And every minuscule cell in her body was telling her she was ready. "Uh…before we go, I'd like to hit the ladies' room."

He gestured. "To the back and then take a right."

Taylor was so high on conversation that she felt almost giddy. As she passed Reno on her way back from the restroom, he stopped her with a hand on her elbow.

"The food was wonderful, Mr. Yates," she said.

"I'm glad you liked it. Now tell me, young lady, how much do you like Jack?"

His question took her by surprise. "I—I like him. He's…a nice person."

"He's more than nice." He pointed to the kitchen. "You see this? I have all this because of Jack."

Puzzled, Taylor peered into the kitchen.

"My beloved wife had cancer for three years and we had no hospitalization. I was going to sell the place to pay for her bills. But Jack organized a group and collected donations to help. They paid for everything. If it weren't for Jack, I wouldn't be here."

And why was he telling her this?

"I don't want nobody hurting him," the man said. His tone was stern, but Taylor saw a twinkle in his eye.

"Oh, I see," Taylor said, realizing he thought she and Jack were closer than they were. "I promise you, I won't hurt anyone," she said. "Actually, we're just…friends. Um…business friends."

The man raised one gray eyebrow.

"Is your wife okay now?" she asked.

His smiled sadly. "Yes, I believe she is. She's with God."

"Oh, I'm so sorry."

"Don't be. We will be together again." He patted her on

the shoulder, "If you always love like there's no tomorrow, you'll have no regrets."

When Taylor returned, she saw Jack heading toward her.

"C'mon, I want to show you something."

He took her by the hand and led her out the side door and down to a dock. At the end, a little boy had just pulled in a giant fish. "It's four pounds," the boy said, beaming. The child's mother was snapping photos. "Here," Jack said, "let me take one of the two of you."

"Oh, thank you," the mother said. When Jack finished, he handed the camera back, but as he did, the boy turned and dropped the fish into the water. "My fish!" the boy screamed. "My fish! It's going to get away."

Instantly, Jack bent down on the dock and reached in, falling halfway into the water as he did. But he came up with the wriggling fish. He stood, then hugging it to his chest, carried it to the shore where the mother directed him to a container of some kind.

"Thank you so much," she said. "But look at you, you're all wet."

Jack waved her off. "I'll dry." He started to walk away, but the boy, tear tracks still on his cheeks, ran over and stood in front of him. "Thank you for saving my fish, mister. No one would believe me if he got away."

Jack ruffled the boy's hair. "Well, they will now, won't they?"

The boy beamed.

Jack smelled like fish.

On the way to the car, he said, "I need to make a stop."

Two backroads later, they drove up to an isolated cabin.

"You know the person who lives here?" she asked.

He pulled out a key and opened the door. "Yes. Me."

"Really?" Taylor said, unable to hide her surprise. She followed him inside and, while he went off into another room, she glanced around. "This is beautiful." A natural stone fireplace dominated one side of a large great room. She smelled cedar and old charred logs. "Have you been here recently?"

"No, I haven't." he poked his head out. "But Cal uses the cabin on occasion. Sometimes we go fishing together."

He was shirtless and her eyes immediately went to his well-defined biceps and the hard-ridged muscles on his stomach. She moistened her lips.

"Here," he said, coming back out to the bookshelf. He stood there for a moment perusing the shelves. She walked over and stood next to him as he reached up to get a book. "Look at the map and see if you can locate where we are." He brought his arm down quickly, clocking her in the head.

She saw stars. Her knees buckled.

"Oh, God." He dropped the book and grabbed her by both arms, pulling her close. "Are you okay?"

Her hand went to her eye. He'd clipped her by her right eyebrow or maybe lower, she couldn't tell, but it hurt like hell. He brought her to the couch and had her lie with her head on a pillow, but she would have been happy just standing there with her head against his bare chest.

"I'll get some ice."

She held her hand over the sore eye. She heard the refrigerator door open, then shut. He swore. Then she heard water running.

"Here." He hunkered down at her side and placed a bag of frozen peas over her eye. "Cal used up all the ice, but this might help."

She could feel the heat of his body.

And her libido was steaming.

He leaned in, one elbow on the couch next to her, and lifted the bag. "It's a big goose egg, but at least you won't need stitches."

She cracked a smile. "Good. I hate needles."

His pupils dilated and he traced a finger down her cheek, then he turned her face to look at the injury. "I'm sorry," he whispered. "I'm glad I didn't mar your pretty face."

Pretty. He thought she was pretty. "I shouldn't have been standing so close."

"Stop that."

"Stop what?"

"Blaming yourself. You do that a lot, you know."

"Really?"

"Yeah, really."

"I suppose it's a habit."

"Why?"

She felt oddly weepy. "When I was growing up, we moved a lot and I was always the new kid trying to catch up. I made lots of mistakes. I was never on the same page as other kids, so I got used to apologizing."

"And now you do it regardless of whether it's your mistake or not."

"I never thought about it."

Carefully, he lifted the cold bag to check her eye.

He smiled, and almost in the same instant, their lips met and the bag of peas fell to the floor. She wrapped her arms around him, kissing him passionately. Want and need seemed to emerge from somewhere deep inside her. *Love like there's no tomorrow.*

Jack knew he should stop, but he couldn't. Her scent had

been driving him crazy from the moment they'd met. Vanilla or whatever, it smelled edible. He slid next to her, half on and half off the couch. The body contact, her warm hand on his chest pushed him over the edge. She was so damned beautiful.

He broke away from the kiss just long enough to say, "I don't want to stop."

"And I don't want you to," she whispered. "Does this cabin have a bedroom?"

That was all he needed. "It has a great bedroom." Scooping her up in his arms, he headed in that direction. He hoped to hell he had some condoms in the drawer.

HOURS MUST HAVE PASSED. It felt like hours anyway, and here he was in his cabin with a naked woman draped across his chest. He would never have thought in a million years she'd be so hot in bed. She'd worn him out, something he wouldn't have thought possible.

Lying here with Taylor, feeling her warm body against his, her heartbeat soft against his chest, he realized he'd trade almost anything for a chance at real happiness.

Being with Taylor was the closest he'd been to that pinnacle in a long, long time.

She shifted position, snuggling into him like a kitten. He touched her soft, silky hair, so unlike his. Everything about her stirred him.

He gently kissed the top of her head, moving just a little to accommodate the surge of blood to his nether regions. Again. She must have felt it, too, because she snuggled even closer, then placed her hand against him.

CHAPTER FOURTEEN

"YOU'RE THE ONE who's always telling me to face my demons. Maybe it's time you face your own," Lana spouted off.

He shouldn't have told her about taking Taylor to the lake yesterday. But she'd known something was wrong the second he'd stepped inside, out of sorts after dropping Taylor off the night before. She hadn't even wanted him to take her to the airport. "I've been facing those demons for thirty some years. I'm tired of it."

"So tired, you finally stopped lying to her?"

"I didn't lie. I just didn't tell her everything."

"Which means she was led to believe something different. Secrets or lies, they're pretty much the same."

"I did what I had to. I just didn't plan on the rest of it."

"And what is the rest of it?"

He shrugged. "I don't know." Jack took a glass from the kitchen cabinet and poured some water. After making love a second time, Taylor had been quiet and then suggested he take her back to catch her flight. He'd wanted to wait with her at the airport, but she refused, saying she had calls to make.

"It doesn't matter now anyway because she's gone. Where's Ryan?"

"He's outside. And quit changing the subject." Lana narrowed her gaze. "It does matter. You care about her. How can that not matter?" She turned, then said nonchalantly, "I think you didn't tell her because you're afraid of commitment and you've got a built-in excuse."

He laughed. "*You're* telling me I'm afraid of commitment?"

"Yes, and don't try to push it off on me. I *know* my shortcomings and why I have them. You just find all these other excuses and gloss over everything else. But the result is the same. You're alone. It's a self-fulfilling prophecy."

"That's bull. I've been in relationships, and I know what happens when you bare your soul. If I was afraid of commitment, I'd be spilling my guts."

Lana glanced out the back door to check on Ryan. "Look, baby brother, we've all been there. You're not the only one who's been given a raw deal or who's been hurt. If you live long enough, you're gonna get hurt, probably more than once. So suck it up and give the girl the benefit of the doubt. You don't know how she's going to feel, and if, as you say, you're not afraid of commitment, the only way you'll find out how she feels is to talk to her."

Maybe. But Lana didn't know what it was like to be torn in sixteen different directions. There was no reason to tell her anything now. The only reason he could see telling anyone was if he wanted to stay in contact with Juarez. He didn't know if he wanted that or not. "You're the one who made me promise not to tell Mom and Dad. Have you changed your mind?"

"If you're serious about her. Don't throw away a chance at happiness for something that may never have a resolution."

He gritted his teeth.

"You could spend the rest of your life trying to find out if Juarez was innocent and it might never happen. And what if you discover you're wrong—"

He stopped her right there. "If you were going to say what I think you were, don't. I need to know." He balled his hands into fists, years of anger coalescing in his chest until he felt as if he was going to burst.

"Jack, it's possible."

In one swift step Jack was in her face. "Don't. Don't say any more."

She stepped back. "That doesn't change what we both know. You care about her. Maybe Juarez is innocent. Maybe he isn't. Either way, you have to make a decision. If it bothers her, then you'll know. But she could just as easily understand."

Precisely what he didn't want. He didn't want anyone's understanding. Anyone's pity. "Don't you think I know that? But it doesn't change anything. I don't want to hurt anyone, and especially not the people I love most."

Jack heard a noise. He turned and saw Ryan coming in. "Hey, tiger. What's up?"

HOLDING UP the scrap of paper to read the address again, Taylor checked it against the street signs. Portobello. That's it. She turned the corner, glancing at house numbers as she cruised down the street in the rental car. When Jack had dropped her at the airport the night before, she'd checked her flight and learned the plane was canceled. So she'd rebooked for eleven tonight. This gave her a chance to talk to Nancy Belamy again. Which would take her mind off the thought that…she might be pregnant.

Making love with Jack yesterday, her breasts had felt

overly tender, and she realized they'd felt that way for a couple of days. But since her period was past due, she'd attributed it to that. Besides, it had been less than a week since she and Jack had made love that first time, and they'd used a condom, even if it had been a little late.

But the nausea she'd felt wasn't as easily dismissed. If it was the flu, it wouldn't come and go. But she couldn't possibly be pregnant. She just couldn't.

She'd told herself making love with Jack didn't mean anything. But, she knew it did. It did because she was falling in love with him.

Except he wasn't in love with her. If she was pregnant, how would she deal with that? If Jack knew, what would he think? Would he want her to get rid of it like Reed? What would she say to him if he did? She closed her eyes. No. She could never do that.

But the fact remained, if she *was* pregnant, she would need to tell Jack, regardless. And if she was pregnant, it would be important to find out more about Margot and Matthew. Her family. Her child's family.

Just thinking about her mother as Margot felt odd. Talking to people about Margot Cooper was even more strange. She felt as if she was discussing a stranger instead of her mother. And when she couldn't think of Margot as a stranger, she told herself that it had been another time, a whole generation ago. Things had been different. If Taylor had been born at another time, she might be different today, too.

She'd certainly changed since she'd arrived in Texas. At home she'd never have dropped everything she was doing to make crazy love in the afternoon. But here, with Jack, it had been the most natural thing in the world…and it had been wonderful.

Jack was a sensitive lover, paying attention to how she felt every step of the way. She'd always been self-conscious of her body, but he'd made her feel beautiful and desired…and that made her want him even more.

She glanced at the next street sign, then looked again at the directions the car rental agent had given her.

Seeing the correct numbers on the house she'd just passed, she drove a little farther, found a place to park, got out and walked slowly toward the house. The scent of freshly mowed grass was a pleasant change from the busy streets in downtown Houston.

The house, an unassuming tract home, in an equally unassuming neighborhood, reminded her of an old song about ticky-tacky houses all in a row.

She rang the bell.

The door opened and Nancy Belamy appeared wearing a bathrobe. It was early, but not that early. "Hello, Mrs. Belamy. I have some new information I'd like to share with you."

At first the woman didn't seem to comprehend, or maybe she didn't remember Taylor. "I'm Taylor Dundee. We talked about Margot Cooper the last time I was here."

The woman nodded. "Yes, I know. But there's nothing left to say."

"This new information that's come to light could affect the case, which," Taylor said immediately, "I'm sure you know, has never been completely solved because the money was never found."

"What new information?" she asked.

"Can we sit?"

Belamy brought a hand to her mouth and worried her fingers over her lips.

"It shouldn't take long."

Stepping aside, she motioned Taylor in. "Have a seat while I quickly change."

As she waited, Taylor wished Jack was there with her. For moral support if nothing else. It wasn't that she couldn't do it alone, she was used to that. But being with him, working together, had made her feel as if she were part of a team. A duo. She liked the feeling.

It also made her acutely aware of her solitary existence. She lived alone, she ate alone, she managed her shop alone, she bought groceries alone. And if she was pregnant, she was going to have a child alone. She didn't want Jack feeling he was railroaded into being a father to a child he never wanted. She closed her eyes.

It wasn't how she'd envisioned having a family. It wasn't the way she wanted it to be.

"I hope this doesn't take long."

The woman's voice jolted Taylor from her reverie.

Belamy sat across from Taylor. She'd changed clothes and wore a pair of brown slacks and a white blouse. "I have no interest in reliving the most horrible day in my life," she said. "Just tell me what this is about and what you want from me."

But she didn't fool Taylor. She was interested…or worried…enough to change clothes.

"Just to recap…you were the one who found Sunny Hawthorne, and you thought she'd fallen…you thought it was an accident."

She lifted her chin. "Yes."

"Can you tell me why you hired an attorney if you thought it was an accident?"

Belamy pressed a hand against her lips, and after a long

moment, she said, "He was a friend who told me not to speak without him there because anything I said could be misconstrued."

"But you were Sunny's assistant for many years, and you got along very well. Isn't that right?"

She nodded. "I wasn't just an employee to her. We were friends. I would have done anything for her. She knew that."

"If you were such good friends, why would your attorney worry about the police thinking anything else?"

She glared at Taylor. "If you're inferring Mrs. Hawthorne and I weren't getting along, you're way off base. We had a professional relationship, but it went beyond that."

Afraid the woman would ask her to leave, Taylor said, "I'm sorry. You must've been devastated when you found her."

"To say the least." The woman's chin quivered.

Taylor waited, then asked, "When did you see Henry Juarez at the house?"

Her shoulders came up sharply. "I never said I saw him. I said I knew he was working late and that I knew he'd been reprimanded by Mrs. Hawthorne earlier that day when he had his young son there."

That was new. "What was he doing with a child at work?"

"The man's wife was sickly and he brought the child with him a lot. Mrs. Hawthorne was understanding to a point, but the boy could get rowdy."

"And that's why the police thought Juarez had a motive?"

"He had a lot of medical bills and needed money."

"And Margot Cooper?" She flipped through her tablet as if looking for notes. "When did you last see her in the house?"

"I don't know what time it was. Maybe an hour before."

In the five minutes they'd been talking, the woman had

shifted in her seat, crossed and uncrossed her legs, clasped and unclasped her hands. And now she was rubbing her palms on her thighs.

"What was Margot doing when you saw her?"

"Well, I...didn't actually see her. She was with Emily."

"So Emily told you that? When did you see Emily?"

Belamy abruptly rose to her feet. "I don't know where this is going, Miss Dundee, but you still haven't told me what new information you have."

"What would you say if I told you Margot Cooper has been found?"

The woman gasped. Finally she repeated in a voice so soft Taylor could barely hear her, "Margot has been found?"

"Yes. You seem disappointed."

"I—" She placed a hand on her chest. "The police couldn't find her, neither could the investigators Mr. Hawthorne hired. Has she said anything about...the accident?"

Taylor tried to interpret Belamy's reactions. "No, not that I know of."

Looking away the woman said, "I told you before I didn't know her very well. She was devoted to Emily and would have done anything for her."

"Anything?" Taylor's muscles went rigid.

"No, of course not," Belamy snapped. "Devotion only goes so far. Margot was upset over her son's death, but I don't believe she would have hurt anyone."

It sounded as if she was saying Margot thought Sunny had something to do with her son's death. Taylor shook her head. "I don't understand. What does one have to do with the other?"

"Margot had heard rumors that Sunny didn't like her son being with Emily. When Matt was killed, some idiots suggested Mrs. Hawthorne might have had something to do with it. Then when Margot Cooper was fired…" She moistened her lips. "Well…you can't blame Mrs. Hawthorne for that when the woman she trusted was having an affair with her husband. I hope Margot isn't trying to say Sunny fired her because of Matthew or she thinks—"

Taylor's chest felt tight. "Oh, no, nothing like that." Good Lord, it seemed like everyone in the world had a reason to hate Sunny Hawthorne. "When exactly was Margot fired?"

Belamy's hand went to her throat. "I don't recall. It might have been the same day as the accident. I know Sunny gave her time to gather her things."

"What about records?" Taylor asked. "You kept records for Mrs. Hawthorne? Wouldn't you have had records on Margot Cooper? Her family, previous employment, references?"

"I did, but the police took all that. I don't know if they ever returned it. And if they did, it would go back to the family."

"I thought I'd read that Emily had been away from home for a few months before the accident?"

The assistant nodded but didn't elaborate.

"Do you know where Emily was staying when she was gone? There was some speculation that she'd been in trouble."

"She was always in trouble," Belamy snapped. "Sunny sent her away to stay…with friends."

"And this was because of her relationship with Matthew Cooper?"

The woman's gnarled hands curled into fists. "Yes, it was."

Taylor leaned forward, resting her arms across her

knees. Then she said, matter-of-fact, "What I don't understand is why Sunny sent Emily away when Matt was already...he was gone."

"Because," Belamy sputtered, picking at her collar. "Sunny would never allow Emily to have that boy's baby in her house."

Taylor heart quickened, "The child was Matthew Cooper's?"

"Sunny thought so, but Emily said different. Then the accident made it a moot point."

"But Emily gave the child up for adoption anyway?"

Frowning, the woman looked away. "It was a terrible time. Without her mother, Emily couldn't handle much of anything, much less care for a child."

"Where did Emily go?" Taylor repeated.

But almost before the words left Taylor's lips, Belamy said, "I don't know! And I don't want to answer any more questions. What difference does it make? Why does any of that matter now?"

Taylor bolted to her feet and faced the woman head-on. "It matters because Margot Cooper is my mother. Matthew would have been my brother."

Belamy gasped and reached for the arm of the chair. Taylor reached to help, but the woman quickly pulled herself together, then ordered Taylor out of her house.

With a quick change in plans, Taylor took the rental car back to the airport, then hailed a cab and headed back to the Marx Hotel. She couldn't believe Emily Kittridge had lied about the child being Matthew's.

God, she was gullible.

Taylor's head felt about to explode. She didn't know what to do, but she knew she couldn't leave just yet. She hadn't booked out of her room yet, so she called and canceled her flight.

What Belamy had said put a whole new color on things. She pulled out Jack's card and punched in his number. He wasn't there, so she left a message for him to contact her as soon as he possibly could.

Feeling nauseous again, she took a sip of water and wondered how soon a person could tell if they were pregnant? She took out her laptop, did a quick Google search and discovered that she'd be able to tell as soon as the next day after a missed period. There was a drugstore down the street so she put her shoes back on and went out the door.

Funny how her whole life could change depending on the results of one little stick.

In ten minutes she returned, a dozen questions without answers racing through her head as she went into the bathroom. She couldn't imagine what Jack would think. She couldn't imagine what she'd do. Just hearing about Emily having a child she gave up for adoption sent a chill up Taylor's spine. She could never do that, either.

But right now, she had to know whether she was pregnant or not. She went into the bathroom, her hands shaking. She followed the instructions and waited, trying not to think about anything. She studied herself in the mirror.

Would a child of hers and Jack's look like her or him? Or a combination of both?

She picked up the stick, then let out a long breath. In less than nine months, she would know.

IT HADN'T TAKEN Jack's friend long to get information on Kevin Darnell, including his address and some photos of him buying drugs. It didn't take Jack long to anonymously drop off the photos to the Houston P.D., either. He hoped that would be the end of it, but there was no way to know until he was told the guy was in custody.

After that, he debated whether to stop and thank Juarez for giving him the information on Darnell, or just leave it alone. He got out his phone and saw the message from Taylor saying her flight was canceled and that she'd gone back to he Marx and had to talk to him.

He grinned from ear to ear. She was still here. He slapped his hand against the wheel. "Hot damn." He'd finally convinced himself that having Taylor go back to Arizona was the best thing for both of them, but his excitement at knowing she was still here made him realize how much he'd been lying to himself. He wanted her to stay, as impossible as that might be.

He drove directly to the hotel and found a note with Taylor's new room number waiting for him at the concierge. He knocked on her door. No answer.

He knocked again. "Taylor, it's Jack."

"Hey," he said, when she opened the door.

She gave him a half smile. "Hey."

"I thought you'd left. What happened?"

She motioned him in. Barefoot, she was wearing a pair of workout shorts and a purple tank top. Her hair was disheveled, her eyes red, as if she'd been crying.

"It's complicated."

He was about to go over and pull her into his arms and ask what was wrong, but she turned abruptly and went to the window, standing just about as far away from him as she could get. "Anything you want to share?"

She shook her head.

"Well, I have good news," he said, hoping it might help. "The police found out the identity of the guy in the car and they have a warrant out for his arrest. Apparently he'd been one of Juarez's cell mates and apparently he thought your mother had the money."

"Juarez told him my mother had the money?"

"No, I think he and Juarez talked a lot and when this joker got out, he came to that conclusion because all the old newspapers said the police were looking for Margot and the money."

"How did the police find him? Did someone get his license number at the scene?"

This would be the time to tell her. Lana was right that if he wanted any kind of a relationship with Taylor he'd have to be honest. "Taylor, can you sit please?" With a gentle hand on her arm, he guided her to the chair. "I have something I need to tell you and I don't know how you're going to feel about me when I finish."

Her eyes grew big. "What is it?"

He stood in front of her but had trouble looking at her directly. He strode to the window, hoping a little distance between them might make it easier. He wouldn't be able to see the disappointment in her eyes.

A loud knock on the door brought them both around. "Who would come so late?" he asked.

"I don't know." She went to the door and looked out the peephole. Her mouth dropped open.

She opened the door.

Taylor couldn't believe the man at the heart of this murder mystery was standing in front of her.

"I'm sorry to disturb you," Henry Juarez said. "But I

knew your mother and I hope you'll give me a few minutes of your time."

She turned to look at Jack. His expression was as shocked as she felt.

Juarez stepped back when he saw Jack.

She didn't know if she should let the man in or not, but then he said, "Jack. I didn't know you would be here."

Jack? They knew each other? She looked at Juarez, more confused than ever. "I'm sorry, did I miss something?"

"My son was worried about you," Juarez said. "So I thought if I told you that the man who ran into you in the garage was in custody, you'd feel better."

His son? Taylor turned to Jack, staring incredulously. What the—nothing made sense. "What's... I—I don't understa…" Blood pounded in her ears and she couldn't even get words out. Nothing made sense.

Jack looked at Juarez, then back to Taylor.

"Son?" She had to have misheard.

Somber, Jack looked away. "Yes."

She felt as if her lungs had collapsed, her knees weak. She reached for the table next to the door for support.

This was the man she'd made love to—the man she thought she knew, whose baby she was carrying…

She couldn't breathe. Her heart felt as if it had been ripped from her chest.

"Taylor," Jack said, reaching her in one long stride.

Blood pounded in her ears. She sidestepped away from him, then ran blindly out the door.

"Taylor, wait. I can explain." Jack took off after her. If she wanted to tell him to go to hell, he wouldn't blame her. But he couldn't let her go without telling her how he felt…and why he hadn't told her about his father.

Catching up to her at the elevator, Jack placed a hand on her shoulder to stop her from leaving. She turned on him like a viper, clearly hurt and disappointed.

"Please don't leave like this, Taylor. At least hear me out. I'm not going to justify anything, but you have to know that no matter what secrets I've kept, it has nothing to do with us."

"Really?" she lashed out, her words sharp. "I could have sworn yesterday had something to do with us."

"I'm saying it's not how it looks."

"No? It looks to me as if you've been lying to me from day one. I don't know who you are, Jack. How is that *not* how it looks?"

"I didn't deliberately lie to you. I withheld personal information."

She turned away, as if she could no longer look at him.

He shoved a hand through his hair. She'd hate him no matter what he said, so he might as well get it all out. He steeled himself, then blurted, "My biological father is Henry Juarez. I didn't know that until I started searching for him. I was only eighteen when I found out, and I was devastated. I'd never spoken a word to him until two months ago when I learned he was getting out. I'm not writing a story. I started out to learn something about the man who fathered me and then it seemed that he might've been wrongly imprisoned for a crime he didn't commit. I had to learn more."

He braced an arm against the wall to keep her from getting on the elevator when the door opened. "When I met you, you had such loyalty to your mother, I couldn't tell you I thought she might be Sunny's murderer. I didn't think you would talk to me then. I didn't tell you my relationship to Juarez because I didn't want anyone to know. I still don't. I had no idea I'd end up feeling the way I do about you, and by the time I realized I did, it was too late."

The elevator closed. Taylor leaned against the wall for support.

Then she raised her chin and, though she tried to look calm, he heard the tremor in her voice when she said, "I believed you. I believed *in* you."

Her words dripped with hurt and betrayal. "Is Jack Parker even your name?" She laughed hysterically for a moment. Then, she threw up her hands. "Hell, I might as well have picked up some stranger in a bar and gone to bed with him."

"Jack Parker *is* my name," he shot back. "That's not a lie. I lied about writing a story."

She looked at him, her gaze narrow. "Y'know, this is really funny. My mother never lied to me, either," she said bitterly. "But she left out one small fact—that she was really someone else. What's one more imposter in my life? I should be used to it by now."

Tears began to slide down her cheeks. Jack reached out.

She jerked away and punched the elevator button. She kept punching and watching the lights above the door until it came to their floor and slid open. She stepped inside. "I'm going downstairs and when I come back up, I want you gone. Both of you."

As soon as the doors shut in his face, Jack took out his cell phone and called Taylor's cell number. He let it ring and when the voice mail picked up, he hung up and called again. Dammit. She had to listen. This time he left a message. "I'm sorry, Taylor. Truly, truly sorry. I know saying I'm sorry doesn't make up for anything, and I know saying I understand how you feel sounds hollow, too. But it's true. I also can't change my feelings for you, Taylor, no matter how much you might hate me. And no matter what you're feeling right now, I believe you care about me, too."

He hung up, dialed Taylor's hotel room number and left the same message. But he might as well be talking to the wall. So, he added, "I'm invested in this and I'm going to get to the bottom of the murder. I have to know. Whether Sunny's murderer is Henry Juarez or your mother or the man in the moon, I have to know. I'll welcome your help, no matter how you feel about me."

He closed the phone and, waiting to get on the next elevator going down, he felt a presence. He turned. Henry Juarez stood directly behind him.

CHAPTER FIFTEEN

AFTER SITTING in the atrium for a half hour, Taylor went back to the room and found both men gone. She listened first to the message Jack had left on her cell, then the one he'd left on the hotel phone. She was invested, too. The irony of it was, both Juarez and her mother were the grandparents of the baby growing in her stomach. If either one was guilty, then her child had a horrible legacy to live with.

It seemed pointless to put herself through such torture, just to find out in the end that her mother might be a murderer. But, like Jack, she had to know. So she could protect her child.

She took a quick shower, threw on a robe and sat on the edge of the bed, feeling overwhelmed.

Seeing the stick turn blue had been both disturbing and wonderful at the same time, something akin to seeing a tiny rose on a wall of thorns you had to climb. Having a child, however that life had been given to her, was a miracle.

Jack deserved to know. There really was no decision there. He also needed to know that having an abortion or putting the child up for adoption were options she'd never consider.

In his messages, Jack had said he cared, but he hadn't said anything about the future, nothing about love, and who *would* say those things after only knowing someone such a short time?

The one thing she was sure of was that she didn't want him making a commitment to her just because she was having his child. He'd feel trapped. He'd feel he had no choice.

She flopped back on the bed and stared at the light on the ceiling fan. She didn't have to plan for the baby right this minute. Her first decision had to be whether to work with Jack or not.

No matter what anyone said, she couldn't believe her mother had had anything to do with what happened to Sunny Hawthorne. She would never believe that.

And because of that, she understood what Jack must be feeling. Except *his* father had been found guilty and he'd gone to jail. And hadn't she lied to everyone about Margot being her aunt? She was no different than he was when it came to getting what she wanted.

The difference between the two of them was that she did believe her mother was innocent. And Jack didn't know. He had no frame of reference except finding out his biological father was in prison for murder. How awful that must have been.

A larger question loomed. If Sunny Hawthorne's killer wasn't her mother and it wasn't Jack's father, who then?

The phone rang again, but she didn't get up. She couldn't hear whether someone left a message either because it went to the hotel answering service. Roxi would call her cell phone. Jack was the only one who'd call her at the hotel and she couldn't bring herself to talk to him right now.

She felt so weary. Physically as well as emotionally. Must be the pregnancy.

She closed her eyes, hoping to drift off and that sleep might give her a fresh perspective.

It seemed as if she'd just fallen asleep when she heard

a loud knocking and bolted upright. She tried to focus. Was she dreaming or was there really someone at the door? How long had she slept?

The clock said two hours. Another loud knock, then a series of knocks. She got up and looked through the peephole.

Jack. She caught her breath.

"Taylor, I have to talk to you. I'm going downstairs to the bar and I'm going to wait for you. Please come. I have something important to tell you."

How could she know whether he was telling the truth? But even as she asked herself the question, her gut told her he was. Jack was intrinsically honest. He'd shown her that on more than one occasion.

Taking her time, she went to the bathroom and splashed water on her face. She brushed her teeth and combed her hair. Then she went into the room, sat in a chair and flipped on the television.

But all the while, she couldn't get Jack's face out of her mind. How long would it have taken him to tell her if Juarez hadn't come to the hotel? Would he have told her ever?

She'd never even had the opportunity to talk to Henry Juarez. If she agreed to work with Jack they had to have an understanding. As if on remote control, she rolled off the bed, dressed in white shorts, a black T-shirt and flip-flops, finger-combed her hair, then took the elevator downstairs.

Jack was sitting in a booth toward the back. A waitress chattered like crazy to him. No big surprise. He stood when he saw Taylor enter the room and waved her over.

"I really don't know why I'm here," she said, sitting opposite him.

"Do you want to order now or wait?" the waitress said.

"Now," Jack said. "I'll have a Bud and a hamburger. Taylor?"

She was starving, so she ordered the same with milk instead of beer.

When the waitress was gone, she said, "If we're going to work together, I have some requirements."

His eyes lit up. "And they are?"

"I want to know everything. I want to know what happened and why you believe your father is innocent even though he was proven guilty. I want to talk to him and ask questions about my mother and anything else that might seem relevant to me."

His lips thinned. He said softly, "Okay. I'll see what I can do."

She shook her head. "Not good enough."

He stared at her. "You're a tough cookie."

"Will you ask? Will you tell him it's important?"

He nodded, then held out his hand. "It's a deal."

When she reached out, he clasped her hand in both of his. His were warm, just as warm as when they'd slid over her body when they'd made love. He had gentle hands. They didn't touch, they caressed. She felt like crying again. Biting her lower lip, she asked, "So what's the next step?"

"What do you think?"

"Emily Kittridge lied to us and I want to know why. I have this nagging feeling that there's more to her lie than keeping quiet about an illegitimate child."

"A feeling?"

"Intuition. And I'm usually right."

The waitress brought their food and Taylor dug right in. He smiled. "Are you feeling okay?"

She looked up. "I'm fine." She took another bite, trying

to ignore the fact that he'd cared enough to ask how she was. "So, since we agreed on the conditions, tell me why you believe your father is innocent when a jury found him guilty."

Jack picked up his beer and took a swallow. He'd never really talked to anyone about his father, not even Lana. Not beyond the obvious, anyway. "I was three when it happened, so I don't remember any of it. All my life I knew I was adopted and I had this yearning to know who my parents were. I don't think anyone can know what it's like not to have your own identity except someone who's been adopted. Even then, some people never have a problem with it. Anyway, Lana made me promise when we were teenagers that I'd never tell my parents, because they'd be terribly hurt."

He set the bottle down, but kept holding on to it, unable to look at anything else. He hated that he needed validation for who he was, but somehow, talking about it felt like a release of sorts. "They still don't know I know. At eighteen, I put my name on all the lists and when I finally discovered…" He stopped to get control. Then he looked at her. "I was stunned. And instead of answering all my questions about who I was, I knew. I was the son of a murderer. I joined the military not long after and never went to see or talk to Juarez until, like I said, I learned he was being released."

"That's when he told you he was innocent."

"Yes and no. I started looking into his life a year ago because I still had this feeling of being adrift. The more I found out about him, the more I wondered about his guilt. When I discovered he was going to be released, I went to see him. The whole time we talked, he never said he was innocent. Then right before I got up to leave, I asked him. That's when he told me. I asked why he didn't say anything right away, and he said because he knew I wouldn't believe him." Jack grimaced. "And I didn't."

He bit into his burger. When he finished chewing, he said, "He later told me that when he was arrested, my mother was fired, too. And she died six months after my dad was found guilty. I guess I went into foster care and a couple of months later, the Parkers adopted me."

Taylor stopped eating. "It's almost too much to comprehend."

He nodded, biting back his anger. "I couldn't back then. From the time I was eighteen and learned who he was, I was convinced he was a murderer and I was the son of a murderer. I hated him and blamed him for my mother's death, among other things."

Taylor had put her burger down and was listening intently. He didn't want to go on, but now he couldn't seem to stop.

He pushed his plate away. "For years, I believed he was guilty. I never once went to see him. And even when I was looking into things, I still couldn't bring myself to believe in his innocence."

Swallowing a huge breath, he said, "I think I was wrong."

But realizing he was wrong couldn't bring back the years they'd lost. "When I started my search, I thought that finding answers would help, but it can't. I talked to him earlier when you left and told him what I wanted to do. He got angry and told me to back off. He said *he* knows the truth. He said his life had been taken away and nothing could change that. He doesn't want to spend the rest of his days fighting the system, and he doesn't want me involved. He just wants to live out his life without making any waves."

"So what are you going to do?"

He gritted his teeth. "If he's innocent," he said quietly, "it's a gross miscarriage of justice."

"And what if he's not innocent?"

"Then nothing will be any different." The sympathy he saw in her eyes unnerved him. Juarez didn't need her sympathy. He didn't need anyone's. All he ever wanted was to know who he really was. He could never get the life he would've had back. "He said I'd be doing it for myself. Not him. And maybe he was right."

He shrugged. "So, that's the story. He's told me to leave it alone and I'm not going to. I can't."

"What about your family? Your promise to Lana?"

"Somehow, when the time is right, I'm going to have to tell my parents."

She nodded. "I won't say anything."

"Juarez may not want to talk to you, you know."

"But he came to tell me the other man was in custody. How did he know about me or where I was staying?"

Jack shoved his hands in his pockets and felt the photo from his childhood. "After the accident, I went to his house and that's how I found out about his cell mate—I may have mentioned you…. I guess he came here because he felt responsible and wanted to put your mind at ease."

His phone rang. He pulled it from his pocket and checked the number. "Lana. What's up?"

"Some guy named Manny Ortega called here. He said to tell you Juarez is gone."

"He's gone?"

"He left a note for Manny to tell you he was sorry he caused you trouble. He said he didn't want anyone to come looking for him."

"That was it?"

"No, he said he's worried because Juarez seemed despondent the past few days. And he took Manny's brother's gun."

Jack's chest constricted. "Did Manny say where he thought he might have gone?"

"No, but he heard him talking to a guy who'd been in prison with him. Manny left his number for you to call."

"I already have it. Thanks. I gotta go." He hung up and punched in Manny's number. No answer. "Dammit."

"Can I help?" Taylor asked.

He looked up as if he'd forgotten she was there. "No, but thanks." He tossed some money on the table and rose to his feet. "I have to go. I'll call you later."

TAYLOR FOLLOWED Jack from the restaurant to the parking garage under the hotel. "Can you at least tell me what's wrong?"

"A friend of Juarez's called and said Juarez was gone and that he left a note saying not to look for him."

"So you think that means something bad?"

"Yeah. I don't think he knows what he's doing."

They stopped next to Jack's SUV. "He's an adult, and he has a right to go where he wants, doesn't he?"

"Not if he plans to blow his brains out. Or rob a bank."

"Oh, God. You think that's what he's going to do?"

"I don't know. That's the problem. I just have to find him." He banged his hand on the hood of his vehicle. "Dammit! I don't even know where to look."

"Do you know where he usually hangs out when he's not working?"

He clenched his jaw, his expression disturbing. "I don't know a damned thing about what he does. I wish I did."

Taylor knew the feeling.

"Manny heard him talking to someone he met in prison."

"Do you think he's going to do something...wrong?"

"People will do just about anything when they're backed against a wall."

Taylor saw the guilt in Jack's eyes. He felt responsible somehow. "I'd like to come along."

He looked at her blankly. "Why?"

"Because I want to help." Because *she* felt partly responsible. If she hadn't come to Texas and started poking into everyone's past—

"Get in," Jack said quickly.

As she was fastening her seat belt, Jack tore out of the garage like a NASCAR driver.

"I feel like...if I hadn't shown up, maybe none of this would be happening."

He turned the corner and then accelerated onto the freeway. "It's not your fault. *I* showed up in Prescott. Remember? That's why you're here. And the reason my father left has nothing to do with you."

That was the first time Taylor had heard Jack refer to Juarez as his father.

"The note said he was sorry for disrupting so many lives. He...he has a gun."

Taylor grabbed his arm as he drove. "Careful."

"Sorry," she said. "If you find him, what will you do?"

"I don't know. I just know that if he does anything, I'm probably responsible."

Jack exited the freeway and took a sharp right onto Calico Street.

"You're taking a lot on yourself. Lana, your parents and now Juarez."

He glanced over, then back at the road. "What do you mean?"

"You feel responsible for helping Lana and acting as a surrogate father for Ryan. That's great, but did you ever think that she may never find someone else to do it while you're plugging the gap?"

He looked at her strangely. "She has issues she has to deal with."

"And your parents should want what's best for you," she added.

"They do. They always have."

"Then why do you think it would be so awful for them to know you want to find out about your heritage? It's nothing against them."

His grip tightened on the wheel. She saw a muscle in his jaw twitch. She'd hit a nerve. "It's complicated, Taylor. You can't possibly know."

Taylor felt as if he'd slapped her. "I...can't...possibly know?"

He looked over. "I didn't mean it that way. I just meant—dammit, I don't know what I meant. I just know I have to find him before something happens to him."

He was right. This wasn't about her. Just because she was having his baby didn't mean she was a part of his life. Or had any say in anything.

She watched the scenery as he took an underpass to the exit. A ragged homeless man held up a sign asking for help. A woman wearing several dirty sweaters, one over the other, pushed a shopping cart full of cans. Two more turns and they were in a neighborhood that resembled an area in South Phoenix. An area she tried never to drive through. She locked her door.

Jack studied her. "Nervous?"

"No. Precautious."

He gave her a tight smile. "Next street and we're there."

When they arrived, two men stood in front of a house that looked more like a garage than a house. The older of the two men walked to the car. "Stay here," Jack said as he got out.

Taylor rolled down the window. Suddenly, she felt nauseous again.

As she watched, Taylor realized how much she didn't know about Jack. She'd fallen in love with him and she barely knew him.

"Manny," Jack said, shaking the large man's hand. "Did you call anyone?"

"No, I didn't want to make trouble."

"I can look for him, but I don't know where to start."

"I don't know, either. If he didn't get work, then he has *no* money."

"What about this guy he talked to?"

"Richard answered the phone. He knows the guy from prison. His name is Oscar Devereaux, and he heard Henry asking where Oscar was."

"That's it?"

"He said something about a shelter."

"Why do you think he took the gun?"

The man shrugged. "I don't know. Here's the note."

Jack took the paper, glanced at it, then stuffed it in his pocket. "Why don't you two call everyone you know who might have seen him," Jack said. "I'll cruise the neighborhood."

Taylor placed a hand over her mouth.

"Are you okay?" Jack asked. "You look pale."

She gave him a wan smile. "I'm fine. Just a little queasy."

The guy still standing on the steps of the house shouted, "Once he finds out he can't do much without money, he'll come back."

Jack glared at him, then said to Manny, "If we wait until that happens, it could be too late." Jack came around the SUV. "I'll call if I find anything," he said over the hood.

Once inside, Jack placed a hand on her shoulder. "You don't look well. I had better get you back to the hotel."

His touch was gentle and the small gesture brought home the need to tell him she was pregnant. But he needed to be sure his father was okay first. The father he'd finally acknowledged, whether he knew it or not. Not wanting to slow him down, she agreed to go back to the hotel.

A silent car ride back to the hotel gave Taylor time to think. She'd reached a standstill. She'd found out things about her mother and her brother, but nothing definitive. Nothing to prove her mother had no part in Sunny Hawthorne's death or the theft. Nothing to help her know who her mother really was. Or her brother.

Jack dropped her off and left right away. On the way to her room, she decided the next day she'd talk to Emily Hawthorne Kittridge.

Henry Juarez was still one of the people she wanted to talk with, too, but with this new wrinkle, just finding him would be a challenge. She hoped for Jack's sake he'd be okay.

Once in her room, she went to the nightstand and pulled the phone book out of the drawer. She could at least make phone calls to hospitals and shelters. Quickly, she found the phone numbers and addresses for all the shelters near the barrio, picked up the phone and began calling. An hour later, the man who answered at the Turning Point Shelter said he thought he recognized the name but couldn't be sure.

She punched in Jack's cell number, but didn't get a connection. Weird. Knowing time was of the essence, she called the desk for a cab and then hurried down to the hotel lobby. It was raining when she went outside to wait. She could feel her hair frizzing up. "I hope the rain will cool things down," she said to the valet.

"Wishful thinking, ma'am. Around here, rain just makes it feel like you're in a sauna."

The cab pulled up. She got in and within a half hour, they drove up in front of a one-story building that looked as if it might have been a grocery store at one time. Squinting through the rain she could see the sign across the picture window in front. Turning Point Shelter. The window was opaque so she couldn't see inside.

"Are you sure this is where you want to go?" the cabbie asked.

Several men were huddled under the overhang in front of the building. Others sat on the sidewalk or meandered up and down the street, wet and bedraggled. "Yes, I'm sure," she said. "Can you come back for me in a half hour?"

"You're my last customer, ma'am. I'm going home after this." He handed her a card. "Just call the company ten minutes before you're ready. There are lots of guys sittin' around just waiting for a pretty lady like you to call," he drawled.

A shiver crawled up Taylor's spine. If he was trying to be flattering, he'd missed the boat. "How much?"

"Twelve dollars."

She handed him some cash, told him to keep the change and went to the door. She didn't know whether to knock or walk right in, so she did both. An older man with a beard greeted her.

"Can I help you, miss?"

The man's smile was friendly, but the acrid scent of wet clothes and body odor permeated the room. Her stomach rolled and she thought she might be sick. "Yes." She coughed. "I...I'm looking for a Mr. Henry Juarez."

"He's inside on the end bed, ma'am. He's helping a friend he brought in."

"A friend. He's not staying here?"

The man shook his head. "I can get him for you. There's a room around the corner where you can wait."

"Thank you, she said, then started for the room. The place looked more like a flophouse than a shelter. Having only seen such a thing in the movies, she realized there may be no difference between the two.

Someone started coughing and couldn't seem to stop, and for a second, she realized what a germ-laden place this might be. She covered her mouth with her hand and pretended to cough herself, then found the room and went inside.

She opened the door and flipped on a light. The room was spare with a threadbare couch and a small card table and two folding chairs. She reached into her purse for her phone to try Jack again, but as she stood there, she heard someone come up behind her. She turned. Juarez. Up close, the resemblance between Jack and his father was uncanny. They had the same solid chin and expressive eyes, though not the same color. Both had shiny dark hair, but Jack's father's was threaded with silver.

"Hello. We haven't met formally, Mr. Juarez. I'm Taylor Dundee. Do you have a few minutes to spare to talk to me?"

His back straightened. "I'm sorry. I can't help you."

Taylor moistened her lips. Not knowing what Jack had told him, she wasn't sure how to approach the subject. Obviously he knew something about why she was there.

"This isn't about what you think. If you can just listen for a minute—"

He nodded.

"First, I have to say Jack is really worried about you. He thinks something happened or that you're…well, he's really worried."

At first he looked surprised, but the emotion was fleeting. "Then you'll tell him I'm fine and that he should leave me alone."

"I will. I'd appreciate it if you'd hear me out, too."

He smiled, a smile so like Jack's it took her breath away. "You're a determined woman."

"I've only recently learned that my mother once lived in Texas and went by the name Margot Cooper. And, I'm sure Jack told you, she passed away," she said softly. "When I went through her belongings, I found information that led me to believe…all kinds of things and now I'm just trying to find the truth."

"I'm sorry for your loss," he said.

He was taller than he'd seemed before, but he wasn't as tall as Jack. And though Henry Juarez was much older than his son, he was still a very handsome man.

He took another step back and she wondered if he was going to bolt. "I'm going to have a child of my own and it's important to me to find out about my family."

He nodded to the table. "Then let's sit."

Juarez went over and pulled out a chair for her. He sat in the other chair and placed both hands flat on his thighs. He tilted his head and looked at her intently. "How old are you?"

"I was thirty in June. Why do you ask?"

He shook his head. "No reason. Is this your first child?"

She nodded.

His gaze went to her hand. "Are you married?"

She was supposed to be asking questions, not him. "No. I'm not."

"You should be. A child needs a father."

He didn't need to tell her that. "I know that's ideal, but it doesn't always work out that way…" Her words trailed off. He probably knew that better than anyone.

"My son should have a wife."

Oh, my. Was he trying to set her up with Jack?

"Only I hear he's too busy to find one. He's successful, but he has no time to marry."

Taylor cleared her throat. "I came here to ask some questions about Margot Cooper. Do you mind if I go ahead?"

He shifted in his seat. "I don't mind. She was a very nice person."

Taylor couldn't help but smile. "So, you knew her pretty well then?"

"My Maria knew her much better than me because they worked in the house together. My job was outside."

"Maria?"

"Maria…my wife."

The soft, loving way he said the woman's name, rolling his tongue over the *r*, wrenched Taylor's heart. "Did Maria know Margot well?"

"Yes, they were friends and Maria always talked about her friends."

"Did she tell you about the…" Taylor cleared her throat. "The affair?"

When he didn't respond right away, she added, "The affair between Margot and Seymour Hawthorne."

He readjusted himself in his chair and crossed his arms. "I only know what Maria told me."

"Did she tell you about the affair?" she repeated.

"Only a little. Maria knew I wouldn't approve."

"How did Maria feel about her friend…doing this?"

"Maria was a loving, forgiving person. She didn't believe it was her place to judge others."

Taylor had to ask the one question that had been bothering her. "Did your wife ever say anything to you about Margot being pregnant?" Because if Margot had been having an affair with Hawthorne and was pregnant when she left Texas, it could mean that Hawthorne was the father. Taylor's father.

Juarez shook his head. "No. She never said anything like that."

Relief mingled with Taylor's disappointment. On one hand she didn't want to think her mother capable of having an affair, but on the other, it was obvious her mother had lied about who Taylor's father was. And she desperately wanted to know.

"Did you know Margot's son, Matthew?"

"The boy used to come and talk to me when I was working. He was a good boy. Very polite and well mannered."

"You liked him, then?" Taylor smiled. Learning anything about her brother made him more of a person, someone Taylor could imagine as her family.

"Yes. I remember telling Maria that I would be proud if our boy turned out like Matthew."

"Do you think he did?" She shouldn't have asked but couldn't help herself.

He got a wistful look in his eyes. "Yes. Maria would be very proud."

She wondered if Jack had any idea what his biological father thought of him.

"So, Matthew was a nice boy, and yet, Sunny Hawthorne didn't like him?"

The man's expression hardened. "Mrs. Hawthorne didn't want her daughter being with someone she considered beneath her. She considered all the help beneath her." He lifted his chin. "But her daughter did what she wanted anyway."

"Do you know anything about Matthew's death?" she asked, eager for any tidbit.

"Only that he was riding a friend's motorcycle when he shouldn't have been. A car hit him near the gate of the Hawthorne estate and took off. Many rumors went around that Mrs. Hawthorne had something to do with the accident."

Taylor bit her lip. "I heard that somewhere. But…the police would have found out if that was true, wouldn't they?"

He waited a moment before saying, "The police don't always do what they should."

Taylor figured he was talking about his own situation now. And as she looked at the man, her gut told her Henry Juarez couldn't kill anyone. If somehow he had, it must have been an accident. "How hard that must have been for Margot. How did she survive after her son's death?"

"She was devastated. Any parent would be. It's a terrible thing to lose a child."

Her hand automatically went to her stomach. She could only imagine the heartbreak. Not to mention that Matthew's death made the events she was trying to figure out even more confusing. "I still don't understand something. If Matthew was gone, then why did Mrs. Hawthorne send her daughter away?"

Henry scoffed. "Maria told me Mrs. Hawthorne was going to disinherit Emily if she kept the baby. So, Emily told her mother the child wasn't Matthew's, but Mrs. Hawthorne didn't care. She was a hard woman."

Emily Kittridge had also told Taylor that the child wasn't Matthew's. But if Emily had lied to her mother…if the child really had been Matthew's… The idea that Taylor may have a niece or nephew out there somewhere, that her unborn baby would have a cousin… Not exactly the family she'd longed for, but it was something. "Do you know where Emily went to have the baby?"

"Emily didn't give the child up right away. Maria said Emily brought the baby home to see her mother, hoping she would have a change of heart once she saw her. The baby was a girl."

At least that information was the same. "And then what happened?"

"Mrs. Hawthorne told her she couldn't keep it." Juarez scratched his head. "I don't know if anything I've told you is true. It's just what I've heard."

"So, then, Emily put the child up for adoption."

"That's one story."

"What do you mean?"

"There were all kinds of stories at that time."

"Like what?" She inched forward, elbows on the table.

"Stories that Margot was involved."

Taylor stood. "Involved how?" She had to believe anything Margot…her mother…might have done would have been with good reason or because she had no other choice. "Please tell me what you heard."

He drummed his fingers on the top of his leg, his expression thoughtful. "One story was that Margot took the money."

"I've heard that story. I don't believe it's true."

He smiled widely. "I never believed it, either." He paused, then looked at her. "Another story was that Margot took Emily's child."

Taylor turned. "She took the baby back to the adoption agency?"

"No." His brow furrowed. "Some people said she took the baby and disappeared."

Taylor stared at him. "She took the baby…and…" Her words came out in stops and starts as she attempted to process the information. If Margot took the baby…what had she done with—

As the realization hit, Taylor felt as if she'd been sucker punched. She couldn't breathe. Oh, God! She bolted to her feet, but the second she put one foot in front of the other, the room swirled around her.

Light faded to dark. Her knees buckled.

CHAPTER SIXTEEN

"She fainted." Taylor heard voices—a woman's, then a man's—whispers fading in and out. They sounded far away, but she felt the heat of bodies, as if a crowd surrounded her. Something warm and wet touched her forehead, fingers touched her cheek.

"The doctor from the clinic next door is coming. She has a bruise by her eye," one man said.

Then another man asked, "What happened?"

She knew that voice. "People faint because there's something wrong," he said. *Jack*. It was Jack's voice.

"I don't know."

Taylor struggled to pry her eyes open, but her lids felt glued shut.

"We were talking. She stood up and that's when it happened. I caught her so she didn't get hurt."

"Taylor....please wake up." She felt warm fingers brush through her hair, then touch her cheek again. It had to be Jack.

"Do you know her?"

Taylor willed her eyes to open and felt her lids flutter. Something soft cradled her head. Something soft and warm. She smelled Jack's scent. Like a fresh ocean breeze.

"She wanted to know about Margot Cooper and her son."

"Did she say anything else?"

Taylor's eyes flew open.

"Taylor," Jack said, immense relief in his expression. He placed his palms against her cheeks, cradling her face in his hands. "Thank God."

She blinked. "What happened?"

"It looks like you fainted. Just stay still. Someone called a doctor."

Taylor pulled herself to a sitting position. She brushed back her hair. "I was standing and I don't know what happened."

"We need to get you checked out," Jack said.

"No. I'm okay." Struggling to get up, she took the hand Jack offered. He didn't let go and kept his arm around her, steadying her.

"I think—" Her gaze fell on Henry Juarez. "Oh!" She gulped air as what he'd said came back to her.

Jack guided her to a chair. "What's wrong?"

Before she answered, a young man came in. "Hello. I'm Dr. Rydecker from the clinic next door. Someone told me there was an emergency."

"No emergency," Taylor quickly asserted. "I fainted. That's all."

"Do you mind?" he said, reaching to take her pulse.

She shook her head.

"Do you faint often?"

"No, I don't. This is the first time ever."

The physician asked Taylor a couple more questions—questions she didn't want to answer with Jack there. Apparently Jack realized the same thing because he cleared his throat and said, "Uh, we'll step out and give you some privacy."

A gaggle of people had gathered in the doorway, too,

and they moved back when Jack and his dad went out. "Your pulse is erratic," the doctor said. "Not knowing your history, I can only recommend that you make an appointment with your physician to see if there are any underlying causes."

Underlying causes? She knew the cause. "I think I fainted because it got a little close in the room, and...I'm pregnant."

He smiled. "Congratulations."

"Thank you."

"First trimester?"

"I guess." She felt funny talking to a stranger about it.

The doctor frowned. "Have you seen an obstetrician?"

"No, I only did the test today. But I'll make an appointment when I go back to Arizona."

"Well, don't put it off."

The edge in his voice made her think there was something he wasn't saying. "Do you think there's something wrong with the baby?" Whatever her pulse rate had been before, she felt it multiply.

"It's just a recommendation, Miss—"

"Dundee. Taylor Dundee."

"Miss Dundee. It's always a good idea to see a physician as soon as you can when you're pregnant. That way if things do come up, they can be addressed immediately."

She nodded, relieved. His soothing bedside manner made him seem much older than she'd first thought. "I will. Thank you for the advice."

Taylor watched the doctor leave and, on his way out, she saw him stop and talk to Jack. As they spoke, Jack turned to look at her, his eyebrows forming a V. His expression went dark, then he looked at the doctor again.

Oh, God! The doctor wasn't telling him she was

pregnant, was he? When she saw Jack's mouth turn down, she knew the answer.

She placed her arms on the table, then rested her head on top. This couldn't be happening. She pulled in a lungful of oxygen. She couldn't deal with Jack right now. She just couldn't. She had other things to think about. Things that couldn't possibly be true.

Taylor raised her head.

Jack was gone. And she couldn't blame him.

CONGRATULATIONS. Jack shouldered open the door, hitting it so hard it sent a jolt of pain up his neck. But it didn't hurt nearly as bad as the pain in his chest. Yeah, he should be congratulated all right. For being a total fool.

He walked a few steps, then stopped and leaned against the side of the building, rain pelting him like bullets.

Taylor had made love with him. She'd given him reason to believe she cared about him. And all while she was pregnant with another man's child. He whirled around and smacked the wall with the palm of his hand.

He couldn't believe he'd been so stupid.

He stuffed his hands into his pockets and stalked toward his SUV parked down the street. Well, this time he wasn't going to compound his mistake by asking for an explanation. If the time they'd spent together didn't mean anything to her, it didn't mean anything to him.

"Jack, wait."

He turned to see Juarez running toward him.

"I need to talk to you," Juarez said as he reached him.

As much as Jack wanted to keep going, he couldn't. He waited until the man caught up, then he started walking again, Juarez at his side. "I'm sorry, I'm not in the mood to talk." he said, reaching the door and opening it. He felt his father's hand on his arm.

"I need to tell you something."

"Fine. You can tell me on the way home. If you don't want to go home, then I don't want to hear what you have to say. I've got other things on my mind."

"What about Taylor?" his father asked.

The vein at Jack's temple pulsed. "What about her?"

"I saw how concerned you were and I thought—"

"I was concerned because she'd fainted. That's all."

"No, I saw the way you looked at her. The way you touched her. You care for her."

"It's not a point of conversation. Are you getting in or not?"

They stood facing each other, neither saying a word. Apparently Juarez was just as stubborn as Jack was. Finally, Juarez said, "I think she needs you right now."

Jack, furious, got in behind the wheel. The irony was almost laughable. Juarez scrambled to climb into the passenger seat. Almost immediately Jack hit the gas. "She doesn't need me for anything. And if you knew more about her, you wouldn't be saying that."

Juarez looked at him sharply. "Son, I know who she is and I know why she's here. I also know what you've been doing. That doesn't change anything."

Son. Juarez called him son. He couldn't find his voice. Finally he said, "She told you what I'm doing?"

"She didn't tell me anything, but I told her some things. That's why she's going to need your support."

"What did you tell her?"

"Who her mother is."

BACK IN HER HOTEL ROOM Taylor felt chilled, even though it was like a jungle outside. She took a long hot shower. As she finished toweling off, she stood in front of the mirror again. Just because Juarez saw Margot—her mother—leaving the house with Emily's baby didn't mean anything. She could have been taking the baby back to the agency. Henry wouldn't have known that. Or... Margot could've been taking the child somewhere else, to another family even. There was no reason for Taylor to think otherwise.

She turned sideways, wondering when her flat stomach would get bigger. It was hard to believe a life was growing inside her. Her child.

Growing up without a father, Taylor had longed for what she didn't have. Was it fair to impose that same kind of life on a child who had no choice in the matter? Right now she didn't know what Jack thought—other than being angry. Visions of Reed flitted through her head. No, Jack wasn't Reed, that much she knew. But what then? Oh, man. Could he think she'd already been pregnant when she arrived? It had never occurred to her. The phone rang, startling her. She answered it while walking to her suitcase for her robe.

"It's about time," Roxi said. Her friend's slightly nasal tone sounded even more so now that Taylor had been hearing Texas accents twenty-four seven.

Hearing her friend's voice sent a wave of relief through Taylor. Or was it thankfulness? She needed a friend right now. "Hey, Rox. What's up?"

"What's up with you? You don't call, you don't write, what's going on?"

Taylor laughed. "I was only doing what you told me to do. Now you're complaining?"

"Actually, no. I'm delighted you could forget about us for a while."

"How are things going at the shop?"

"Perfect. Couldn't be better. You'll see when you get back."

"Okay."

"When might that be?"

"I don't know. Things here have gotten a little strange." Lord, it was good to talk to Roxi.

"Strange? I hope you mean kinky strange with the hot guy."

"No, I don't." She sighed deeply, then sat on the edge of the bed. "I took a test. I'm pregnant."

There was a long silence. "Oh, man. I'm really sorry."

Taylor gulped and wiped her eyes with the back of her hand. Crazy hormones. She'd never, ever, been this weepy. "Don't be sorry. I'm very happy about it."

It took a few seconds before Roxi said, "Yeah, uh, you sound very happy."

"I am. I'm just…hormone challenged. I really am happy about it." She might be even happier if she knew how Jack felt about her. And if there weren't so many other things going on.

"Good. If you're happy, then I'm happy. Hey, we need some kid blood around here, anyway." She paused, then said, "I didn't know you'd been seeing anyone before you left."

Taylor swallowed. "I—I wasn't. This happened right after I got here."

"Hot guy? Wow. I guess that means you took my advice." She blew out a breath. "Are you sure? It's what… about a week. Your eggs must've been just waiting to bust out."

"I took the test, but I suppose it could be wrong. I'm going to do it again in a few days."

"Does he know?"

Taylor rubbed her hands over her face. "Yes. But he doesn't know he's the father. It's complicated. I've got a lot to think about, and I'm a mess."

"So, come home. We'll take care of you."

God, she wanted to do that. More than anything. But she needed to know if what Juarez said was true. "Soon. Maybe a couple of days. I'll call and let you know." She started sniffling again.

"What? Do you not like him? Is he a jerk?"

"No, it's just that I'm so stupid when it comes to men. Everything is so screwed up," she said, and within seconds, she'd related the whole story about finding out who Jack was, making love with him and meeting his family and finding out about the pregnancy. She told Roxi everything, including what Henry Juarez had told her not more than a couple of hours ago. By the time she finished talking, she was more angry than upset. "So, that's the whole ugly story in a giant bombshell."

"I—I'm speechless," Roxi said. "Literally."

"I was, too. All these people are ruining their lives and trying to ruin mine, too. I'm tired of being a puppet who gets jerked around when someone else pulls the strings. I've had it, and I'm going to do something about it."

"What do you mean?"

"Before I leave here, I'm going to have answers."

She heard a knock at the door, light at first, then louder. "I gotta go, Roxi. I think my dinner is here." What she really needed was a drink, but she couldn't have one because she was pregnant. Peeking through the security hole, she didn't see anyone, so she opened the door a crack with the chain fastened.

Jack stood off to the side.

She was about to shut the door when he thrust his hand in the opening. If she pulled it shut, she'd squish his fingers.

"We need to talk."

The last person she wanted to see right now was Jack. When he was around, she couldn't think. Hell, she couldn't breathe. And that reaction made her want to run. If she let it go any further, if she let herself go emotionally, it would tear her apart when it ended—like all relationships did, sooner or later.

But she couldn't avoid him and opened the door for him to come inside.

He strode purposefully to the minibar and took out a bottle of beer. "Do you mind?"

"Just leave the money on top."

He looked at her, one eyebrow raised.

"Kidding." She had to do something to lighten the moment. If she didn't, she'd fall apart. "What do you want?"

"Juarez told me what he said to you. We need to figure out what to do next."

"Juarez? Is everything fine with him?"

"I don't know if fine is the correct term."

"What about his leaving and all that?"

"He's not leaving right this minute. So, forget that. We need to get busy."

She couldn't believe he just wanted to go on as if nothing had happened. That he'd ignore the fact that she was pregnant. Well, she was tired of pretending. "Aren't you going to ask me about the baby?"

He looked away. "I figure that's between you and the kid's father. If you wanted to tell me, you would."

Her heart thudded. Oh, Lord. He *did* think it was someone else's baby. She didn't know if that was better or worse. "Well, I do, and I will."

His surprise gave her the courage to go on.

"I'm just barely pregnant. You're the first person I've been with in a year. I don't know how it happened, I just know it did, or so the test kit says. But rest assured, I don't want anything from you. I'm not going to hit you up for money or anything else. I'm perfectly capable—"

He held up a hand, astonishment on his face. "Are you saying that I'm…"

She nodded, unable to tell if he was shocked, disgusted, angry, or all of the above. "It probably happened in the shower when we didn't get the condom on right away. I was supposed to get my period right after that, but I didn't. I'm only telling you because you have a right to know. I don't have any expectations, and I'm perfectly capable of handling this myself. It won't be that big a deal. I'll just go home and take care of—"

Before she finished, he was in her face, his hands on her arms. "Take care of it? You expect me to just walk away? What kind of person are you?"

She shook her head, not understanding.

"I spent my life wondering who the hell I was. There's no way I'm going to allow you to walk away with my child and…God knows what you plan to do."

Did he think…oh, God. "No. You're wrong. I'm not going to do…that. But I'm not going to saddle you with a child you never planned on or don't want any part of."

He took off his hat and ran his hand through his hair, more

incredulous than ever. "You think I could just walk away and never see my own child? You think I'm that uncaring?"

His face was inches from hers and she could see the veins popping out on his neck, his face red, his hands curled into fists. "You don't know me at all, do you?"

"That's just the point. I do. I think you are responsible. You feel obligated to take care of everyone. I don't want the father of my child to feel obligated. I don't want you in my child's life because you're responsible."

"I think you mean our child," he ground out.

She truly had no expectations of Jack. Her only expectations were for herself. Things worked best that way. If she had no expectations, no one had to live up to them and she didn't get hurt. How could she convey that to him?

Right now, she couldn't. Not with emotions at fever pitch. "I'm tired, Jack. I'm not trying to brush this off, but I need to go to bed and get some sleep. I'd rather talk about this with a clear head."

He just stood there, his eyes roaming over her, her face, her breasts, her stomach.

"Fine," he snapped. "Tomorrow then. And don't even think about leaving town."

He stormed out the door.

Calmly, Taylor latched the safety chain, then rested against the door and cried. He was happy about the baby. Or, if not happy, accepting. But what she really wanted was for him to love her. He wasn't going to let it go. He was going to make things even harder. Her chest tightened, her knees buckled and, as she slid to the floor, she began to sob.

CHAPTER SEVENTEEN

"GOOD EVENING," Seymour Hawthorne greeted Taylor at the door with a smile. "Was I expecting you?"

Taylor stared at the man who might be her grandfather. "I'm sorry to disturb you this late, but it's important that I talk to Emily. Is she here?"

He raised his thick white brows in question. "Yes, she is. I'll have Benjamin round her up. Please come in."

She stepped inside the marble-floored foyer and the butler appeared, eyeing Taylor warily. "I found a very pretty young lady at the front door," Hawthorne said to him.

"Answering the door is *my* job, sir," Benjamin said through pinched lips.

Hawthorne dismissed the comment with a wave of his hands. "I enjoy answering the door, so there's no need to get your shorts in a twist. Now off you go."

Taylor liked Hawthorne. She noticed the slight head tremor that Jack had mentioned.

"Oh, Benjamin. Please tell Emily to come down. She has company."

A thin man with a narrow nose, Benjamin nodded stiffly and all but clicked his heels before he walked away.

Hawthorne led Taylor into the library, the same room

she'd been in before. He went over to the ornately embellished mahogany bar against one wall. "What can I get you to drink?"

"Nothing for me, thank you."

Hawthorne took a bottle of Perrier from the bar refrigerator, took out two glasses, filled them with ice, then poured the water. He set them on the table between two chairs. "Please sit down and tell me what you wish to talk to Emily about."

"Not a chance," Emily's voice rang out. The tall blonde stood in the doorway, eyeing Taylor suspiciously. "What do you want now?"

Taylor cleared her throat. "It's about Margot Cooper."

Emily shook her head and turned to leave.

Hawthorne's eyes narrowed. "Where are your manners, Emily?"

"Father!" She swung back around and glared at him. "This isn't any of your business."

Hawthorne shrugged nonchalantly. "Last I heard, this was my house." Smiling, he looked at Taylor. "And, by golly, it still is."

"Well, I'm not staying," Emily snapped. She stalked out the door.

"I want to talk to you about the baby girl you gave away thirty years ago."

Emily froze. Slowly, she walked back into the room.

Blood thundered in Taylor's ears. She didn't want to do this. But if she didn't, she'd never know. She forced out the words, "I w-w-want-t—" She stopped abruptly. Dammit. Every time she had something important to say, she couldn't do it without stuttering.

She tried to remember how she'd felt with Jack's arms around her, his strength channeling into her.

She took a deep breath and began again. "I…want…the truth. About Margot Cooper."

Emily blinked. "What are you referring to? I told you I didn't believe she took the money."

"Did Margot Cooper kidnap your baby?"

It got so quiet in the room, Taylor could hear her heart beating.

Kittridge stared at Taylor. Then her gaze shifted, first to her father, then to the door. Her hand went to the chain at her throat. After a long second, she seemed to regain her composure and, raising her chin, she said, "I gave my child up for adoption. Why would anyone think otherwise?"

"Because Henry Juarez told me some people saw Margot Cooper leaving the house with your baby on the night your mother died. And she never returned."

"Henry? Henry Juarez? You spoke with him?"

The muscles in Taylor's shoulders cramped. "I did."

Emily hovered near the door. "I can't talk about this. It doesn't matter what happened that night. It was thirty years ago."

"It matters to me," Taylor said, suddenly realizing what she had to do. "My mother died recently and it turns out Margaret Dundee wasn't her real name. Her name was Margot Cooper."

Kittridge's mouth fell open. She stared blankly at Taylor. After a long moment, she said in a hoarse whisper, "Margot was…your mother?"

"Margot, Margaret, whatever her name really was… Yes. She was my mother."

Emily walked over to them and sat on the couch. "You're—" Her hand went to her mouth.

The elder Hawthorne looked confused. Understandable.

She'd told him she was Margot's niece. He had no reason to make a connection between Taylor and Emily. She didn't know if he did now. But Emily knew the truth—and Taylor wasn't going to leave without hearing the whole story. "Tell me what happened," she demanded.

Emily covered her face with her hands and moaned, "It's not what you might think."

Taylor crossed her arms. She'd been hearing a lot of that lately. "Then tell me, so I don't need to find the answers somewhere else."

Emily looked up. "Father, I'd like you to leave."

Taylor glanced at Hawthorne. "Please," she said.

He looked confused but left the room anyway.

Alone with Emily, Taylor perched on the edge of her chair across from her. "Now! Tell me now."

"I barely know where to start."

"How about your relationship with Margot Cooper." Despite what Juarez had said, she had to make sure of that one thing. She wanted facts, not conjecture. "Can you tell me where Margot was going with your baby on the night your mother died?"

Emily bit her bottom lip. She bowed her head, her fingers twisting the chain at her neck. "It's hard to explain. There was the…argument, and I gave Margot the baby to hold and then…then it happened and everything was so mixed up after that." A tear slid down her cheek. She swallowed. "Margot left and I had to go to London. I thought…" She shook her head. "I thought everything would be okay, but it wasn't."

"Are you saying you left and don't know what happened to your own child?" Taylor asked, incredulous.

"I had to leave," she sobbed, tears streaming down her

face. "I couldn't stay. I didn't mean for any of it to happen. Only my mother wouldn't listen to me. She just wouldn't listen... and I pushed her. Not hard, just barely, and—and I gave Tiffany to Margot and—"

Taylor's heart stopped. "Oh...my...God!"

Emily shook her head wildly. "No. No, no, no. You don't understand. She hit her head. It was an accident. Nancy called 911. Everything was crazy after that. My mother was in the hospital and she was okay when Nancy sent me to London. I didn't know she was going to—"

Emily's face contorted in anguish, her voice became a squeak. "I didn't know she was gone until my father called. Then I couldn't come home because no one except Nancy knew what had happened and she said someone might find out and blame me."

Taylor stood, leaning heavily on the chair. "You were responsible for the accident that sent your mother to the hospital," she said flatly. "You were responsible for her death."

Panic shone in Emily's eyes. "No. You don't know how she was. My mother wouldn't let me keep my baby. We were in love and she made him leave. I loved him so much, and our baby was all I had left." Her eyes glazed over when she looked at Taylor again. "I knew Margot would take care of her. I didn't just give my baby away. I would never do that."

Emily spoke of her baby as if there was no connection to Taylor, and her voice seemed to get smaller and smaller until she sounded almost childlike. "He was the love of my life. My mother ruined our relationship like she ruined everything. When he was gone, I didn't want to live anymore."

"So, Matthew was...the father?"

Emily hiccupped. "I hope so."

"You hope so?" Even more confused, Taylor said, "What does that mean?"

"I was in love with Matthew. But when my mother broke us up, I was…with other boys to get back at her. I'm not very proud of that, but I was so young…I didn't know what to do."

Oh, God. Taylor was too stunned to make sense of anything anymore. "Did you *ever* try to find Margot to see your child?"

Emily dabbed at her cheeks and eyes with the corner of her blouse. "I couldn't. Nancy wouldn't let me. I was only sixteen."

"What about your father? He could have helped you."

. "Oh, no." Emily said. "He didn't know about any of it. I couldn't tell him. I can't ever tell him."

Suddenly Taylor felt drained of all emotion. *You never tried to find me.*

Emily shook her head. "Two years later, I got married and then I had Sienna to think about. I couldn't do something that would ruin her life. She was an innocent child."

"You loved the baby's father so much you couldn't give up your child, yet you did anyway," Taylor scoffed. "And you never once tried to find her."

Emily looked at Taylor, her eyes red and watery. "I didn't have a choice. I was only sixteen. I didn't know."

Another horrible thought struck Taylor. "And what about Henry Juarez? How do you explain letting him rot in prison for thirty years for a crime he didn't commit?"

Emily started crying again. "I didn't think that would happen, and it took so long for the trial… By that time, I had Sienna. I couldn't tell or Sienna would be all alone."

"You didn't think! What about after it happened? You didn't think to go to the police then?" Taylor felt like hitting something. "If it was an accident, nothing would have happened to you. And yet you let an innocent man go to prison!"

Emily dried her cheeks with her hands. "I did what Nancy told me to do. I didn't know any better. She told me everything would be okay."

A wave of nausea swept over Taylor, but it wasn't because of the baby she was carrying. "And how about a year later? Five years later? Ten? Didn't you know any better then?"

"As I said, it was too late. I had my husband and Sienna, a home and responsibilities."

And Henry Juarez had nothing. Bile rose in Taylor's throat. She had to leave.

When she reached the door, Emily said, "You're not going to tell anyone, are you?"

"I don't know."

"But…I'm your mother."

The word had never seemed so hollow. Taylor ran out of the room.

Hawthorne was hovering outside the door. "I believe I deserve an explanation, young lady."

Taylor stopped in her tracks. What could she say? I just discovered I'm your granddaughter? The woman I thought was my mother "might" be my grandmother? My father could be any number of guys Emily slept with, and my birth mother let an innocent man rot in jail for thirty years? "I really need some air."

He lifted his chin. "I might be old, but I can still pull a few facts together."

She bit her bottom lip. "It's not something I can talk about." She pulled out her cell phone. "Please excuse me. I have to call a cab."

"No need for that," he said, motioning for her to put the phone down. "I'll have Benjamin drive you."

Hawthorne was a nice man. She wished she could get to know him. But there was no way that would happen because, right that minute, she realized what had to be done. "Thank you. I'd appreciate that."

"I'll be right back," he said. "I'll round up the car."

When he left, Taylor turned right around and went back into the library. Emily was standing at the window. Taylor slammed the door behind her.

"You have to go to the police," Taylor said without preamble. "Nancy has to go to the police, too, and you both have to tell them everything."

Emily stared blankly at Taylor.

"I'm leaving here and going back to the hotel. I'll give you until midnight. If you don't go to the police by then, I will."

Emily clutched the chair at her side. "You can't mean that."

"I've never meant anything more in my life."

The door opened and Benjamin peered inside. "Miss Dundee, the car is ready."

Taylor looked at Emily again, hoping she hadn't just given the woman reason to leave town. She wanted to say something to that effect but couldn't.

On the way out, Seymour Hawthorne caught up with her. "Are we ready?"

"We?"

"I'm going to ride along with you. It isn't often I get to keep company with a pretty young woman."

Taylor doubted that very much. He was charming. And he was rich.

"And we also need to talk," he added.

Outside, Hawthorne opened the limo door for her and she slid inside. Benjamin pursed his lips. Hawthorne went to the other side and got in. Once Taylor had given directions and they were on the road, Hawthorne said, "Why did you lie about Margot being your aunt, Taylor?"

She stiffened. "I didn't think Emily would talk to me if she knew." And now she understood Jack's dilemma.

"Well, I would like to talk to you about your mother. As you probably know, she and I were...good friends."

Taylor nodded, but didn't know what to say.

"Actually—" he sighed "—I was very much in love with her."

Taylor was glad he admitted it. Even though it was hard to picture her mother in that light, she was glad to know she'd had the experience of loving someone and having him love her. She couldn't remember her mother having any male friends while Taylor was growing up. Margaret— Margot—had always said one great love was enough.

"I'm sure you've discovered that already, and I can't blame you if you think badly of me."

She moistened her lips. "It was a long time ago. It would be hard for me to think badly of you for something I know nothing about."

They were both silent. As the car sped along the freeway, she could hear herself breathing.

Finally Hawthorne said, "I'd like to know who your father was."

She turned to look at him. "What difference does it make?"

"It shouldn't make any difference since I was the one

who couldn't make a decision back then. But it bothers me that she found someone else so soon. I really thought we were—" He stopped, then shook his head. "I didn't know there was someone else. But, you're right. It doesn't matter. She deserved all the happiness she could get."

Oh, boy. She wanted Emily to be the one to tell him she hadn't given up her child for adoption and that Taylor was her daughter—his granddaughter. "I don't believe there was someone else," Taylor said. "I never knew my father. I was told that he passed away. Except now I know that's probably not true."

He looked confused for a moment and, rather than letting him draw the wrong conclusions, she said, "I finally discovered I was adopted."

He didn't smile, but Taylor could see by his expression that he was pleased there hadn't been someone else.

"I imagine it was difficult to grow up without a father."

He'd get no argument from her on that.

The limo pulled up to the hotel. "Ask Emily about my mother when you get back," Taylor said. "She knows all about it."

"She knows all about what?"

"She knows how Margot became my mother." Taylor quickly opened her door and got out. "I've got to go. Thank you so much for the ride."

Benjamin had come around to open the door and gave her a look, so she left it open for him to close. It wasn't her place to tell Hawthorne. It was Emily's. Then he could do what he wanted with the information.

More than anything, she hoped Emily would tell her father the truth and then go to the police. But based on past behavior, Taylor didn't have high hopes.

The woman who gave birth to her had until midnight to
do the right thing. If she didn't, Taylor would do it herself.
Mother or not.

CHAPTER EIGHTEEN

HENRY JUAREZ IS INNOCENT. The truth was finally sinking in. Taylor glanced at her watch again. Eleven-thirty. Another half hour to wait. Unable to bring herself to go up to her room, Taylor had gone to the twenty-four-hour snack bar, but overcome by nausea, she couldn't eat what she'd purchased. To distract herself, she walked from one hotel shop to another until they closed. A half hour ago, she'd finally dropped onto a bench in the atrium adjacent to the lobby.

The water trickling over the rocks in a mini-waterfall above the koi pond reminded her of the trip she and Jack had taken to Lake Conroe. She closed her eyes to summon up the almost spiritual feeling she'd had when making love with Jack. The memory of his gentle touch, his tender and yet passionate kisses would soon be all she'd have of him.

The thought of everything his family had been through made her sick all over again. Things that never would have happened if Emily had been honest in the beginning. And the irony was, if it was truly an accident, nothing would have happened to Emily.

Jack needed to be told. If Emily went to the police, he would hear that way. If Emily didn't go to the police, then Taylor had to decide what to do. Should she tell Jack first? Or his father? Or the police and let them do the job?

Henry deserved to know immediately, but it was because of Jack's relentless quest that the truth had come out. If it weren't for him…

It had to be Jack who told Juarez, she realized. And she had to tell Jack. He'd been right and she'd been wrong. The outcome had affected them both in life-changing ways. But oddly, she felt at peace with it. And she was ecstatic for Jack.

Margaret Dundee may not be Taylor's biological mother, but if DNA tests showed Matthew to be Taylor's father, Margaret Dundee was her grandmother. Margaret hadn't committed any crime, she'd simply provided a safe harbor for a child she believed was her granddaughter. The worst thing she'd done was deceive Taylor. And as Taylor had always believed, she'd had a good reason. She'd been right to believe in her mother. But for some reason, being right didn't make her feel any better.

Perhaps it was knowing that her real mother was the kind of person who'd give up her child and then never think twice about it. The kind of person who'd let an innocent man go to jail.

She looked at her watch again. Almost midnight. Emily wouldn't go to the police. Still, she'd hoped. She always hoped. That had always been her downfall.

The only bright spot in all of it, besides being happy for Jack and his father, was that she'd discovered Seymour Hawthorne was her grandfather. She liked him very much. And she had a half sister. Sienna, whom she'd glimpsed just once.

She touched her stomach. Her baby would have an aunt and a great-grandfather.

But if Taylor had to go to the police about Emily, she could forget about anyone being a part of her baby's life.

"Taylor?"

She looked up to see a young woman. Her blond hair was pulled back in a ponytail and just as Taylor recognized her, the woman said, "I'm Sienna Kittridge. We met at my grandfather's house."

"Yes…" Taylor braced for a verbal assault, sure Emily had told the girl Taylor had all but blackmailed her. "I remember."

Sienna sat on the bench next to Taylor.

She didn't seem angry. Not even upset. "Did you come here to see me?" Taylor asked.

"Actually, I was in the bar with friends when my mother called. She was upset after your visit, so I was leaving to go home. Then I saw you."

Taylor could only imagine what Emily had told her. "I'm sorry. I know she was upset, but I never expected—"

"Oh, don't worry about her. She's always upset, and she gets over it quickly. I'm glad we've finally had the opportunity to talk."

Apparently Emily *hadn't* told her everything. And that could only mean Emily wasn't going to the police. But what did she mean about an opportunity to talk? "You wanted to talk to me?"

Sienna smiled. "For a long time, actually. But not because my mother told me about you."

Taylor frowned. "How then?"

"When I was young, I heard my mother talking on the phone and I kept hearing references to 'the baby.' She never told me she had a child she gave up for adoption, but people talk, and over the years I pieced things together. When I left for college, I asked her point-blank and she finally told me about it. Later, I tried to find you. Eventually I came to the conclusion that there had been no adoption."

For Taylor, with everything else that had happened,

this news was almost anticlimactic. "Did you ask your mother about it?"

"No, not then. I knew she wouldn't tell me, and I was just getting involved in college and stopped looking. But a year later when I came home on break, my mom and I were talking about her nanny, how close she and Margot were. I decided if anyone knew what had happened to the baby, Margot would. I let my mother know I was going to find Margot and that's when she told me. But before she did, she made me promise I wouldn't share the secret with anyone...or try to find you."

"So, you didn't?"

"Not immediately. And when I did, I couldn't find anything. No old addresses, no nothing. Margot seemed to have vanished."

"Did you tell your mother you'd begun to look for me?"

"There wasn't any point. I'd hit a dead end. Then, not that long ago, I placed an ad in several major newspapers looking for Margot Cooper."

Oh, God. Taylor remembered the ad her mother had torn out and kept. "Did my mo—Margot ever contact you?"

"About six months ago. She was angry. She said I'd be ruining many lives if I persevered."

Six months? That was close to the time of the accident. "Do you remember when she called? What day? What time?"

"I do, kind of, because she called so late. Not the date or anything but I know it was a Saturday night, and I'd just come home from a party. It was about two o'clock in the morning. Why?"

Could the call have been made the night her mother went off the road? Had she been upset and talking on the phone while going around the treacherous curves....

"Are you okay?" Sienna asked.

"Uh…what? Oh, yes. I'm fine," she said absently. "How…did the call end?"

Sienna wrinkled her brow. "She was really upset and made some harsh remarks. Then she just hung up." The young woman bowed her head. "I felt terrible afterward. I knew all she'd done was help, and she thought I was going to ruin everything. But I wasn't. I just wanted to know."

Now it made sense. There was a reason for the crash. She didn't know that for sure, but it was something to hold on to. A reason. Just knowing made her feel better somehow. Closure in a way.

How strange that something that happened thirty years ago was still affecting lives. Taylor realized how little control she had over the things that had happened in her life. The only thing she was able to control was how she handled what came her way.

The thought buoyed her. How she handled things was her choice. Would always be her choice.

"Are you sure you're okay? You look pale."

"I'm fine." She glanced at her watch. Maybe she could give Emily a while longer. It had to be hard making this kind of decision. "Did your mother tell you anything else?"

"About what?"

She hadn't. And now Sienna would hate Taylor if she went to the police. She would destroy Sienna's family. It would be *her* fault and…and dammit, she was making excuses again. Jack was right. She excused everyone, making herself the scapegoat. The recognition gave her a small shot of courage.

Just then, Taylor's cell phone rang. "Excuse me," she

said to Sienna, then got up and walked a few steps away to answer it. She didn't recognize the phone number. "Hello?"

"Is this Taylor Dundee?"

"Yes, who's calling?"

"William Macfarland with the Macfarland and Chase law firm. I represent Emily Kittridge."

Taylor's stomach dropped. Emily had hired an attorney! "What is this about?"

"Emily requested that I let you know I'm accompanying her to the police station. She would have called herself but she's busy settling her affairs."

Taylor staggered back. What should have been happiness that Jack's father might be exonerated was tempered by the knowledge that Emily could go to jail. What the woman had done was unconscionable, and yet…Taylor felt sad for her. "Thank you," she said. "I appreciate the call."

"I bet you do," he said with no small note of sarcasm. "Just don't plan on this maneuver bringing you a windfall."

Shocked, Taylor closed the phone with a snap. He couldn't really think that's what she was after, could he? Did Emily?

Sienna waited patiently as Taylor put the phone in her purse. "Sienna, I think you should go find your mother. She might need you right now."

Especially right now.

"HERE'S YOUR MORNING PAPER," Jack said as he dropped it on Lana's kitchen counter. "It's heavy with Saturday ads."

Lana almost dropped the cup she'd just got out of the cabinet. "What's going on?" he added.

"We're late. I'm sorry I told you to come over. I forgot about Ryan's ball practice."

"I can take him."

"No, you can't." She poured two cups of coffee and handed him one.

"Why not?"

"Because you have to stay here. Taylor called looking for you. Is something wrong with your phone?"

He shook his head. "I think I accidentally shut it off."

She raised her eyebrows. "Well, I told her you were coming over and I'd give you a message. But she said she had to see you. She asked me to keep you here until she arrived."

"Taylor's coming here?" He leaned against the counter, watching Lana buzz around. She tossed some oatmeal and water in a bowl and stuck it in the microwave. "And she didn't say why?"

"Let's see. Since she wants you here, I think it's pretty obvious she wants to talk to you." She gave him an impish smile.

"Funny. Your mouth is going to get you in trouble one of these days."

Lana laughed. "It already has, baby brother. More than once."

"How did Taylor sound?"

His question got an are-you-kidding look. "How did she *sound?*"

"Yeah. You know…was she serious? Perky? Matter-of-fact?"

Lana took a swig of her coffee. "You've really got it bad, don't you?"

He wasn't going to get into his love life with Lana again. "I've got things to do, that's what I've got. Is there any real reason I need to stay?"

"She said it was very important and that it was good news."

At this point, he didn't know what that could be. "Was she leaving right away?"

"Yes. I figure if she caught a cab immediately, it'll any minute."

Jack glanced at the time. Cal had called and wanted to see him, but he knew Taylor wouldn't be coming here if it wasn't important. He sat at the table and took a sip of coffee.

"Ryan, get a hustle on," Lana called out to her son. "You're going to have to fill me in later."

As was her style, Lana didn't ask, she commanded.

"Hey, Uncle Jack." Ryan came in and his mother gave him his breakfast. "Oatmeal again. Why can't I eat regular cereal like other kids?"

"Don't whine," Lana directed. "It's good for you, now hurry up or you'll be late."

Lana sat next to Jack and sipped her coffee.

"You think you need more coffee? You're already hyper."

She smiled. "Cal called and said he's buying a ranch near Bandera. He sounded excited. I'm excited."

"A ranch? A working ranch?" Before she could answer, he said, "You mean he quit the circuit?"

She nodded. "He thinks it's time to settle down."

"That's hard to believe." But his buddy had said the trick to getting what you want was all in the deciding.

You just decide how you want it to go and you do it. That's all it takes.

"Apparently, this is something he's been planning for a long time. I'm surprised you didn't know," Lana said.

"He'd talked about it, but he always said he'd wait to do it until he had a reason. I thought he meant something like being injured and unable to ride." Jack smiled. "But I guess he has another reason." He looked at his sister, then poked her on the shoulder.

Lana actually blushed. "I hope that's the reason."

He gave her a big bear hug. "Be sure to let me know as soon as he pops the question."

"Let's not get ahead of ourselves. It could be wishful thinking on my part."

Jack shook his head. "No, when Cal decides he wants something, he goes after it. And he wants you."

"Does this mean I'm gonna have a real dad?" Ryan piped up around a mouthful of oatmeal.

A real dad. He was going to be a real dad. The idea made him smile.

Lana ruffled Ryan's hair. "No, like I said, it could be wishful thinking on my part."

The doorbell rang. "That must be Taylor." Jack stood, his nerves on edge.

"We're leaving right now," Lana said, nudging Ryan to get up. "I'll take my time if you want me to." She grinned at Jack.

He glanced at her and started for the front door. "The sooner the better."

At the door, he took a deep breath. When he heard the back door slam shut, he turned the knob and gave one quick tug. The morning sun shone behind Taylor, back-lighting her sun-kissed hair like a halo. "Hi."

"Hi."

Her expression was dead serious. Dark circles made half moons under her eyes, and her jean shorts and red T-shirt looked as if she'd slept in them. Suddenly he felt guilty. She was pregnant and her whole life was crashing down around her. He should've stayed, he should have held her in his arms. He motioned her inside, then closed the door.

"Whatever—"

"I'm sorry—"

Then they both said, "You go first." He couldn't help laughing.

"Can I sit?" she finally said.

He made a wide sweep with one arm. "Wherever you want. Would you like something to drink?"

"Kitchen—" she said. "And a glass of water, please."

He led the way, took a bottle of water from the fridge and handed it to her along with a glass. He still had his coffee.

"So," he said when they sat. "What's up?" He tried to be casual, nonchalant even, but it wasn't working.

Facing him at the table, Taylor took a drink. "The police know your father is innocent."

He leaned closer. "What did you say?"

"The police know your father is innocent. I thought you should know so—"

He shook his head. "No, I heard what you said, but I don't know what you mean. What exactly are you talking about?"

"I went to see Emily Kittridge. I wanted to know the whole story about how I ended up with...my mother. I had to know. It was an emotional exchange. In the end I discovered that Emily had an argument with her mother. Her mother tried to stop her from leaving and Emily pushed her. Sunny Hawthorne fell and hit her head."

Jack heard the words, but it seemed almost impossible. A cruel joke.

"Last night Emily and her attorney went to the police with the information."

Jack launched to his feet, spilling his coffee. "I'm not getting this. If it was that simple, why did my father spend thirty years in prison? Why didn't this come out during the investigation?"

She made herself busy mopping up the spill with one of the napkins on the table. "It's complicated. Emily was a teenager at the time and she left the country. Apparently she didn't know your father had been incarcerated until she came back to the States. Nancy Belamy covered up for her."

Two people knew Juarez was innocent and had kept quiet? Years of anger and rage churned inside him until he literally shook. "And when was that?"

"I don't know exactly. But I do know that she went with her attorney to the police station around midnight last night, and I expect your father will hear something today. I just thought you would want to know and maybe tell him yourself."

"That's why you came here," he said, more or less talking to himself now, because he didn't know what else to say or do. He paced from one side of the kitchen to the other. "You came here to tell me that. I appreciate it."

"Where's your father?"

He threw his hands in the air. "Oh, God." He could barely hold back tears. "I don't know. Work maybe. Day labor, which means he could be anywhere. Different companies pick up workers on street corners and take them where the work is. If not at some job, he's probably back at Richard's."

"If he's not there, then you could call the day labor office. Maybe they'll tell you."

"You know this for sure…she's at the police station? If I went there, she'd be there and they'd tell me what you just did?"

"That, I don't know. The police have procedures to follow."

As he moved past Taylor for at least the tenth time, she reached out and touched his hand. He stopped on a dime, then closed his hand around hers and, taking the other one, too, he pulled her to her feet. Her face was mere inches from his, her body so close. "Is it true? Really true?"

"It's a lot to absorb," she said, her voice low and soft. "I know you don't want to count on anything without knowing for sure, but—"

The next thing he knew, she was in his arms and he kissed her. He needed to kiss her. He wanted to share his happiness with her.

Her lips were so soft and so warm and, to his surprise, she kissed him back, deeply and passionately. He didn't know where any of this was headed, but he didn't care. Right now he didn't care about anything except that Juarez—his father—might be exonerated, and he wanted Taylor. With all his heart he wanted her. Forever.

He was just going to tell her that when she pulled back. "I'm sorry," she whispered. "I guess I got caught up in the excitement of the moment."

"I liked it. I—"

She turned and started to walk away. Before she got out of the room, she stopped. "I can't, Jack. Please understand. I—I just can't."

He crossed his arms, but his pulse was still pounding triple time. "Okay," he said. "What exactly is it that you can't do?"

"I can't keep getting my hopes up. I can't handle another disappointment. Another…heartbreak."

"And you believe that's inevitable in any relationship?"

"So far, I'm batting a thousand."

"Me, too," he said. "But I'll be damned if I'm going to let it ruin the rest of my life. I love you and I can't let you go without telling you. But—" He stopped. He knew if she couldn't trust him, there was no future for them. "But you have to feel it, too."

The door slammed and he heard Lana call, "I'm back!"

He looked at Taylor. At her belly.

"I have to find Henry. I can't tell Lana before him. C'mon, I'll give you a ride to the hotel."

She shook her head. "I have a car. But thanks anyway."

Taylor heard Jack making an excuse to Lana, so she took the opportunity to leave.

Back at the hotel, she was tossing her clothes into a suitcase when the phone rang. Who now? She didn't want to talk to anyone. But what if it was the travel agent about her flight back to Arizona?

"Hello?"

"I'm calling for Taylor," an elderly man said. Her stomach dropped. Mr. Hawthorne.

"This is Taylor." She steeled herself. He had to be feeling horrible and he had to know it was her fault.

"I'm in the lobby. Shall I come to your room?"

He was there, at the hotel. Oh, man. She wanted to run away. She didn't know what Emily had told him… "Okay. It's room six twenty-five."

When he hung up, Taylor felt paralyzed. It was too much. It was all too much. She sat in a chair and waited. A few moments later, she heard a knock on her door.

Zombielike, she went over and opened it.

Mr. Hawthorne looked terrible and his hands were shaking very badly. "Please, come in," she said.

She directed him to a chair. "Can I get you something?"

He looked at her suitcase on the bed. "Are you leaving?"

"I think it's best."

He went over to sit, his steps heavy. "I'd like you to reconsider."

She wasn't sure she'd heard right. She sat on the end of the bed nearest him. "Reconsider what?"

He reached out and took her hand. "Staying in Houston. If you leave, how will I get to know you? I'm not a young man anymore and I'm not as healthy as I was. If you leave now, we may never have the opportunity."

Taylor frowned. "You want me to stay?" She couldn't believe he'd even talk to her, much less want her to stay.

"Come to the house. Stay with me."

"I—I can't. I have a business in Arizona. I have—"

"Two weeks then. At least stay that long. We have to get to know each other. Sienna would like that, too."

"Y-you don't... She doesn't..."

"This is a horrible mess, but it's not your fault. No one blames you, my dear. My God, you're the most innocent person in all of this. If anyone should take some blame, it should be me. Emily has always done what she wanted, and I wasn't there to guide her. Now she has to take responsibility for her actions. It should've happened years ago." He shook his head. "That poor man."

"You can't think—"

"Yes, I can," he said sternly. "I wasn't a good father. I worked all the time. Had I been there, things might have been different." He heaved a sigh, his voice husky. "I'm not proud of that, but there it is." He shook his head again. "That poor, poor man."

Taylor felt sorry for Hawthorne, too. So many lives affected by a few selfish people. She felt warmed by Hawthorne's compassion. "I'm sorry, I wish I could stay longer, but I have things that I have to take care of."

"Things more important than family?"

She didn't feel like she had a family. And what she had biologically wasn't exactly the *Leave it to Beaver* kind. Families were built through a lifetime. You didn't make a family by just saying it. "My mother was my family. And I'm going to have a baby who'll be my family."

His eyes brightened. "A baby? You're married?"

"No, I'm not."

"Where's the baby's father?"

"Gone," she said, not wanting to get into it. "For good reason."

"Mr. Parker?"

She looked down.

He cleared his throat. "We're family by blood and we can become family if you give it a chance. We can't do that if you go away."

He was right.

"I'd like to be your family, Taylor," he continued. "And if I'm going to have a great-granddaughter, I'd like to be in her life."

"But what about Emily?"

"She knows where I stand. I'm her father and I'll help her as much as I can, but ultimately, she will have to take responsibility for what she's done."

Taylor felt a tightening in her stomach, her emotional needs warring with logic. "With a baby coming, I have to make sure my company is running smoothly. I can't risk my child's future."

"I wouldn't want you to. But rest assured, you and your child will never have to worry about the future." He stopped and put his hand over his chest.

When Taylor started to get up, he waved her away. "Just

heartburn." Then he went on, "I understand your concerns, but if I've learned anything in this life, it's that we have to take risks. Sometimes that means not doing the sure thing. Sometimes it means we screw up. Sometimes we simply have to take a leap of faith and trust our own instincts."

The knot in her stomach grew tighter. Her baby would need a family. Even if they were far away. She could handle a week, couldn't she? Maybe even two. She took a deep breath, then smiled. "I'll consider it."

CHAPTER NINETEEN

TWO WEEKS LATER, Taylor was packing her suitcase again. It had taken almost that long to get comfortable with the idea that she had a grandfather and a sister. Sienna, unfortunately, had had to return to graduate school a few days earlier, but they'd promised to keep in touch.

In the short time Taylor had been there, her grandfather had shown her numerous photo albums with pictures of relatives dating back to the Civil War, and had told her many stories of his adventures. Even with the whirlwind of activities, Taylor couldn't stop thinking about Jack.

He'd called, but she'd told him she was taking this time to get to know her new family. Her grandfather had continued to lament the fact that such an injustice had been caused by his own flesh and blood and had given Henry Juarez a large sum of money. Money could never make up for the time the Juarez family had lost, but it was something. She hoped Jack was getting to know his father, too.

But after looking at photos and hearing people talk about Emily, Taylor was almost at the point where she understood that Emily had only been a child when she'd gotten pregnant and set off this disastrous chain of events. She'd gone to see Emily twice. She didn't know why, but they seemed to have found a level of understanding, and

Taylor had begun to realize the decisions Emily had made were a child's decisions. Belamy had been arrested immediately, and the police soon discovered she'd taken the money so it looked like a robbery. She'd since spent it all, but still had the jewels. Belamy was more to blame than anyone. Taylor couldn't imagine how the woman could live with herself. Jack was outraged.

In the end, Taylor had had the best mother she could possibly have had. She wished Jack could've met her mother. He would have liked her.

After packing the last pair of shoes, she went downstairs for breakfast. She had a little time before she went to the airport, so she went into the breakfast room where her grandfather sat at the table. She was going to miss their breakfasts.

"You can still change your mind, my dear," he teased.

"I'll be back often. And you can visit me, too."

"And what about your friend?"

She looked at him, realizing he meant Jack. "I imagine he's going on with his life now that his father has been cleared."

Her grandfather looked serious. He tapped the newspaper next to him. "Well, I don't expect he's going to be happy with the newspaper this morning."

She leaned over to look at the headline. Newspaper Editor Son of Falsely Convicted Murderer.

"Oh, no." She snatched up the newspaper and read more. "That's horrible. How could his own newspaper do that?"

"It's the nature of the beast," he said.

"I suppose so. I'm just sorry it happened to Jack. He didn't deserve that." She stood. "And I better finish packing."

In her room, she took out her cell phone and punched

in Jack's number. No answer. When the voice mail kicked in, she hung up. What would she say? It would be better if she just went home and forgot about him.

It was all she could do to shower and finish getting ready. Soon she'd be home, and she had a million things to do and think about when she got there. She had to see an obstetrician, make a nursery and—

A knock on her door startled her. Benjamin, ready to take her things down. She swung open the door. "I'm read—"

For a moment, she couldn't move. "Jack. I—what—"

"I saw your number on my caller ID and I was nearby, so I thought I'd stop and see what you wanted."

She stepped back so he could come inside. "Well, I called because I saw the paper and I wanted to say how sorry I was. I had no idea they'd do that and—"

"You're apologizing again."

She stopped. "I am?"

He nodded.

"But if it weren't for me, it wouldn't have happened."

"You know, that's a big ego you've got there."

"Excuse me?"

"You think you're responsible for everything. Well, you're not. Other people screw up, and some things just happen. It's not your fault and you can't take credit for it."

"Take credit. What are you talking about?"

"It makes you feel more important to take credit for things whether they're bad or whatever."

"It does not."

"Well, then stop it. Because you don't cause everything. I'm responsible for what's in the paper. I told my boss. It was my decision. I knew what would happen and I knew he had to do it. I don't regret it. Not for one minute."

She opened her mouth, but nothing came out.

"The thing is," Jack said, his face lighting up, "since learning who my father was, my biggest fear was having people find out who I really am. I was afraid of what they'd think. But I realized that if I told the world who I was, I would no longer have to be afraid. It turns out that my biological father isn't a murderer, but even if he were, he's not me. How I live my life, how I treat other people—that's who I am."

She was speechless.

"And you're not who people thought you were growing up. You don't have to apologize for everyone and everything. You're you. You're unique and I love you very much."

She swallowed over a lump in her throat.

He brushed her cheek with his fingertips. "I think we can have a future together, Taylor. I want to marry you."

A leap of faith. Sometimes it takes a leap of faith.

"But…there's my company. The baby."

"It's a package. I love the whole package."

"It's time to go to the airport, Ms. Dundee."

Benjamin stood at the door.

"If you have to go home to take care of business, if you need time to think and sort it all out, I understand," Jack said. "If you love me, we've got a little over eight months to get married. Love is enough for now. We can figure out the rest later."

She couldn't think of anything she'd want more than for her and Jack and the baby to be a family.

"I love you, Taylor, and I want to be with you always. I want to marry you and have more babies. We can be a family. A real family."

It was what she'd always wanted. And yes, they did need time, but when she looked into his eyes, she knew that he was right. Love was enough for now.

HARLEQUIN®

Super Romance®

*Welcome to our newest miniseries, about five
poker players and the women who love them!*

Texas Hold'em

When it comes to love, the stakes are high

Beginning October 2007 with

THE BABY GAMBLE

by USA TODAY *bestselling author*

Tara Taylor Quinn

#1446

Desperate to have a baby, Annie Kincaid
turns to the only man she trusts, her ex-husband,
Blake Smith, and asks him to father her child.

Also watch for:

BETTING ON SANTA *by Debra Salonen* November 2007

GOING FOR BROKE *by Linda Style* December 2007

DEAL ME IN *by Cynthia Thomason* January 2008

TEXAS BLUFF *by Linda Warren* February 2008

Look for THE BABY GAMBLE *by* USA TODAY
bestselling author Tara Taylor Quinn.

Available October 2007 wherever you buy books.

REQUEST YOUR FREE BOOKS!
2 FREE NOVELS PLUS 2 FREE GIFTS!

HARLEQUIN®

Super Romance®

Exciting, emotional, unexpected!

YES! Please send me 2 FREE Harlequin Superromance® novels and my 2 FREE gifts. After receiving them, if I don't wish to receive any more books, I can return the shipping statement marked "cancel." If I don't cancel, I will receive 6 brand-new novels every month and be billed just $4.69 per book in the U.S., or $5.24 per book in Canada, plus 25¢ shipping and handling per book and applicable taxes, if any*. That's a savings of close to 15% off the cover price! I understand that accepting the 2 free books and gifts places me under no obligation to buy anything. I can always return a shipment and cancel at any time. Even if I never buy another book from Harlequin, the two free books and gifts are mine to keep forever.   135 HDN EEX7 336 HDN EEYK

Name _____ (PLEASE PRINT) _____

Address _____ Apt. _____

City _____ State/Prov. _____ Zip/Postal Code _____

Signature (if under 18, a parent or guardian must sign)

Mail to the **Harlequin Reader Service®**:
IN U.S.A.: P.O. Box 1867, Buffalo, NY 14240-1867
IN CANADA: P.O. Box 609, Fort Erie, Ontario L2A 5X3

Not valid to current Harlequin Superromance subscribers.

Want to try two free books from another line?
Call 1-800-873-8635 or visit www.morefreebooks.com.

* Terms and prices subject to change without notice. NY residents add applicable sales tax. Canadian residents will be charged applicable provincial taxes and GST. This offer is limited to one order per household. All orders subject to approval. Credit or debit balances in a customer's account(s) may be offset by any other outstanding balance owed by or to the customer. Please allow 4 to 6 weeks for delivery.

Your Privacy: Harlequin is committed to protecting your privacy. Our Privacy Policy is available online at www.eHarlequin.com or upon request from the Reader Service. From time to time we make our lists of customers available to reputable firms who may have a product or service of interest to you. If you would prefer we not share your name and address, please check here. ☐

HSR07

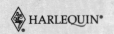

EVERLASTING LOVE™

Every great love has a story to tell™

An uplifting story of love and survival that spans generations.

Hayden MacNulty and Brian Conway both lived on Briar Hill Road their whole lives. As children they were destined to meet, but as a couple Hayden and Brian have much to overcome before romance ultimately flourishes.

Look for

The House on Briar Hill Road

by award-winning author
Holly Jacobs

Available October wherever you buy books.

Ria Sterling has the gift—or is it a curse?—
of seeing a person's future in his or her
photograph. Unfortunately, when detective
Carrick Jones brings her a missing person's
case, she glimpses his partner's ID—and
sees imminent murder. And when her vision
comes true, Ria becomes the prime suspect.
Carrick isn't convinced this beautiful woman
committed the crime...but does he believe
she has the special powers to solve it?

Look for

Seeing Is Believing

by

Kate Austin

Available October
wherever you buy books.

#1446 THE BABY GAMBLE • Tara Taylor Quinn
Texas Hold 'Em

Desperate to have a baby, Annie Kincaid turns to the only man she trusts—her ex-husband, Blake Smith—and asks him to father her child. Because when it comes to love, the stakes are high....

#1447 TEMPORARY NANNY • Carrie Weaver

Who would guess that the perfect nanny for a ten-year-old boy is Royce McIntyre? Not Katy Garner, that's for sure. But she has no other choice than to ask her handsome neighbor for help. Never expecting that Royce might be the perfect answer for someone else...

#1448 COUNT ON LOVE • Melinda Curtis
Going Back

Annie Raye's a single mom who's trying to rebuild her life after her ex-husband, a convict, tarnished her reputation. But returning home to Las Vegas makes "going straight" difficult because she's still remembered as a child gambling prodigy. And it doesn't help when Sam Knight costs her a good job. So she sets out to prove the private investigator wrong.

#1449 BECAUSE OF A BOY • Anna DeStefano
Atlanta Heroes

Nurse Kate Rhodes mistakenly believes one of her young charges is being abused by his dad and sets in motion a series of events that jeopardize the lives of the young boy and his father, who are forced to go into hiding. To right her wrong, she must work with Stephen Creighton, the legal advocate who's defending the accused father, and find the pair before it's too late.

#1450 THE BABY DOCTORS • Janice Macdonald

When widowed pediatrician Sarah Benedict returns home after fifteen years in Central America, she wants to set up a practice where traditional and alternative medicine work together. And she hopes to team up with Matthew Cameron, the friend she's loved since she was eight. Loved *and* lost, when he married someone else. Except now he's divorced...and she doesn't like the person he's become.

#1451 WHERE LOVE GROWS • Cynthia Reese

Becca Reynolds has a job to do—investigate the suspicious insurance claims of several farmers. Little does she realize that she "knows" one of the men in question. Could Ryan MacIntosh really be involved? And will she be able to find out before he figures out who she is?